1·9

eighth shepherd

BOOK EIGHT

A.D. CHRONICLES®

eighth
shepherd

Tyndale House Publishers, Inc.
Carol Stream, Illinois

BODIE & BROCK
THOENE

Visit Tyndale's exciting Web site at www.tyndale.com

TYNDALE and Tyndale's quill logo are registered trademarks of Tyndale House Publishers, Inc.

A.D. Chronicles and the fish design are registered trademarks of Bodie Thoene.

Eighth Shepherd

A.D. Chronicles series designed by Rule 29, www.rule29.com

Interior designed by Dean H. Renninger

Edited by Ramona Cramer Tucker

Library of Congress Cataloging-in-Publication Data

Thoene, Bodie, date.
  Eighth shepherd / Bodie & Brock Thoene.
    p. cm.—(A.D. chronicles ; bk. 8)
  ISBN-13: 978-0-8423-7528-3 (hc)
  ISBN-10: 0-8423-7528-7 (hc)
  ISBN-13: 978-0-8423-7529-0 (sc)
  ISBN-10: 0-8423-7529-5 (sc)
  1. Jesus Christ—Fiction.   2. Bible. N.T.—History of Biblical events–Fiction.   I. Thoene, Brock, date.   II. Title.
  PS3570.H46E35 2008
  813'.54—dc22   2007039162

Printed in the United States of America

14 13 12 11 10 09 08
 7   6   5   4   3   2   1

~Psalm 15~
This book is dedicated with much love
to our dear friends and Good Shepherds in London,
Rod and Julie Anderson!

You stand in the gap to pray for us and for the nations. In such a time
as this the Lord has raised you both up. You have blessed our lives
and our ministry more than words can express.

the middle east

FIRST CENTURY A.D.

Mount Hermon +

Caesarea Philippi

GALILEE

Mediterranean Sea

Chorazin
Capernaum • Bethsaida
Magdala • Sea of Galilee
Tiberias

Jordan River

SAMARIA

Jericho
Jerusalem • + Mount of Olives
Bethany
Bethlehem •
Herodium

PEREA

JUDEA   Dead Sea

IDUMEA

N

← to Alexandria, Egypt

Prologue*

It was a night unlike any other night recorded in the memory of man.

Perched high on the rim of the Valley of Lepers, I could see Yeshua of Nazareth far below in the gathering gloom. Yeshua sat on a table of rock beside an old man. The light of a bonfire glowed like a lantern in the evening shadows.

Three times the blast of a ram's horn resounded in the hills, announcing to the lost sheep of Israel that their Shepherd had come to save them, to heal them, to heal them and to carry them home at last.

As the echo of the third blast died away, the Valley became alive with the light of torches as the lepers emerged from caves and hovels. Those dwelling in darkness and despair flowed in thin rivulets, like the molten ore of first creation, toward Yeshua, the source of First Light.

It is written that the pit of human anguish was, for the Son of God, a wondrous mine of human souls. Throughout the night the cauldron of Messiah's love glowed golden, promising new life.

The people of Mak'ob drew near to Yeshua. One at a time they approached: those hobbling on crutches, the sightless, the lame. Half hands. Faceless faces. Legless stumps.

* For more of the story, read the previous books in the A.D. Chronicles series by Bodie and Brock Thoene . . . especially *Second Touch* and *Seventh Day*.

And Yeshua embraced each one, called each by name. One at a time He healed them all—rebuilding limbs and features, renewing blind eyes with radiant revelation, restoring lips with which to praise the God of Heaven.

One by one the residents of Mak'ob ascended the switchback trail, returning to the world that had cast them out. The glow of torches illuminated beautiful visages where, hours before, decay and living death had been etched. They were evidence of Yeshua's resurrection power among those counted as dead among the people of Israel.

If Yeshua of Nazareth could work such a wonder as this, what more was He capable of?

Torches bobbed up the crooked path to where I, Peniel, the man born blind, stood watch.

A few spoke as they passed me on their way out of the valley of despair.

"Where are you going?" I called cheerfully.

"Home!"

"My mother and father!"

"My children!"

"To show myself to the priest as Yeshua commanded!"

It was almost dawn. The deep shadows of the mountain relinquished their hold on Mak'ob.

Among the last to be healed was a pretty woman, about thirty years of age. Her lively brown eyes were the color of freshly turned, rich earth. Brown hair was thick and cropped short. It curled softly around her face. Skin was sun-bronzed. Still dressed in the rags of her disease, she climbed the path with certain strides. She seemed not to notice me as she reached the top.

"One last look," she whispered.

I coughed, alerting her to my presence. "Shalom," I said when she smiled down at me with surprise.

"Oh. I didn't see you there."

"Sorry. Didn't mean to startle you."

"Shalom. Shalom . . . been here long?"

"All night," I answered, moving over as she sat beside me. "A long night, eh?"

"Twelve years for me." She was breathless from the climb. She looked up as the last stars faded, then down into the shadows where

Yeshua was embracing the lepers of Mak'ob. "But now . . . look . . . the sun is rising."

Musing, I said, "He is healing them all."

"Mmm." She hummed with contentment. "Were you one of us? I don't recognize you. But then, I don't recognize anyone from below . . . now that we all have faces. Everyone . . . so beautiful!"

"I used to beg in Yerushalayim. I was blind," I explained.

Sunlight seeped under the dome of night.

"You saw everything?" she asked, smiling down at the few lepers who remained clustered around Yeshua. "We need a witness."

"I saw the lights. Torches as they flowed to him. I heard the singing. What is your name?"

"Shimona," the woman replied, gazing at her own hands in delight. "Shimona the Leper."

"But you're healed now. No need to call yourself a leper anymore."

"I want everyone to know what happened here last night. To me. To all of us. We waited so long. Besides what we had already lost, some of us lost still more as we waited. There were so many rumors. Some went out to find him. Then he came here to find us. I want to remember what I was and remember what he has done for me. I want to tell them all. Show them all. Suffering is at an end."

"People outside don't want to believe." I shrugged. "Just a warning. I was born blind . . . healed . . . then they threw me out of the synagogue. Even my mother and father disowned me. You see, everyone with human power is afraid of Yeshua's power. They have a lot to lose."

"Lose? But . . . people have been climbing out of the Valley of Sorrow . . . up and up the path all night. They are healed. Whole."

"I was from Yerushalayim . . . before. Begged for years at Nicanor Gate."

"I remember the gate."

"Sometimes the high priest himself dropped coins into my begging bowl . . . before." I felt sorry for Shimona. She had suffered so long she couldn't understand that there were many outside who would look at her and resent Yeshua for the miracle that had brought a leper back from the grave. "So. Where are you going?"

"Home. Jericho."

"Family?"

"I think so. Many years ago. Maybe still there. My father was the Chazzan of the synagogue when I was a girl. Before I was a leper. Before they found the spot on my hand and I became dead to them. I was the daughter of the Chazzan before I was sent to this place."

"How many years? I mean, since you last heard from them?"

"I don't remember. A very long time, I suppose. After a while time no longer existed here in the Valley of Sorrows. No hours or days. No weeks or months or years. Only one endless night until he came . . . last night."

I agreed. "Yes. The Light."

"Out of the darkness," she said quietly.

"Where will you go if your mother and father aren't in Jericho? Or . . . if they don't recognize you?"

"They can't have forgotten." She frowned for the first time as a doubt crept in.

I cleared my throat and said cheerfully, "If your family is gone, you could come with us. Follow Yeshua. There are lots of women among his disciples."

She gazed toward the lightening sky. "He told me, 'Go home, Shimona.' He told me to show myself to my father, who is a Chazzan. Like in the Torah. And be purified. Then wait there until he comes."

"If that's what Yeshua says, then of course there's a reason. He never says anything without a good reason. Everything he says and does means something important. Look." Yeshua embraced the last of the lepers.

Shimona shielded her eyes as the sun burst over the eastern rim of the chasm. "That's Lily . . . my friend. The last. So. It is finished."

Shimona and I rose to our feet.

"Will you wait for her here at the top?" I asked.

"She'll go home a different way than me."

We stood together for a long moment. I remarked, "It will be remembered. He healed them all . . . all the lepers in Israel."

"Yes," Shimona agreed, turning away from the Valley of Sorrows. "And how he prophesied about Israel and about his Kingdom as he laid hands on us. And our wounds vanished."

"Did he speak over you?"

Smiling enigmatically, she did not answer for a time. "The old tree in Jericho. You know the story?"

I was silent as I searched my memory for the details. "The Amos tree? That one?"

She nodded and gazed into the western sky. "Rabbi Ahava always says, 'Everything means something.' So . . ." Shimona's eyes seemed warmer than ever, as though vitality was restored with every passing minute. "Shalom, Peniel! Maybe we'll meet again?" She raised her hand in farewell.

"Sure. Sure! Shalom!" I called after her. "We'll meet again, Shimona, daughter of the Chazzan of Jericho!"

PART I

This is what the Sovereign LORD says: Woe to the shepherds of Israel who only take care of themselves! Should not shepherds take care of the flock? . . . You have not . . . healed the sick or bound up the injured. You have not brought back the strays or searched for the lost. You have ruled them harshly and brutally.

EZEKIEL 34:2, 4

1

There was a hawk soaring high above Bethany that day. It was the flight of the raptor that made Peniel remember Shimona the Leper and the Valley of Mak'ob for the first time in many months.

Where had they all gone? he wondered. All those leprous sons and daughters of Israel, rejected and forsaken by all but other lepers, had been embraced by Yeshua. In His arms they had been healed, made whole.

Ten fingers and ten toes. Noses. Ears. Lips. At the command of Yeshua, all had returned intact and better than before.

He had sent them to the priests as a testimony. From there? Where had they all gone? He had healed them all, yet it seemed they had vanished into the landscape without a trace.

For the first time Peniel wondered how many had been silenced by the enemies of Yeshua.

Now, once again, a miracle beyond comprehension had occurred. Today El'azar of Bethany, beloved friend of Yeshua of Nazareth, had been raised from death. More than that, he had been restored—resurrected from rotten decay that clung to the nostrils and stung the eyes of the living who had gathered at his tomb.

Eternal things have come to earth, Peniel thought as he watched El'azar of Bethany embrace his sisters.

The celebration of El'azar's resurrection was unlike any Peniel had witnessed. The gates of the Bethany estate were besieged by hundreds and then thousands who heard the news that El'azar was alive and flocked to see.

Inside the walled compound a great feast was prepared for Yeshua and His band of followers. The talmidim looked proud of their Master as they sat at the table with the family. They seemed more confident now than at any time in their travels with Yeshua.

"Let them come," Thomas boasted with his hand on the hilt of his sword. "And even if they kill us, what of it?"

John agreed. "They're beaten now for certain. What can Rome do? Or Herod Antipas? Caiaphas, the high priest, and his puppets are beaten. Yeshua will raise us up again, though they kill us a hundred times!"

Peniel's father, a potter by trade, agreed with all and rejoiced at the miracle, yet he said this to his son: "It is a bright, clean cup we drink from today. A new way of looking at life and death. And yet, here is the dark crack that runs through the cup of our joy: They will fight harder, I think, to kill the man who has returned from death. They will plot secret ways to kill Yeshua, who we know now is the source of life. Be careful, Son."

Peniel embraced his father at the gate. "What do you mean, Father?"

"You know well how they put you out of the synagogue when Yeshua gave you eyes. I have heard that in other towns lepers healed by Yeshua's command and returned home from the Valley of Mak'ob have been banished as well, put away as though they are still be: There is a rumor about the daughter of the Chazzan ished, though she is plainly healed. They don't want . what Yeshua is capable of."

Peniel peered at the circling hawk and wondered "He tells everyone he heals not to speak of it."

"Too late. The cat is out of the bag, as they say. ⁊ of the tomb. The secret is shattered like a clay pot and . . . Everyone!"

"I don't know how long we'll stay in Judea," Per

"Send word to me in Yerushalayim when you are returning, my son. You know you and your Master will always have a home."

Peniel stood on the parapet and watched as his father made his way up the road against the flow of thousands coming to see El'azar, the dead man who now lived. He searched the sky, but there was no further sign of the hawk.

Cut into a solid rock face in the Kidron Valley beside the eastern flank of Jerusalem, the tomb of Ra'nabel ben Dives was modest by comparison with its neighbors. The simple rectangular portal boasted no columns and only half as much ornate facade as the nearby tomb of the priestly Hezirs.

Still, Bera ben Dives, oldest of Ra'nabel's five surviving brothers, and now head of the Dives clan, was proud of his family's monument. Located on the lower slope of the Mount of Olives, not far from the sepulchres of kings and facing the grand eastern wall of King Herod's Temple platform, it was a fitting memorial for men of wealth and power.

Inside the quarried space were a preparation room and four burial chambers. There was also an ossuary vault where dried bones would eventually be collected. At the moment only two of the vaults were in use. One contained the remains of Bera's mother and father, while his brother's fresh corpse occupied the other.

The brothers Dives were gathered in the open air of the forecourt, just outside the tomb's narrow opening. A pair of servants grunted as they used wooden poles to lever a heavy round stone into place, sealing the entry.

"Cut down in his prime," Bera intoned to the solemn nods of his siblings. "A man of vision and leadership, with the heart of a servant."

Murmurs of agreement all around.

"High Priest Caiaphas sent a personal note of condolence," one of the brothers observed.

"Ra'nabel was held in the highest regard by Lord Caiaphas," Bera said, lifting his chin and tilting his head to the side. "Since the time of our grandfather, every high priest has welcomed our family's advice."

This was an exaggeration—actually, an outright falsehood—but one understood and accepted by all the brothers. Their paternal grandfather had been a leather tanner, a dishonorable and despised profession, but one in which he had accumulated great wealth from curing the hides of sacrificial animals. He had split the profits with the high priest and so began the association.

Bera continued, "Naturally we all assumed Ra'nabel would fill that role for our generation. But since the Almighty has seen fit to cut him down, I will do my best to meet the need." Then Bera added with modestly downcast eyes, "I will try to uphold the honor of our family."

Ezra, the youngest ben Dives, inquired, "Is it true that Ra'nabel was investigating the charlatan Yeshua of Nazareth?"

"You are not to mention that name!" Bera rebuked Ezra sharply. "Wild stories! Rumors! Gossip! That deluded blasphemer El'azar of Bethany returned to life when our worthy and noble brother lies here?" Bera put the palm of his hand on the sealing stone in a dramatic gesture of bereavement. He betrayed no sense of irony when in almost the same breath he accused Yeshua of trickery and then credited the man with bringing the dead back to life.

"They say he works miracles," sixteen-year-old Ezra persisted.

"Superstition! Poison, more likely!" Bera exclaimed. "Perhaps El'azar and the Nazarene conspired to kill our brother. From perfect health to stone-cold dead? Is it reasonable? Is it likely?"

"I-I had a dream," Ezra said. "Ra'nabel appeared to me. It was a warning, he said."

Led by Bera, the four senior ben Dives spat between their fingers and made the gesture against the evil eye. "Childish nonsense!" Bera chided. "Anyway, you are too young to meddle in such things. I will present myself to Lord Caiaphas. Neither El'azar of Bethany nor the Galilean will trouble our house much longer."

The one-room stone hut where Shimona the Leper lived was proof that even after happy endings, the road of life continues with unexpected twists and turns.

Shimona's father was still Chazzan of the synagogue in Jericho. He was an upright man, a righteous man, respected by all in the community.

The citizens of Jericho had almost forgotten that the Chazzan's grown daughter and her husband were lepers living in the Valley of Mak'ob.

The Chazzan had been surprised to see his daughter on his doorstep after so many years of believing she was among the living dead. Shimona's mother wept to see her face but did not embrace her. The Chazzan did not allow Shimona's sisters to come near her.

She had stayed in the shed behind the house until nightfall. After dark she followed her father to the rabbi, and they called the Levite priest. At the side of the synagogue in Jericho they had listened patiently to Shimona's story about Yeshua coming to the Valley of Mak'ob and healing everyone.

"You say he healed them all?"

"Yes! He healed us all!"

"Everyone in Mak'ob?"

"Every one," Shimona declared. "Yeshua is Mashiyah! He is the Son of the Living God!"

This declaration shocked the Chazzan, the rabbi, and the priest. The rabbi made the sign against the evil eye and turned his back on Shimona, commanding her to be silent.

The officials conferred together in the synagogue by lamplight while Shimona waited outside beneath the stars.

When they emerged at last, neither Shimona's father nor the rabbi nor the priest in Jericho believed her story. Every word must be tested, they declared. Shimona had been irrefutably pronounced unclean—she and her leprous husband. Had her husband not perished horribly in the dying cave of Mak'ob?

How could Shimona, so near to death, have been healed? Though she had returned home in the stinking rags of a leprous beggar, the dread disease did not seem to be evident.

Was there a possibility that Shimona had indeed been healed by Yeshua of Nazareth? And that the one some proclaimed a charlatan was actually a miracle worker? Yet the high priest himself had declared Yeshua a fake Messiah in league with the devil.

What if this was a trick? What if Shimona the Leper was not truly healed? What if the eyes of those outside the Valley of Lepers who beheld her were bewitched and blinded to the truth by a demon? Perhaps Shimona the Leper had been sent back to Jericho by Yeshua to infect all who came near her!

The rabbi of Jericho had said, "Perhaps . . . just perhaps . . . Shimona is like a fireship in a battle, sent among our ships by the enemy to set us on fire."

Shimona's father had stared at her in fear as he considered his other children, his home, and his reputation. "What shall I do with her, Rabbi? How can we be sure?"

The rabbi considered the danger for a moment before he replied. "Torah and Mosheh command that anyone suspected of leprosy be isolated from the congregation of Israel. How could we know for certain, unless she is isolated for a time? Say, perhaps a year or so? Does Torah not command Shimona the Leper to live apart until her wellness can be proved without any doubt?"

"But where can she live, Rabbi?"

The rabbi held up a crooked finger. "Chazzan, you hold lease tenancy on a grove of sukomore fig trees from Zachai the Publican, whose soul is like that of a leper. I remember there was a stone cottage there."

The Chazzan concurred. These were the facts. "The old gardener who cared for the figs died recently. The stone house is vacant. The grove of sukomore fig trees needs a caretaker."

The rabbi snapped his fingers. "Blessed are you, O Lord, who gives us answers for troubling questions! So, figs. Perfect! The very fruit by which Lucifer, the great serpent, tempted Eve. Then, after the Fall, they covered themselves with its leaves. But the Lord saw through their deception. Yes! Eliminate all deception! Shimona must live in the grove of fig trees."

"This property is outside the city walls about half a mile," the Chazzan volunteered. "It is the perfect place for Shimona. The stone cottage will be her dwelling."

The rabbi added, "Warning signs must be posted: 'Shimona the Leper lives in this place.' She must remain confined to the orchard. For her to cross the boundaries and enter the company of normal, healthy people will result in stoning. Agreed?"

Shimona's father raised his eyes heavenward in relief. Then he considered the fruit of the orchard. "But what about the fig harvest? How will I sell it if anyone knows it is tended by . . . ?"

"Sell it in Yerushalayim," the rabbi had declared. "Figs is figs. Shimona will live in isolation until such time as Yeshua is proved a prophet or a devil, and she is pronounced free from leprosy or sent back to the Valley of Mak'ob!"

Less than a year had now passed since that meeting of the elders of Jericho. Shimona the Leper had not seen her father or mother since that night. She lived in isolation in the cottage and tended the fig trees for her father.

It was, to her, as it must have been for Adam and Eve in Gan Eden before the Fall. Once a week someone came with an oxcart to collect baskets of fig cakes that she harvested, prepared, and left at an appointed place. Supplies were left behind for her. She had chickens in a pen, two goats for milk and cheese, and a small garden beside the house where she raised vegetables and food enough to live on. She wore the cast-off clothes of her sisters. There was a stream on the downhill side of the property that marked the border. She did not cross it to leave her verdant prison, nor did anyone from the outside come in.

There was a fine well in the yard in front of her little house. The water was clear and good for washing her body and her clothes.

Each day she woke up before dawn and said, "God who hears my prayers and sees to every need, I love it here!" Then she sang songs of praise that she made up as she went along.

Each morning and night she looked at her smooth skin and knew that she was indeed healed—whole, well! And she thanked the Almighty One for sending Yeshua into the Valley of Mak'ob.

Of course, there were small irritations, including the army of field mice that lived in the grove. Shimona called the rodents "Philistines" and fought a constant battle against them. Sometimes they snuck into the house and spoiled her flour. They chewed her clothing as she slept. She set traps and captured a great number every day. But there were always more.

She prayed, "Blessed are you, O Lord, God of the Universe. You hear my every prayer. You know my needs before I ask. So, Lord of Heaven and Earth, if you will not banish the Philistines from this suko-more grove, please send me a cat! Please. Lord who hears all my prayers and knows my needs, please, O Lord! Send a cat to keep me company. A cat with sharp teeth and keen eyes to hunt and catch the horde of Philistines who are my enemies and the enemies of this orchard, which my father has rented."

But no cat came to the orchard.

Day after day, month after month, Shimona expected and looked for an answer to her prayer. She did not stop hoping, though she lived alone with the chickens and the goats. She fought the army of Philistines on her own.

"Lord, is it so much to ask?" The heavens seemed like bronze in the matter of cats.

Shimona sent word to the Chazzan, her father, and begged him to send a feline to help her defend the fig grove. He did not heed her request. She heard from him less and less as time passed.

Undaunted that her family seemed to have forgotten her and abandoned her in the fig grove, Shimona never lost hope.

She remembered her Father in Heaven, for whom nothing was impossible. She prayed that one day, perhaps, the Messiah would cross the creek and enter the sukomore grove with His disciples. She could see it plainly in her mind. Yeshua, the Deliverer of Israel, and His band of holy men would accept Shimona's offering of cakes of figs, and she would feed them all a hearty meal.

In preparation for that possibility, Shimona composed a song about a gray-striped cat riding on the shoulder of the Messiah. She decided that if Yeshua ever came to the sukomore grove, she would sing Him the song. Then perhaps Yeshua, who healed lepers and fed five thousand with only five loaves and two fish, would see her need for help and answer her request.

Zachai of Jericho was a son of Abraham, yet he was the most hated man in all the territory of Judea. He was more despised than Tetrarch Herod Antipas, more hated than Governor Pontius Pilate, more loathed even than the common Roman soldiers who prowled the streets of Jericho looking for someone to harass, arrest, or torment.

Herod, Pilate, and the Roman soldiers ranked high in ability to strike terror in the hearts of everyone who lived in the shadow of their power. At bedtime the mention of those names conjured nightmares: *"Be good, little Dan, or the demons will take you away!"*

Images of crucifixions along the roadsides haunted the dreams of Jericho's children.

The royal faces of the Herodian family, glimpsed in broad daylight in passing processions, became the demons who peered out from the dark corners of rooms. Soldiers' voices, shouting in the marketplace, were transfigured in memory into howling wolves waiting outside the windows to devour little ones.

Fear, it was believed by Rome, was a good thing, engendering respect and submission from citizens young and old.

Hatred alone was not enough for Rome.

The great Tiberius Caesar often proclaimed, "Hatred flowing from the people, when untempered by Fear, becomes a wide river upon which the warship of Rebellion will sail to attack the Empire."

The name of Zachai, the chief tax collector, conjured only disdain and insults in the hearts of all within the district of Jericho. He was short of stature and had a big voice and a jovial laugh. He might have done well as a jester in the court of Herod or as a comic actor in a Greek play. He was cocky in his manner, wore a perpetual smile, and exhibited no shame when making a demand for overpayment.

Loathing and earnest curses for Zachai were woven into the bedtime prayers of little ones taught by their parents.

"Blessed are you, O Lord, who hates thieves and liars and extortioners and collaborators and tax collectors. Blessed are you who hates Zachai, who is all these things and more. Please crush our much-loathed enemy, Zachai the Tax Collector, who stole my father's vineyard. Do unto him what he and his fathers before him have done to our father and his fathers. Omaine!"

The Jewish elders of Jericho were counting on the fact that the God of Israel heard and answered the prayers of children. Like the citizens of Jericho, Jewish Zealots who met in secret and carried daggers beneath their cloaks hated Zachai more than they feared him. He and his fathers before him had grown wealthy by betraying their own people, had they not?

Collaboration with the enemy made Zachai very rich and, therefore, a greater enemy than the Gentile overlords he served. Little wonder rebels covertly watched the bronze gates of Zachai's estate and took down his every move. They plotted and waited for their opportunity to murder Rome's chief tax collector in Judea.

This reality made Zachai a man who sensibly lived in fear for his own life. He came and went, surrounded by four Nubian bodyguards, all related to each other and utterly fearless. Zachai's four Nephilim—prehistoric giants, as they were called by the rabbis—had been purchased in the gladiatorial slave market of Damascus. Ebony titans, they towered over all as they passed, concealing their diminutive master and protecting him from death. Their shining backs absorbed the black looks and spit of the mob. On his way to the Customs House each day Zachai felt as safe as a little duck in their shadows.

The bodyguards could not be coaxed or bribed. What did they care about taxes and oppression of the *am ha aretz*? Zachai's slaves were well fed, kindly treated, and loyal. They were grateful their master had saved them from death in the Roman arena. Zachai gave each man an Ethiopian wife and a room in his mansion. Soon there were little Nephilim toddling about the slave quarters, increasing Zachai's wealth and control over his servants. Without Zachai's precious life to protect and serve they would certainly all be auctioned off and doomed. Fear of losing their positions and their families made the four a living fortress around their master.

As the entourage passed, rebels in the souks fingered the hilts of their daggers and calculated how best to divide four Nubian giants from one small publican and still have living assassins left over.

As of now the problem remained unsolved. But hatred demanded retribution.

"It is only a matter of time," the Zealots whispered.

Jericho, the City of Palms, was actually two villages located between Jerusalem and the Jordan River. Old Jericho was downhill in both geography and economics. Ramshackle, home to shifty-eyed importers and overeager caravan promoters, it was a place where beggars congregated because the climate was kind. Alms from outward-bound travelers, eager to secure the blessings of heaven on their journeys, likewise made it attractive to lepers, cripples, and the blind.

In any case, beggars were not permitted inside the gates of the new city. Clustered around the palace and gardens built by Herod the Great in a wadi west of the old city, New Jericho continued to be the winter retreat of the wealthy.

The Customs House for the district of Jericho was located midway between the new city and the old. A mud-brick wall surrounded an expanse of hard-packed earth, and another such wall bisected it, forming two expansive compounds. Caravans arriving from east of Jordan entered the northern enclosure. Those coming from Jerusalem went into the southern space. Merchants caught circumventing this arrangement were arrested and their goods confiscated. By this simple device, smuggling was discouraged and the collection of duties soared.

Chief Publican Zachai's office sat along the central barrier. Roman auxiliary legionaries—Syrians and Samaritans—controlled the gates and patrolled the grounds. Since detecting contraband was rewarded, the guards were diligent in carrying out their assignments.

So much wealth passed along the Jericho route—spices and perfumes coming in, oil and wine and balsam going out—that the guards had no time or interest in harassing the beggars or other bystanders.

At either end of the compound there were always knots of casual laborers looking for temporary employment. Some of these would sign on as additional caravan drovers. Others were paid to help pack and unpack the goods being inspected.

The day was pleasantly warm, though spring had not yet arrived on the calendar. A group of two such unemployed workers squatted outside the eastern gates. One was slightly built, but the obvious leader was sturdy and muscled. His hair, long and shaggy, hung so as to conceal his face, already masked by a thick, coarse beard.

"See there," the slender companion suggested, pointing to the Customs House where Zachai the Publican was just arriving. "Never goes anywhere without them guards. Comes from home with 'em. Goes to meals with 'em. Behind and before on his way at night. Hedged in proper, he is, sure as my name's Lamech. This is a waste of time, if you ask me."

"Shut up," the captain growled. "Who cares what you think?"

"Listen, bar Abba," Lamech returned. "I—"

The rest of the opinion went unspoken as the point of a concealed dagger reached from under Amos bar Abba's cloak to press against Lamech's left kidney. "Breathe my name aloud like that and you'll never breathe anymore," bar Abba hissed.

"Sorry . . . sorry!" Lamech returned in a hoarse whisper. "Won't happen again!" After recovering his composure, he continued, "But you see what I mean. Guards go first even when he goes to the necessary. They run everyone else out before he goes in, wait outside 'til he finishes. Stick to him like they was chained together. Like a galley slave chained to his bench."

"Shut up and keep watching!"

Beside the highway between the old and new cities of Jericho, not far from the customs plaza, was a throng of beggars. Most of them were either crippled or blind. Deaf-mutes could still find employment as gatherers or piercers in the groves of sukomore figs.

Those who lived on the charity of others often moved with the seasons if they could. Jericho was a good choice as a winter retreat, but with warmer weather it grew too hot and too dry. In summer and fall Jerusalem was preferred both for the climate and for the generosity of its pilgrims.

Some beggars supplemented their meager income by acting as informants for the Romans, or for Chief Publican Zachai, but such men either did not live in Jericho for long or, if they tried to stay, did not live very long at all.

There was one beggar known to all the residents of both Jerichos. He had been a fixture of the settlement forever. He kept his place just where the road connecting the two villages curved around a rocky outcropping and ascended the hill of Lord Zachai's villa. The incline made travelers slow down, giving the beggar additional opportunity to make his plea. Years before the man had fought with teeth and jagged fingernails for such a prime location; now it seemed to belong to him permanently.

He was called, as everyone knew, Bartimaeus. What his covenant name might be, no one had a clue, perhaps not even Bartimaeus himself. Nor was Timaeus his father's name, as was proper, for the phrase meant "Son of Defilement."

Some said he was the son of a prostitute and a Roman soldier, others that he was the abandoned whelp of a highborn lady and a foreign slave. Either might be true, or neither. Bartimaeus had no family nearby, and if he knew of any still living, he kept the knowledge locked in his heart.

Bartimaeus was in the sixth decade of his life—almost a record for a blind beggar. His body and features were gaunt. His beard, which might have been white, was the color of smoked parchment. The amber whiskers contrasted with his leathery, ochre-colored skin. A thin fringe of dirty yellow hair encircled his head just above his ears. The rest was smooth as an egg . . . a very old, mottled ostrich egg, abandoned in hot sand for many a long year, withered and wrinkled as a result.

The most remarkable characteristic Bartimaeus possessed was his blind eyes. Wide-open and staring, they were the pigments of a marbled sky: bright blue with streaks of clouds. He had not been born blind, he once said, but had become so at such an early age he did not recall ever having sight.

Encountering Bartimaeus for the first time made pilgrims uncomfortable. The fixed gaze he unerringly turned toward any footstep or spoken word seemed uncanny. Even if a group of several passersby approached, he managed to stare at each of them in turn, crying out in a high-pitched voice: "Good sirs, have pity on a poor, blind man. Have pity! A copper or two for the good of your soul, eh?" This he continued without ceasing, but at an ever-increasing volume and intensity.

Only the sound of coins jingling on the cloth of his cloak made him stop shrieking and staring. His voice then fell to a normal level, with which he called down the blessings of heaven on the giver and turned his attention to the next traveler.

Most locals whose business carried them on that road had a penny in hand before they ever reached where he sat. To do otherwise was too nerve-racking.

Bartimaeus' only possessions were his walking stick and cloak. Tattered and threadbare, the cloth sheltered him from the sun with its tail propped over his head. It became a blanket at night. Spread to catch the fall of coins, it was an indispensable part of his occupation.

Blind Bartimaeus was the folklore of Jericho. It was believed to bring good luck to give him a gift; bad fortune followed refusal.

No one believed this more fervently than Zachai the Tax Collector.

As the evening sun sank lower and the stars appeared in the eastern sky, Shimona stood awhile within the verge of the sukomore grove and gazed at the walls of the new city of Jericho. She could plainly see where the house of her father and mother was. The lamps of distant houses shone until Shimona could not tell what was heaven and what was earth.

It was always this hour of the day when the shadow of loneliness crept over her heart. She thought about her mother and father and sisters sitting together and sharing a meal. It had been so very long since she had eaten a meal with any human company. The last time she had partaken in pleasant conversation had been the night she left the Valley of Mak'ob.

She sighed deeply, hoping that perhaps her father would feel some longing for her company as well. But she knew it had been so long . . . so very long . . . that he had probably gotten used to her absence. Daily life had flooded in where her place had been. It was as though she had died in Mak'ob and never returned home, as though she were never coming back.

Shimona walked slowly through the gloom of the fig grove to her dwelling. The scurry of mice scampering away from her footsteps reminded her she was not alone.

"God who hears my prayers . . . always . . . a cat. Remember? Most of all I would like a fine cat."

She took one last look up at the stars, then gathered an armload of wood, entered the cottage, and bolted the strong wooden door behind her for the night.

The one room in Shimona's stone house was compact and neat. The window opening was high, with wooden bars to keep out intruders, but also open to the air so birds could freely roost and sing on the sill. The floor was earthen, beaten hard by years of use from the previous caretaker. Shimona swept it every day and congratulated herself that it was as clean as any stone pavement. In the corner was a bed of rushes she gathered new from the creek each month and dried in the drying shed. A large sheep fleece and a ragged blanket covered the mat. Nearby on a low table were a clay bowl, a cup, a basin, and three pots for cooking. A three-legged stool was close to the embers where the remains of a fire built from gathered fallen sukomore branches now smoldered.

She roasted vegetables from her garden and melted cheese to drizzle on the squash. She sang a prayer of blessing over her supper and then ate in silence.

Was her family eating together even now? Did they look at the empty place at the table and think of her here in the sukomore grove? Or had they forgotten her?

"O God who always hears my heart, always loves me . . . bless my father, the Chazzan of the synagogue of Jericho. Strengthen him as he prepares to sing at Sabbath. Make his voice . . . oh! So beautiful!"

She often thought of her father's voice as the wind passed through the trees. His songs had carried her heart to the throne room of the Most High! How she had loved to hear him sing.

As a child Shimona had played the harp quite well. As a leper without fingers the talent had been useless, so she sang throughout her waking hours to help retain her sanity. The habit of song had come away with her when she left the Valley of Lepers. There were times, like tonight, when she studied her ten fingers in the firelight and wondered if they might easily pluck the strings of a harp again.

"Lord of Heaven and Earth, Lord of song who dances with the angels, someday perhaps when my father the Chazzan remembers me and brings me home, I will play the harp again. Lord who hears my prayers always, I implore you to remind my father that I am here, waiting. Make some old tune he hears bring my face to his thoughts, please, Lord. And then I will play the harp for him and sing such a song of joy for you . . . such a song of coming home and embracing my family as I have dreamed for so long."

The loneliness might have crushed her except for the hope that one day soon her father and the rabbi and the priest would come to the grove and pronounce her well and healthy. Perhaps they would come soon and she would be free again, like other women. She imagined sitting by the well of Jericho, drawing water and talking about the weather and their children. How she missed the sound of human voices this time of night!

"God who hears my prayers . . . oh! God of Heaven and Earth . . . free again," she sighed, gazing through the bars of the window to the starry sky.

achai concealed himself behind the rooftop lattice intertwined with jasmine. Below him in the street the congregation of the Jericho synagogue gathered, greeting one another with joy and news.

There was Barucha. She walked between two sisters in front of her father and mother. She held her skirts up from the mire of the road. One of her sisters caught her shoulder and whispered in her ear. Barucha leaned her head close and replied. They both laughed and linked arms as if they were bound by some shared secret. Inexplicably, she turned her face up toward Zachai's rooftop perch and frowned.

He instinctively stepped back a pace. Did she sense his longing? Did she somehow feel his gaze upon her? Was she secretly drawn to Zachai? Or at least to the opulence of his existence? Could such a thing be true?

God of Israel who cannot hear my prayers: Oh, how I long to marry this woman and bring her home to fill my wide, but empty, house.

But she glanced away quickly, as though by looking at the vast house of such a sinner she had also sinned.

Zachai's blood bounded through his veins. He became almost dizzy at the thought of such a tall, elegant creature in his arms.

Jacob the patriarch must have felt this way when first he laid eyes on Rachel. Was anything too much to give to possess such beauty?

Barucha seemed to shimmer in the soft light of morning. She leaned close to her sister and whispered behind her hand. Then both women looked up at the same instant, fixing their eyes on the lattice where Zachai hid. Could they see him there?

Barucha shook her head in an unmistakable gesture of derision, then laughed in a voice that sounded like breaking glass.

Zachai's chin dropped. Whatever Barucha had said to her sister, the comment was directed at Zachai. He flushed with embarrassment as though his desires had been revealed, ridiculed, and rejected in an instant.

His fists clenched and unclenched. He closed his eyes in resignation, trying to blot out her expression of disgust as she had turned her eyes toward him. *God who does not hear me, I am the most hated man in Judea. I am a fool to love or ever think I could be loved. I am a fool to think it could be otherwise.*

"Shimona!"

She heard the woman's voice whisper her name on the wind. It woke her from a deep and dreamless sleep.

"Who's there?" She sat up slowly and gathered her shawl around her shoulders. "Is someone there?"

There was no answer, so she called out in a childlike voice, "Mother?"

The night was thick with quiet, like cobwebs hanging from the ceiling of a deserted house.

"Mother?" Shimona cried again, hoping . . . hoping.

She drew in her breath, remembering what it had been like to hear the breath of her husband and the baby in the darkness. Strange how lonely the sound of her own heartbeat had become.

The kindness of lepers had been daily comfort in the Valley. The isolation of this stone house and sukomore grove seemed more painful to endure than the disease that had first separated her from home and kin so long ago.

"Mother?" she called, knowing her mother had long ago forgotten her. The forgetting was so complete that her mother did not want her to come back . . . not ever.

"God who hears me . . . always . . . always you hear me. I am so alone now, God. Did you heal me only to suffer this? At least when there were others sick and dying all around me, we loved one another. Though our bodies had no feeling, our hearts were full of wishing the same wish."

A night bird sang from somewhere deep inside the grove.

"God, Lord! You who hear my every thought. I know you remember what I remember. I knew fear that was like the low, dark entrance to a tomb. Enter the blackness and there was no way out." She covered her face with her hands. "Though I was set free, I am still a prisoner. Trapped in a dungeon. Needing to hear the voice of my mother . . . my mother."

Raising her face to the patch of starry heaven that gleamed through the window, she cried, "I miss Mak'ob! I miss the lepers of the Valley of Sorrows who moved my heart, though I was a disease. Oh, Lord, where are they all now? Where is Yeshua? Oh, please! I don't believe you healed me, Lord, only so I could suffer a deeper wound."

When El'azar of Bethany emerged from his tomb at the behest of Yeshua of Nazareth, the event was witnessed by many more onlookers than just Yeshua's talmidim and El'azar's family. Dozens of mourners were on hand when the miracle occurred.

The news had broken over Judea like a clap of thunder, and its implications reverberated among the ruling classes like an earthquake. Though an hour of wrangling had already elapsed, there was still a stormy session inside the cedar-paneled hall of the Sanhedrin's council chambers on the Temple Mount in Jerusalem. It seemed everyone was speaking at once.

"What are we to do?"

"What *can* we do? The man from Nazareth performs many . . . signs."

"Dead four days! El'azar was *stinking* dead! Widely reported by reputable members of my own sect."

Until now High Priest Caiaphas had maintained a brooding silence.

His graying beard sunk on his chest, almost but not quite obscuring his triple chins. His sausagelike fingers were interlaced and resting on his belly. Caiaphas allowed the furor to spend itself. He was of the Sadducee sect, but before any other consideration, he was a politician.

When Caiaphas spoke it was with a harsh, nasal tone, laden with condescension. Since the high priest had numerous positions of wealth and privilege to dispense, the hall quieted immediately. "Your quarreling accomplishes nothing. We have already looked into the claims of this man. Some choose to believe. But belief or not is no longer important."

"How can you say such a thing? If we let him go on like this, everyone will believe in him! Then the Romans will come and take away both our place . . . and . . . our nation!"

Renewed murmuring swept the chamber, but it was much subdued. Every man present enjoyed wealth and prestige—much of it connected with Temple worship. The Sadducees, like Caiaphas, profited directly.

Imperial Rome appointed the high priests. So long as the emperor received his cut of the profits and the province remained peaceful and profitable, Governor Pilate had no reason to upset the status quo.

But if all the *am ha aretz* truly welcomed Yeshua as Messiah, two dreadful things would happen: The common folk would stop paying exorbitant fees for sin offerings and fellowship offerings and cease buying overpriced lambs for sacrifice. Perhaps Yeshua would lead them all to worship somewhere else completely.

Many in the room recalled the time a couple of years earlier when a then little-known Yeshua had stormed around the Temple Mount stalls, overturning tables of money changers and disrupting commerce.

No, Yeshua of Nazareth could not be counted on to keep the money flowing into the coffers of the priests and the Temple officials. If all the peasants ran after Yeshua, Imperial Rome might choose to deal with Him, rather than with the council at all.

This worry was clearly uppermost in the minds of many.

That the Romans would take away the Jewish nation was added as a patriotic afterthought.

If Yeshua led an uprising against Rome—as most believed Messiah would do to free His people—not one on the council believed such a rebellion would succeed.

It would be a bloodbath, followed by mass executions and deportations into slavery.

And it would be bad for business for a long time to come.

"Then what are we to do?"

At last Caiaphas stood. Unfolding his hands, he touched the tip of a forefinger to his nose. "You know nothing," he said in his most pompous, professorial manner. "None of you. Nothing at all. Don't you understand that it's better for you that one man should die for the people rather than the whole nation perish?"

Behind the dais Bera ben Dives nodded approval.

Silence reigned in the council chambers. There was no doubt in anyone's mind what the high priest was implying: Assassinate Yeshua and the problem would be solved.

"Meanwhile, you will do nothing!" Caiaphas thundered. "Except to see that what is spoken in this room remains in this room. Do you understand? If any of you carry tales from here, I will hear of it . . . and I will address such treason accordingly."

Nakdimon ben Gurion, one of the Pharisees on the council who looked at Yeshua and saw the true Messiah, stood in his accustomed place for the afternoon sacrifice. The elevated walkway beside Nicanor Gate was an ideal location for worship. From it Nakdimon could both observe the ritual within the Court of the Priests to the west and hear the Levite choir assembled just east of the great gate.

The silver trumpets blew and the drink offering was poured out. Nakdimon shivered with anticipation, even though he knew from years of experience what was coming next.

At a clash of cymbals the choir began to sing. As it was the first day of the week, the psalm for the occasion was David's composition number twenty-four. The tenors lifted the solemnity. A bass rumbling underscored the majesty. A lyric treble from the sons of the Levites conveyed a message of the sweetest grace in the first phrase:

> *"The earth is the Lord's and the fullness of it,*
> *the world and they who dwell in it.*
> *For He has founded it upon the seas*
> *and established it upon the currents and the rivers."*[1]

The hair on the back of Nakdimon's neck prickled as it always did for that hymn. What a great privilege was his! To be a worshipper of The One, the Almighty God, in His Holy City, before the Temple of His Name!

"Who shall go up into the mountain of the Lord?
Or who shall stand in His Holy Place?" [2]

Who indeed? Nakdimon reflected. When the high priesthood was bought and sold; when the House of Annas was mocked in street songs for the wealth they had accumulated because of it; when so many family members, including Lord Caiaphas, occupied the office in their turns . . . who indeed?

A latecomer slipped through the throng of local citizens and visiting pilgrims to take a place beside Nakdimon. When the Pharisee glanced at the man's face, he thought perhaps it was someone he knew. He also thought he saw a frown imprinted there, but the neighbor ducked his head and turned away.

The choir, having posed the question, now prepared to answer it:

"He who has clean hands and a pure heart,
who has not lifted himself up to falsehood
nor sworn deceitfully.
He shall receive blessing from the Lord
and righteousness from the God of his salvation." [3]

Nakdimon bit his lip and gnawed his beard. All men stood in need of repentance and forgiveness, but Lord Caiaphas was a habitual plotter and schemer. Nakdimon wondered if the loathing he felt for the high priest was evident in his expression. It must be; the man beside him was regarding him oddly.

He looked familiar, but Nakdimon still could not place him. The fellow's dress was modest. He wore no jewelry and had no distinguishing marks, except the pierced ear of a freedman.

"This is the generation of those who seek Him,
who seek Your face, O God of Jacob." [4]

Nakdimon remembered how he had gone to Yeshua's camp by night. *I am part of the generation seeking the God of Jacob*, he reflected. *Many of the people seek him. Why not the council?*

This was the concluding phrase of the first section of the hymn. As the last of the notes drifted out over the city, the silver trumpets blasted the remnants into thoughtful silence, and all the onlookers prostrated themselves on the stones.

Enough of despising Caiaphas and the Sanhedrin; it was time for Nakdimon to examine his own heart.

"*Pssst!*" hissed the man next to him. "Lord Nakdimon, please listen carefully."

Could this be a trap? Was this man a spy or an informer? Nakdimon grunted to show he had heard.

"I am Gerar," the man continued, muttering so low that Nakdimon strained to hear. "Servant to Joseph of Arimathea. He sends me to you with a message."

Nakdimon stared at the man's features. Even pressed flat against the stone he was recognizable. Nakdimon had met Gerar at his brother Pharisee's home.

At another call of the trumpets the congregation stood again. Once more the cymbals announced the choir.

"Lift up your heads, O you gates,
and be lifted up, you everlasting doors!
That the King of Glory may come in!" [5]

Gerar continued speaking, his mouth now just behind Nakdimon's right shoulder. "My master says ben Dives kept you from the council meeting, at the order of Lord Caiaphas, because they are plotting to kill Yeshua of Nazareth."

"Why didn't Joseph come himself?" Nakdimon growled suspiciously.

"Though he was not kept from the meeting, Lord Caiaphas is having him watched. He could not write to you, for the same reason, so he sent me."

"Who is the King of Glory?
The Lord strong and mighty.
The Lord, mighty in battle." [6]

A battle was indeed coming, then. The high priest of Israel planned to murder the one who Nakdimon, and many others, believed was the Messiah! "So I'm to warn him? send him to safety?"

"Not just Yeshua," Gerar stressed. "They plan to kill El'azar too. A man brought back to life! They fear this power, this fame, Lord Nakdimon. And fear makes them willing to do murder . . . *many* murders."

"I'll see to it tonight."

"Who is this King of Glory?
The Lord of Hosts!
He is the King of Glory!"[7]

The clarion voice of trumpets ordered the onlookers to prostrate themselves again to ponder the conclusion of the psalm.

When Nakdimon lifted his eyes, Gerar was gone.

The furtive tap at the door came just after midnight. Miryam, a follower of Yeshua, blew out the flame of the oil lamp and cautioned her sister, Marta, to keep still. Soldiers would batter down the door without knocking, but whoever was calling at the Bethany estate had crept over the wall and not arrived by the front gate. It was best to be cautious.

"Who . . . who's there?" Miryam called.

"Nakdimon ben Gurion" was the reply. "I'm alone. Miryam? Please open at once. It's important."

Sliding back the bolt that secured the beam across the portal, Miraym allowed the oak door to swing inward. "Come in, Nakdimon. Welcome! It must be important for you to arrive like this."

Once the door was securely fastened again, Miryam relit the lamp. Marta stood in a corner of the room, her eyes wide. In another corner Miryam's aged servant, Tavita, lowered the axe handle she carried.

"You look like you're already expecting unfriendly visitors," Nakdimon noted grimly. "Anyway, I came with a warning: Yeshua, El'azar, all of you must leave at once—tonight! Lord Caiaphas has promised the Sanhedrin he will deal with the 'problem' of Yeshua . . . and that can only mean murder."

Miryam's hand flew to her mouth. She knew from Nakdimon's tone that he was deadly serious.

Tavita brandished the axe handle. "Over me first!" she announced.

Marta appeared shocked. "But everyone is praising Yeshua, Nakdimon! Our brother, given back to us from the grave? Everyone says Yeshua is the Messiah. They're ready to crown him!"

"Not everyone," Nakdimon corrected. "The high priest and his party think if Yeshua is proclaimed, they will lose their position. You know what that means."

Miryam nodded her understanding. For once she was the more practical of the two sisters. "Yes, of course. Not just Yeshua. They'll try to destroy any evidence of his power. Yeshua and our brother must leave at once. Peniel too."

"All of you," Nakdimon added. The Pharisee took Miryam by the shoulders, then made eye contact with each of the other women in turn. "Don't you get it? If they must, they'll hold you as hostages to force El'azar and Yeshua to return. None of you are safe. Now . . . where's Yeshua? There's no time to waste."

"In the vintner's cottage where El'azar . . . where he died." Miryam shuddered at the memory. How could it be that someone would deliberately try to take her brother's life, so recently restored? "They've been there, talking, ever since Marcus came at sunset."

"The centurion? He's here?"

"Came with the same message as you."

When footsteps approached the cottage, Marcus Longinus instinctively stood and laid a hand on the hilt of his sword. The door creaked open and the centurion relaxed when Miryam entered. Then he stiffened again at the sight of Nakdimon.

The two men were rivals for Miryam, though neither challenged the other openly, and Miryam gave neither Jew nor Roman any encouragement.

El'azar stood to greet Nakdimon, grasping the Pharisee's forearms warmly. He instructed the new arrivals to keep quiet. "The Master is sleeping behind the curtain. His talmidim are camped in the orchard."

"Not me," Peniel corrected, stirring amid the blanket in which he was wrapped beside the curtained alcove.

"It's true," El'azar offered with a smile. "Despite the presence of a Roman officer and an elder of Israel, Peniel will not be denied the role of watchdog to the Master's rest." Then El'azar's features creased with concern as he addressed Nakdimon: "But tell me, old friend . . . you did not come at midnight for a social call. Perhaps your visit is the same as Marcus'?"

Gruffly Marcus said, "It's not safe for Yeshua to be in Judea. He should go over Jordan or, better still, to Egypt."

"It's worse than that," Nakdimon said and proceeded to explain the danger to the whole Bethany family.

"And me too?" Peniel concluded, scratching his thin beard. "What kind of priests are these that would murder the Son of God and his friends?"

"They are the false shepherds written of by the prophet Ezekiel and described by Yeshua in the same way," El'azar said. "The Almighty will smite them now that the Good Shepherd has come. I am not afraid."

"But the false shepherds may still slaughter many innocent sheep first," Nakdimon warned. "Yeshua has friends on the council—myself and a handful of others openly, and still more who admire him secretly. But we need more time. And we need safety for those we love."

Marcus saw the glance Nakdimon gave Miryam and witnessed the reddish tinge to the Pharisee's ears.

"Marcus," Miryam pleaded, "can't you do something?"

Marcus felt a mix of pleasure that she asked for his aid and chagrin that his hands were tied. "Pilate wants to prevent any more trouble. If he can accomplish that without bloodshed, he will . . . but he will turn his back on murder if it suits him. He'll not risk another complaint to Caesar. No, Nakdimon is exactly right. All of you must leave by morning."

"Yeshua will never go to Egypt," Peniel added. "But he has said he wants to preach in the hill country."

"Then it's settled," Marcus concluded with a Roman officer's certainty. "North into as obscure a region as he'll agree to. And all of you must stay well away from Jerusalem until either Nakdimon or I send word that it's safe to return."

The wind whistled in the branches of the fig orchard and ruffled the folds of Bera ben Dives' cloak. The ground was damp underneath him. The sky, clear all day, had clouded over since sunset, and now the night was shrouded in inky darkness.

Ben Dives fingered the dagger in the leather sheath at his belt. When he imagined taking his elder brother's place as personal secretary to the high priest he had accepted that he would do whatever Caiaphas demanded. He had not anticipated murder as one of his primary duties, but it was achievable if a man's aspirations reached far enough.

As High Priest Caiaphas joined forces with Herod Antipas to eliminate Yeshua, so Bera ben Dives now associated with a pair of Antipas' minions. An accomplished team of assassins: Shamen was a strangler; Ona, Shamen's wife, a poisoner.

Ben Dives had shuddered when he met them but once again set aside his scruples in the name of ambition. Besides, how wrong could it be if the religious shepherd, Caiaphas, and Herod Antipas, the son of the royal house, both approved this action? This night's work should certainly fix him firmly in the high priest's favor.

The appearance of El'azar's Bethany estate, seen from the knoll behind it, confirmed the marauders had come in time. A single light flickered in the main house and dimly in one of the outbuildings as well. The chimney in El'azar's home revealed a bellyful of stove wood by occasionally belching sparks.

If the meddling Pharisee Nakdimon had arrived with his warning, they had not taken him seriously.

Ben Dives drew the knife halfway out of its scabbard and thumbed the edge of the blade.

Shamen had told him his job was to take care of the beggar-boy, Peniel, the son of a potter. Peniel was the least important target and probably the weakest. Perfect for an amateur like ben Dives.

The Sadducee had not argued.

Something wriggled in the grass behind him. A snake?

Straining his eyes in the gloom, ben Dives stared at a bush. He was certain it had not been there before. Ben Dives jumped when the shrub spoke to him.

"House and orchard all quiet."

It was Ona. "Shamen has found a way in, through a hole in the back wall. Everything is still—no sign of alarm. They must all be sleeping."

Ona had no knife or garrote in her hands. "How can you depend on poison to work so quickly?" ben Dives asked, one killer to another.

Flexing her fingers, Ona replied, "A thumb on each side of the windpipe. Easy, if you've had practice."

Ben Dives could think of no reply to that. The whistle of a night bird floated down on the breeze. It came again a moment later.

"That's the signal," Ona said. "Let's go."

When they approached Shamen, he whispered that no guards patrolled the grounds.

No one shouted at them as the three killers slipped through the fence. No one challenged them when Shamen lifted the weight of a rear door on its pole hinge to keep it from squeaking.

It swung open soundlessly, and Ona led the silent charge into the main house.

It was empty, as were the outbuildings. Their quarry had fled, leaving behind no sign of their destination.

Bera ben Dives, like the two assassins, was left with no course except to return to his master and report failure.

The red-tailed hawk circled slowly over the sukomore grove, searching the ground for signs of rodents. High in a tree harvesting ripe figs, Shimona was startled at first when the hawk wheeled past at eye level. She gasped at the nearness of his course, then simply watched him as he soared away above her.

She smiled up as his shadow touched her hand. He was hunting, seeking his supper in the dry grass on the orchard floor.

Where had he come from? Had he come to drive away the horde of mice that tormented her and threatened to destroy her work?

"O Lord, I asked for a cat, and you sent a hawk to fight my Philistines."

The hawk hovered on the wind, tucked his wings, and dove almost straight down. Landing at the base of her tree with a cry, he caught a mouse in his talons. Then, as though he carried a heavenly message for Shimona, he leapt up to a branch near her. Perching there long enough for her to see the limp rodent in his talons, the hawk looked directly at her with his piercing gold eyes.

"Well done. I didn't see that mouse," Shimona addressed the hawk.

The noble creature ruffled his feathers, seeming to bow his head in acknowledgment, then ascended with his prey.

Hawks were familiar to Shimona. Years ago in the Valley of Mak'ob, Lily's husband, Cantor, had trained a red-winged hawk to hunt pigeons and bring them back to him for supper. The relationship between that enormous bird and the man had seemed a sort of miracle to Shimona when she watched them work together.

Today the whoosh of the raptor's wings was an angel's voice speaking to Shimona's heart: *God cares for you. Though your earthly father did not heed your request for a cat, your heavenly Father knows all your needs. He loves you enough that He has sent His friend to drive away your enemies. . . . The mice in the sukomore grove will not remain to torment you or steal from you. The Lord Himself covers you and your work with the protection of His wings.*

The hawk did not fly away from the grove. He landed on the highest branch of the tallest sukomore. Bobbing on the fragile limb, he devoured his prey in full view of Shimona.

So it will be even with small worries, Shimona thought. *O Lord, who answers my prayers in ways more perfect than I know to pray . . . I thank you for sending this ally, who has come to help me. I never thought to ask you for a hawk.*

Then she addressed the bird. "So, Hawk, it's plain to see you are a friend of the Almighty. The Lord has told you to come here to hunt. I know that. Thank you for listening to his voice. I suppose that men are the only creatures in creation who do not listen to him." She sighed. "So, I need help, but it won't come from man. There's lots of game here in the sukomore grove for you. Stay with me, Hawk," Shimona whispered. "I will harvest the figs, and you will harvest the mice. We will praise the Lord together for his bounty, you and I."

Zachai of Jericho wasted no sympathy on the financial woes of Azarel of Emmaus.

Torvald was a Germanic tribesman and a slave, but the gentle, blond giant had belonged to Azarel the Olive Grower for so long—twenty years and more—that he was like one of the family. When a sandstorm disrupted a caravan en route to Damascus, the slave did not try to escape, concentrating instead on locating his master's missing camels. More than once Torvald had rescued Azarel from bandits. When the family lived at Joppa, on the seacoast, Torvald saved Azarel's only child, Ida, from drowning.

That had been a decade ago, and seven-year-old Ida was now a beauty of seventeen. She was to be wed to the son of the rabbi of Emmaus, near where her father's orchards glistened silver in the sun.

"What would you like for a wedding gift, Daughter?" Azarel inquired six months before the wedding.

Without hesitation Ida presented the reply she had long pondered in the hope the question would be asked. "I would like you to give Torvald his freedom," she said, while the slave listened impassively in a corner of the room.

Azarel blinked rapidly in thought. "I intended to give him to you," he suggested. "He's very valuable, you know."

"More valuable than money!" Ida exclaimed. "Set him free, please, Father! Then if he wants to serve me and my husband, it will be his choice."

Azarel turned to Torvald. "You hear? What do you say?"

"Yah, I hear," Torvald rumbled. "I say, what Lady Ida wants, I do. I put my head against the post; I take the pierced ear; I wear the earring of the freedman, if she wishes, but I serve her either way."

"It's what I want," Ida confirmed. "Papa would never sell you anyway, Torvald, but this makes it official."

That conversation had been five and a half months earlier.

A lot can change in five months.

Azarel had concluded a contract for his entire olive oil crop with an Alexandrian importer. It was an enormous sale . . . Azarel's greatest ever. He watched with pride as the holds of three coasting galleys were loaded with amphorae bearing the clay seal of the House of Azarel.

That night a great wind blew off the desert and carried the galleys far out to sea, away from land.

Two weeks later he got the news that all of his ships, all of his crop, all of the year's income had been lost.

A week after that a message appeared from the chief publican of the Jericho district. It seemed Emperor Tiberius, in an effort to protect the oil dealers of Italy from eastern competition, had instituted a tax on olive groves in Judea. The tax was not large—merely a single bronze coin for each tree—payable immediately.

When Azarel protested that he could not pay until after the next year's crop had been sold, Zachai was adamant.

"That is hardly my concern." The publican sniffed. "What you do and what I do aren't really so different. You farm olives. . . . I farm taxes. You invest in your trees and in pressing the oil with the expectation of a return on your investment. I have to pay what is owed to Rome now. I confidently expect to reap a proper harvest by pressing the . . ." He cleared his throat. "You cannot expect me to take a loss because you have suffered ill fortune."

"What's to be done?" Azarel inquired.

Zachai appeared to relish the question. "For advancing taxes on your behalf I might accept two years' profit of your grove."

"I'd be out of business! What else?"

Zachai's nose twitched as he scanned the room. He seemed unimpressed with the furnishings. His eyes lit on Ida. "You could indenture your daughter. Five years' servitude should cover what's owed."

"Never!"

Zachai backed up a pace as both Azarel and Torvald bristled at the image of Ida scrubbing floors for the likes of him.

"Have you nothing of value you can sell?"

Azarel's gaze locked with Torvald's; of the two men, Azarel was first to turn away.

Azarel sent Ida off to her aunt's in Arimathea the day Zachai came to collect Torvald. Her father did not want her to see her rescuer, her friend, marched off in chains.

Peniel had mixed emotions when Yeshua asked him to remain behind the rest of the group to buy supplies in Jericho. Even before being accepted as one of the talmidim, Peniel had hated being separated from Yeshua for even a short time. But because of the haste with which they departed from El'azar's estate in Bethany, there had been no time to get all the provisions needed. Peniel was proud the Teacher thought him dependable enough to carry out such a task.

"We will see you again, over Jordan, in just one extra day," Yeshua said. "Thank you for doing this for me."

Who would not feel an increase in self-worth to have the Master appoint him for a special task?

Though Peniel was also in some danger, it was thought that apart from Yeshua's entourage he would escape notice. In any case, the feisty Zadok, formerly chief shepherd of Beth-lehem, was detailed to travel with him and keep him out of trouble.

"Strong back and strong legs needed for this job," Zadok explained as they trudged down the hill separating the two Jerichos. "Naught else, eh?"

The rest of Yeshua's band had journeyed by a shorter, more direct route to the northeast. In order to catch up, Peniel and the old shepherd would have to maintain a persistent, rapid motion. Zadok's long strides ate up the miles. Peniel had to trot to keep pace, but youth and eagerness supplied the energy.

Zadok's three adopted sons and his stock dog dashed down the hill in advance of their father and Peniel.

A few yards farther along, Peniel heard Bartimaeus before he saw him. The blind beggar was at his usual spot, screeching for alms. "As I am doubly to be pitied . . . a beggar with no family, and blind besides . . . so a double blessing comes to those who give!"

Zadok and Peniel stopped beside him. His cloak lay spread out before him. A small circlet of copper coins formed a gleaming hoop against the dark cloth.

"I hear you, sirs," Bartimaeus exclaimed. "Two of you. One walks with the step of an older, heavyset man. The other is a youth, barely bearded, I wager."

"Are y' a fortune-teller too?" Zadok challenged. "Can y' tell how many eyes I have, then?"

"A soldier, wounded in the wars?" Bartimaeus cajoled.

"Y' might say so," Zadok agreed. "Though I still have one good eye."

"Brave hearts always give generously, don't you find?" the beggar flattered.

Peniel rummaged in the leather sack of money and produced two pennies. They made a pitifully light-sounding clink on the cloak.

Bartimaeus looked reproachful.

"More is not ours t' give," Zadok explained. "What we have is in trust only, t' buy supplies. And we live on charity ourselves."

"You are wandering beggars, then?"

Peniel brightened as a thought struck him. "No. We are followers of Yeshua of Nazareth. Let us take you to him. It's better than money. He can heal you."

"From Nazareth?" Bartimaeus repeated scornfully. "In the Galil? Ha! Who's he, anyway?"

"He is Messiah," Zadok replied stoutly. "Son of David."

"Son of David!" Bartimaeus mocked. "Another messiah to run after into the desert. I've heard people speak of him. I've also heard—" he lowered his voice—"Herod Antipas wants him dead." Then, louder again, "No, thank you! Better a live beggar, even blind, than a dead fool."

Zadok bristled at the affront, but Peniel still spoke kindly. "You do not know me, but I'm Peniel. I used to be the blind beggar of Nicanor Gate. Yeshua healed me . . . me! Blind from birth. He'll do the same for you. Leave your begging cloak and come with us."

"Leave my cloak?" Bartimaeus said incredulously. "Give up my livelihood to chase moonbeams? Thank you for your pennies, but you may keep your advice. And if you'll take some counsel from me, your best chance of keeping your throats uncut is to keep away from the Nazarene. He's trouble."

Peniel was dejected as he and Zadok trudged away from the beggar and entered Old Jericho. "I can't understand why he wants to stay blind," he lamented.

"There's many has the use of both eyes who are eager t' stay blind in other ways," Zadok reminded, "or so the Master says. Y' cannot force someone t' want what's best for them, eh?"

"Why don't you have Yeshua restore your missing eye, Zadok?" Peniel asked. "You know he can and would."

Zadok replied with a smile, "Aye! He offered it t' me. I told him I made out fine with one, and any roads, as y' know, the other was lost in the defense of my babies. My badge of honor, eh? But I'll tell y' this, lad: If I ever find anything keeps me from following Yeshua, I'll cast it off at once. Two eyes, one, or none a'tall. Makes no difference. If ever some bit of me hinders me from staying close to the Master . . . off it goes! Mark this: Yeshua'll never make y' give up anything y' need, nor leave y' long without filling that need. But a whole lot of folks wander about carrying loads of unneeded things that hold 'em back on their journey."

Peniel pondered that wisdom for a long time on the road.

Using a handcart, Shimona hauled the harvest of dried cakes of figs out to the boundary of the grove. She placed the baskets beside the warning sign facing the highway that kept the curious or the foolhardy from entering.

The placards were written in Hebrew, Greek, and Aramaic:

DEFILED BY LEPROSY!
ENTER NOT THIS GROVE!

Shimona did not regret the stern and horrifying message that marked the boundaries of her life. Terror infused all who read the sign, keeping her safe from thieves, vagrants, and Romans.

Concealed within the thick foliage of the fig trees, she sat down in the shade to await her father's servant, who came once a week to take away the fig crop and leave behind supplies and news of the outside world for her. He was very late today.

Travelers' voices fell to whispers as they approached the grove.

"She may be still tsara, *so they say. Her name was Shimona. A widow. Her husband died a leper. She was the eldest daughter of the Chazzan before . . ."*

"She was healed by Yeshua of Nazareth, they say. But who knows? She came home and they put her away until it is proven she is not unclean."

"What was her sin?"

"Who can say? Perhaps she was too proud. You know, the daughter of the Chazzan. Proud."

"I heard she was very beautiful."

"Who remembers? Leprosy."

"Will they ever let her come out and live among the people?"

"Who knows? Better safe than sorry, I always say. It's not such a bad life for her. A place to live until she dies. Food to eat. Her father, the Chazzan, has done well enough by her in spite of her disgrace."

The passersby trudged beyond the sukomore trees on the far side of the road. Shimona smiled as they retreated in haste. It was something like being dead and hearing what was said at your own funeral.

Hours came and went with no sign of her father's servant. The sun climbed high. Green pools of light formed like dew on the leaves of the tree.

Shimona stretched out her hands. Ten fingers. What a gift. There had been only six fingers remaining before Yeshua had come to Mak'ob. She clenched and unclenched her fists, marveling at the way her body worked.

"God who always hears my prayers, I thank you for my home. I thank you that you know the truth about Yeshua and what he did for me. You know the truth about me, though no one else on earth may ever know. God who hears my prayers and knows my heart, thank you for loving me enough to give me this place as my own."

Birds twittered above her. The mice, little Philistines, stirred in the dry grass.

The afternoon began to cool with the approach of evening, and still the servant did not appear. Had she mistaken the day? Shimona fell asleep with her back against the tree trunk.

The sun had moved from east to west when the scent of decay and death on the breeze awakened her. It was a familiar aroma.

"Lepers!" she whispered, rising quickly to her feet. Through the tree trunks she saw that her father's servant had come and gone while she had been asleep. The basket of provisions for the next week was left in place of the figs.

The smell of diseased flesh came closer. She covered her nose and mouth and hurried toward the road. As she emerged from the suko-more grove, she saw ten lepers clinging to one another as they limped forward.[8]

"Unclean!" rasped a man at the sight of her.

Shimona recognized the desperate beggar. It was Carpenter, leader of the ten lepers who had left the Valley of Mak'ob in search of Yeshua so long ago! With him was the Samaritan Fisherman, the Crusher, the two Cabbage Sisters, the four young Torah scholars from the camp of boys, and one more Shimona did not recognize. Clearly their search for Yeshua the Healer had been in vain.

Shimona cried out as she ran to them, "Carpenter! Crusher! Look—

all of you! It's me, Shimona. Daughter of the Chazzan." She embraced the two Cabbage Sisters, who tried to fend her off.

"Please! We're *tsara*. Unclean. Defiled. Woman, don't touch us!"

Laughing and crying at the same time, Shimona showed them her unmarred hands. "But I was one of you. In the Valley. Yeshua came! He came to us one evening and—"

Carpenter, his noseless features hidden behind a strip of fabric, said, "It is Shimona. I know the voice. But why are you here? And you're restored but . . . what is that sign posted there?"

"The people are afraid their eyes are bewitched. They can't accept that I've been healed. So I'm here. Until, well, I don't know how long. But they want to be certain."

Fisherman muttered, "We've been looking for the Healer. But every time we hear he's one place and go there, he's gone to another place. He was in Bethany. Raised a dead man to life, they say. But then the high priest got wind of it and put a price on his head. They want to kill Yeshua and the man he raised as well."

Shimona's words spilled out in a rush. "Kill him? Kill? Oh, Carpenter, you must find Yeshua. He is life to us!"

Crusher shook his head slowly. "We are afraid they will kill him before we find him. What then?"

The Cabbage Sisters cried, "Our only hope!"

Shimona sighed. "Friends! Yeshua healed everyone in the Valley. Everyone. It's not a fable. Everyone who came near . . . he healed them all. He laid hands on us and healed us and sent us out of the Valley and to our homes. But my family was afraid. My mother wouldn't touch me. The rabbi and the priest and my father . . . they don't believe what they see, even though their eyes tell them I have no spot or sign of sickness. They are afraid it is witchcraft. So I have been here in isolation according to the law of Mosheh for all these months."

"Alone?" asked the Cabbage Sisters in unison.

"It's not so bad. My father rents the grove from Zachai the Publican for a share of the harvest. I have a cottage. I tend the sukomore trees. I wound the figs and harvest them and dry them." She pointed to the basket of provisions left for her. "Once a week my father's servant comes. He takes the figs and leaves me food and such. And the servant brings me news. Only today I missed him. I didn't hear any news from the world. Didn't hear what happened in Bethany. Raising the dead.

Oh, such news! Every day I pray, 'When is Yeshua going to set up his Kingdom?'"

Crusher raised fingerless hands to the heavens. "Omaine to that. Omaine! Oh, that Yeshua would come to Yerushalayim soon! The oppression of Herod and the Romans grows worse every day. Taxes. There's nothing left over to share with a beggar."

Fisherman agreed. "The people are desperate. Hopeless but hoping Messiah will restore the throne of David. So many believe Yeshua will overthrow the Romans. At least they are hoping. Hoping he'll call down fire . . . you know. Like Elijah."

Shimona said, "Please. Come stay with me. Stay here. You'll be safe here."

Carpenter answered, "We must go on. We have heard that Yeshua is hiding from the authorities over the Jordan. The place where Yochanan the Baptizer used to preach. We're going there to find him. Shimona—come with us!"

"I can't. I made a promise to my father. To the rabbi and the priest. I made a vow that I would stay here and work, that I would not cross the boundary and leave the grove. I'm happy. Really." Shimona opened the basket, which contained heaping loaves of bread. "I don't have money, but take what I have. Here. There's plenty to get me through the month. Take it, my dear friends, and go quickly. Cross the Jordan. Find the Lord and you will find life!"

Shimona remained fixed behind the boundary of her vow. She moaned inwardly as her friends left her. Was it a contradiction, she wondered, to say that her heart was filled with emptiness at their going?

The ten topped the rise of the road. Shimona, hungry for one last look, scrambled up the tallest sukomore tree. Clinging to the branches, she stared after them until their individual identities were indistinguishable in the distance. Her beloved friends, linked together by the common bond of suffering and longing, seemed no longer to be ten lepers, but one dark unity, moving forward, searching for Yeshua the Savior. Thus they remained in her vision, framed against the slope of a hill until it was too dark to see them anymore.

"O God who hears our prayers and knows our suffering, my heart travels with them. Though they seem to be only one, you know them each as individuals. You love us one at a time and all together as we search for your Son."

Shimona carefully climbed down from the tree. She groped her way through the darkness to her little house. "O God who sees their suffering, you see that I am also alone and forgotten. Send angels to this sukomore grove. Keep me company in my long, unending night."

6

The rice caravan lay at Bethabara, a handful of miles southeast of Jericho. Fording the Jordan had been accomplished easily, but getting all the barley-laden sacks across without them getting wet and ruined was a time-consuming process. The river was always high at this season, and this wet-wintered year it was especially so. Because so much of the early spring daylight had been used up in the crossing, it was nearing nightfall. Rabshak ben Shebna, the chief merchant, gave orders that the caravan would spend the night where it was. Tomorrow would be soon enough to pass through Jericho and reach Jerusalem.

It was in his tent, as Rabshak was eating lamb and rice and drinking a cup of wine, that Haman, Zachai's steward, found him.

"Shalom, noble ben Shebna," Haman greeted the wealthy trader. "My master, Zachai of Jericho, sends you greetings."

"Don't waste your breath carrying compliments from that worm," ben Shebna said dismissively, his hands clasped across his broad belly. "In fact, tell him exactly that if Jericho is the apple of the trade route, then Zachai the Publican is the worm in the apple."

Haman bowed his face to the ground. "Surely you do not wish—"

"Don't tell me what I wish or don't!" ben Shebna roared, upsetting his plate of rice and knocking over his wine. Two servants rushed in from opposite sides to clean up the mess and sponge their master's clothes.

Haman seized the interruption to hurriedly present his case one more time. In one breath, without a pause, he recited, "Lord Zachai wishes you well. He wants to invite you to dine with him. He recalls that you and he were born in the same village and are kin on his mother's side."

The words exploding from his lips, ben Shebna retorted, "Zachai the worm was never born; he was spawned." The merchant brushed his attendants aside with impatient waves of both hands. "Dinner? You may tell your master, the taste of whose name spoils my food, that I'd sooner eat from the same dish as a leper than sup with him! He is a traitor *and* a thief. I thank the Almighty I deal in rice, where the duty is set by Roman law. He'll get just that many drachmae from me, and not a mite more. Now go away and tell him so!"

Bowing low and sweeping his hand across his chest, Haman backed out the entry. "My master, while disappointed to be correct, has already anticipated what you would say. Rest well, Lord Rabshak."

Using his fingers to claw fragments of rice out of his beard, ben Shebna never saw the enigmatic smile on Haman's face.

The same expression of happiness was on Haman's face several hours later, when in the dead of night he crept round the caravansary. Since it was so close to the garrison at Jericho and had nothing more valuable than rice, no one was on guard, except one drowsy sentry, who saw nothing.

In a matter of moments Haman made his six deposits in a half dozen sacks of rice chosen at random but marked afterward with a bit of frayed string at the mouth. This night's work was certain to bring him Zachai's approval and, more importantly to Haman's thinking, a large monetary bonus.

The man who appeared on the fringes of the crowd there, just beyond the group of Miryam, Marta, and El'azar, had been listening to Yeshua for about a week. Because the fellow hung back when everyone else pushed forward to be closer, Peniel suspected the man of being a spy . . . or worse.

When he pointed this out to Levi Mattityahu, the former tax collector shook his head. "I've also seen him, but he's not a spy. His name is Juniah of Joppa; he's on the city council there."

Peniel studied the fellow. He was young—midtwenties, perhaps. His clothes were expensive in appearance. A best-quality striped woolen robe. The tunic was a much finer, softer weave than the rough, homespun cloth worn by the *am ha aretz*.

Yet the man did not have the appearance of either a Pharisee or a Sadducee. Juniah was not argumentative like the former, not sneeringly condescending like the latter. He listened attentively, nodding as Yeshua emphasized certain key points. Occasionally the man grasped his chin, with one hand over his mouth, almost as if to prevent himself from speaking.

"What is he, then?" Peniel inquired.

"Rich, interested, and shy," Levi replied. "Juniah's heard so much about Yeshua befriending and championing the poor that he's afraid he's not welcome here."

"Why should someone feel that way, just because he's rich?"

With that observation, and remembering how Yeshua praised him for bringing other friends to meet Him, Peniel made his way through the crowd to pluck the young man by the elbow. "Would you like to meet the Master?" he asked. "You look as if you have a question."

Seeming to finally make up his mind in regard to the matter after much internal debate, Juniah nodded vigorously. "Can I? Will he see me?"

Peniel led him forward.

There was some grumbling in the crowd at "rich folks seeking special favors," but most of what Peniel sensed was not resentment but envy.

Yeshua smiled at Peniel as the pair approached, but the Galilean waited for Juniah to speak first.

He finally did so, but only after much throat-clearing and a prod from behind by Peniel. "Good Teacher," Juniah began, "what must I do to inherit eternal life?"

Yeshua's response was not in answer to the question. Instead, He said, "Why do you call me good? No one is good, except God alone."

Juniah, appearing surprised at having his compliment rebuffed, did not reply.

The newcomer might be confused, but Peniel thought he

understood: Juniah was asking a question about eternal life—a question only God could answer. Was the man willing to accept an answer from Yeshua as coming directly from God, or was he just collecting religious opinions?

When there was no response, Yeshua continued, "You know the commandments: Do not commit adultery. Do not murder. Do not steal. Do not bear false witness. Honor your father and mother. Love your neighbor as you do yourself."

Was there a reason Yeshua listed the commandments out of order? Had there been a special stress laid on the next-to-last named commandment? How did it happen that this man, still very young, was already so wealthy?

Could it be that Yeshua was looking into his heart? Peniel watched the young man's expression for any guilt.

The reply was simple—straightforward: "All these I have kept from my youth."

It was then Peniel also got a glimpse into the man's heart. Juniah was blessed by God with great wealth. He acknowledged that his possessions were from God, and he did this by carefully keeping the commandments. It was a bargain. The questioner expected God to keep up His end of the contract too.

But was Juniah ready to keep the commandments Yeshua often cited as the most important: to love God with all his heart, soul, mind, and strength, and his neighbor as himself?[9]

Only this time, after hearing the glib way in which the man had already responded, Yeshua phrased His restatement of the highest law in a different way: "One thing you still lack."

Juniah jerked and backed up a pace, as if he'd been stung. His expression clearly stated, *What else could I possibly need to do?*

"Sell all you have and distribute it to the poor, and then you'll have treasure in heaven; and come, follow me."

The man appeared crushed. *Sell everything?* his features and slumping shoulders demanded.

Perhaps he had anticipated being told, *"Don't worry about eternal life. You've already got the mark of God's favor on you. Just keep doing what you're doing."*

Instead, Yeshua's requirement shattered Juniah's expectations and his own cherished image of the future.

The young man's face fell, and Peniel observed how the sorrow in Yeshua's gaze mirrored that in the man's.

Watching Juniah's dejected departure, Yeshua murmured so that only those nearest could hear, "How difficult it is for those who have wealth to enter the kingdom of God. For it is easier for a camel to go through the eye of a needle than for a rich person to enter the kingdom of God."

Peniel saw what Yeshua meant: the higher the heap of possessions the harder to see over it and recognize the need for a personal, daily relationship with God. It was all about being willing to leave excess baggage behind to follow the Master.

Thomas, seated nearby and who clearly did not get it, interjected, "Not the rich? Then who can be saved?"

Yeshua responded, "What is impossible with men is possible with God."[10]

Later, Peniel overheard Thomas discussing the man with Philip. "The Pharisees teach that wealth and possessions are a mark of God's favor," Thomas said softly. "Don't we all think that's at least partly true?"

Philip nodded. "And if, as the Pharisees teach, holiness requires attention to detail—first washings, second washings, tithing of tiny grains of spice—well, doesn't it seem that only rich men have time for such piety?" Peniel saw Philip glance down at his own well-worn clothing. "Where does that leave us, eh?"

Peniel wanted to say that the answer to Philip's question was not a statement or a declaration or even a book of philosophy. The answer was the person kneeling by the creekside in prayer; the answer was Yeshua Himself: *"What is impossible with men is possible with . . . God."*

Zachai noted the derision on ben Shebna's face from all the way across the customs plaza. It was almost as broad as the man's belly, Zachai thought sourly. The publican brightened with the realization that today he would wipe that smirk of superiority off the merchant's face forever.

A small leather pouch dangled from ben Shebna's outstretched fingers. It jingled as he approached. The small bag of coins was evidently what ben Shebna expected to owe in taxes on his load of rice. Zachai wondered for a moment if the man would actually throw the money at him.

The reality was almost as scornful; the tradesman stopped a few paces away and dropped the sack at Zachai's feet. Ben Shebna was announcing to all onlookers that Zachai the Publican was no better than a dirty beggar. One might owe a mitzvah to a beggar, but no one had to touch one or breathe the same air as one . . . or dine with one.

"Fifty denarii," ben Shebna announced calmly. "The same as last time. I checked before I crossed Jordan. No use trying to pretend otherwise, Publican."

The title was spat out with such a curl of ben Shebna's lip that he had to wipe moisture from his beard afterward.

Zachai smiled at him. "I'm sorry you could not join me for dinner."

Ben Shebna narrowed his eyes. "Except never having to see you ever again or hearing your name mentioned in your obituary, nothing could give me greater pleasure than spurning you, scum."

Zachai shrugged. "You've had a profitable trip, then?"

Ben Shebna, betraying a sudden wariness at Zachai's curious responses, touched the money pouch with the toe of his boot. "Count it, if you wish. It's all there."

Shrugging, Zachai motioned for one of his Nubian bodyguards to retrieve the coins. "No need. We are men of honor, you and I."

Ben Shebna did not even bother replying, but his tight-lipped countenance expressed the conviction that the outcast publican was somehow making fun of him. He turned to go.

Zachai let the man get five steps away, then called after him, "There's just one thing more and you'll be on your way. Purely a formality. My men must make a random search of the rice. Others, not so honorable as you, have tried to import expensive contraband concealed within less expensive goods . . . in sacks of barley or . . . rice . . . for example."

Ben Shebna spun back around. "Go ahead," he muttered. "Your authority may let you delay me, but I'll not lose my temper. After all, I'm going home to my family, while you—" he smirked—"must go home with yourself!"

Zachai dispatched his bodyguards to rummage in the rice sacks.

Ben Shebna was startled when the first alabaster jug of Egyptian perfume was discovered buried within a bag of rice. By the third he was belligerent; at the fourth, apoplectic.

He shook his fists at Zachai but dared not approach because of the drawn stabbing spears of the returned guards. "Those bottles aren't mine! I never saw them before! You'll never get away with this!"

"I?" Zachai returned with arched eyebrows. "It's you who are caught smuggling! Rabshak ben Shebna, I hereby charge you with seeking to avoid Imperial customs through fraud and deceit. The penalty is imprisonment in Yerushalayim. I'm certain it won't be long . . . perhaps no more than a month 'til the governor returns from Caesarea to hear your case."

At a slight motion of Zachai's index finger the guards advanced in a circle around the tradesman.

"Wait!" ben Shebna implored suddenly, images of being tossed into the dungeons beneath the prefecture imprinted on his features. "Be reasonable! There must be something!"

"Well," Zachai drawled, "it is at my discretion to remit the imprisonment in exchange for a suitable fine. . . . How much did you say the rice was worth? That . . . and your camels . . . should just about cover it. You may sign a note for the rest, due in, say, thirty days. After all, we are honorable men."

The office of Zachai's steward, Haman, was not in the Customs House but in a separate building near the back wall of Zachai's estate. Zachai had decided long before not to allow Roman officials a casual glance at his personal accounts. For their visits, infrequent as they were, there was a separate set of scrupulously correct and orderly records.

Every morning Zachai stopped in to consult Haman before leaving for his official duties. Passing through his garden, Zachai stooped to pluck a handful of mint leaves from the bed of kitchen herbs. He crushed them between his palms, appreciatively inhaling the sharp, sweet tang. Zachai popped a couple sprigs in his mouth to chew. This particular mint was a new variety, imported from Egypt, with a flavor reminiscent of green apples.

Haman was already at work when Zachai arrived. Scrolls of rents collected, loans outstanding, and foreclosures to be enacted occupied tables on three sides of the room. In the center, seated on a stool at a raised workbench, was the steward. At his master's arrival Haman slid quickly from his seat, bending and bowing as he ushered Zachai in.

A head taller than his diminutive employer, Haman had a trick of stooping his shoulders and tucking his head down to his chest that made him appear shorter. "Welcome, good master. A beautiful day."

Zachai dropped the crushed mint leaves on a window ledge and rubbed his hands briskly. "Anything especially needing my attention?"

"A question for you, my lord," Haman responded. "When Elijah the Vintner sent off the last shipment of wine for the drink offering, was there any . . . issue . . . about paying the duty?"

"Now that you mention it, yes. He griped more than usual about how miserly Lord Caiaphas was and how the duties ate up all the profits."

Haman nodded, bending even lower and squinting at his feet. "This confirms something I've heard. The winemaker is in some financial difficulty."

"Oh?" Zachai responded with barely concealed interest.

"A shipment of wine for Damascus miscarried in the desert. I have heard that Elijah is behind in paying the potters and some of his other suppliers."

"The taxes on his property are due at the first of next month," Zachai mused. "And if the duty on Temple wine were to suddenly increase yet again . . . ?"

Haman nodded vigorously. "Elijah the Vintner would almost certainly have to sell the vineyard . . . and quickly at that."

A broad smile crept across Zachai's face. "Haman, you are invaluable to me. We'll speak more of this tonight. Now I'm off to Yerushalayim."

Haman bobbed obsequiously, tugging at his forelock as he bowed his master out of the office.

After Yeshua was through teaching for the day and the crowds had departed, the band of talmidim rested under an ancient sukomore tree. Perhaps there had once been a farmhouse beside it, but now only abandoned foundations and the lone tree marked the spot. The sukomore stood alone atop a grassy knoll, and the disciples gratefully sprawled in its shade.

Looking up at the trunk, Peniel noted it was covered with figs.

The fruit, untended and unpierced, was not ripe; it was hard as rocks. Peniel reflected how like the tree the wealthy young man seemed. Yeshua had tried to challenge him—to pierce the man's complacency and self-satisfaction—but apparently without result. The fruit of the fellow's life might remain forever useless, like the tree's inedible growth.

The point Yeshua had made about how difficult it was for the wealthy to enter the Kingdom of God was still being discussed among the talmidim. Peniel overheard Philip and Thomas continuing to trade verbal jabs.

The subject was apparently on the minds of others in the band as well, for Shim'on Peter suddenly blurted, "Master, that man you told to leave everything to follow you? Well, we've left everything—homes, professions, families—to follow you. . . . That is, every one of us left something behind when you summoned us."[11]

Glancing at Levi, Peniel understood what Peter was saying. Levi had been a tax collector and a well-to-do man, especially for the Galil. The others, while not coming from wealth, had certainly surrendered possessions, professions, and ambitions to follow Yeshua around the countryside.

Why had they dropped oars or ledgers or shepherds' staffs and put the remainder of their lives on hold? Would Peter ever own a fleet of boats, or Levi have his own counting house?

Why were they here, on a hillside in the middle of nowhere?

For Peniel, the answer was easy: Yeshua had given him his sight. After seeing Yeshua, Peniel wanted to see Him every day for the rest of his life. Besides, what had Peniel given up? A begging bowl by Nicanor Gate and a hovel behind his father's pottery shop. It was a life in which Peniel had managed to find little joys, but how much better now?

But what about the others? Why were they still here?

Had they decided to take a chance that Yeshua was going to be crowned king in Jerusalem? Did they expect He would reward His closest followers with wealth and social position?

Peniel studied the Zebedee brothers. Had a desire for power and fame been behind their decision to follow Yeshua?

Peniel's gaze fell on Judas. The man's face was sour with disapproval. Judas hated it when Yeshua said things that encouraged the *am ha aretz* to cluster around, while seeming to make it difficult for the "better classes" to join the group. Judas probably thought it was Yeshua's fault they were stuck out here in the hills instead of being wined and dined in Jerusalem.

And as for being pursued by Herod Antipas or Caiaphas, spending every night in a new location, never having a single place to call home . . .

Yeshua smiled at Peter, then let His gaze seek out each questioning visage in turn. "Truly," Yeshua said, "there is no one who has left house or wife or brothers or parents or children for the sake of the Kingdom of God who will not receive many times more in this time, and in the age to come . . . eternal life."[12]

Eternal life! The words glowed like the warmth of a pleasant fire in Peniel's soul. No fear of death . . . no fear of anything! A permanent home, truly permanent. Not like the decaying foundations under the sukomore tree.

Peniel saw Mary, Yeshua's mother, beaming at her son. He also heard Judas hum with approval. It was clear from Judas' expression, exuding pleasurable anticipation, that he had completely misunderstood.

What Yeshua had just promised was all about the Kingdom of God. What had they given up? Family. What had He just vowed? That they would all have greater family ties in His everlasting Kingdom than the ones they were born to.

But Judas? Judas was clearly seeing brocade robes, mahogany-paneled offices, and hordes of servants to do his bidding. A Jerusalem mansion and a villa by the sea.

Peniel shook his head. How could any of that dream compare to eternal life?

Yeshua spoke again: "Peter, I also promise you this: I will never ask you to leave behind anything you still need, only the things you don't. And when new needs arise, you'll have no lack. Of that, you can be sure."[13]

Exactly what Zadok predicted Yeshua would promise!

His eyes locked on Yeshua's face, Peniel discovered he already had all he needed . . . or ever wanted.

Zachai waited nervously in the courtyard of Governor Pilate's Jerusalem palace. He stood before the platform where formal audiences were held, alone except for a pair of Roman legionaries flanking the stage. Zachai offered one a smile, received a sneer in return, so he retreated into his thoughts.

The complex of towers, reception halls, royal residence, and gardens was on the Holy City's western hill. It had been constructed by King Herod the Great but for the last twenty-five years had been the property of Rome.

Zachai had heard that the gardens in particular were fabulous. Marble statues stood amid limpid pools; fountains shot their jets twenty feet into the air; artificial streams mimicked the papyrus-cloaked banks of the Nile and the willow-draped canals along the Euphrates. All this was nurtured by precious water brought at great expense through aqueducts originating as much as thirty miles away.

All financed by duties and taxes collected by men like Zachai and his predecessors.

Was there any wonder Rome was the master of the world? Herod had achieved this magnificence by being a friend of Caesar and endeavoring to out-Rome the Romans. Now that he was dead and gone, his architecture proved Rome could take whatever it wanted, even reshaping nations and nature at its whim.

Zachai had heard of the legendary splendor, but he had never seen it for himself. Though summoned to the palace on several previous occasions, he had never been admitted farther than where he stood right now.

The publican straightened his back and raised his chin. None of the *am ha aretz* had even been allowed this far, except on rare occasions when a deputation brought a grievance to the governor.

And the last of those events had ended badly, Zachai reminded himself. It was in this very courtyard that the Passover riot had erupted, ending in the deaths of scores of Jews.

Best not to dwell on that.

Today's occurrence was a happy one, of which Zachai was proud. Today he would be honored for having set a new record as the Chief Publican of Jericho. For twenty previous reporting terms the revenue collected had increased. No publican had ever achieved as much before.

Zachai was to receive a commendation for his service. That's what the note read. Of course, it was penned and signed by Pilate's secretary, but the governor's seal of office was affixed.

Perhaps Pilate had pressed his ring into the hot red wax with his own hand?

In any case Zachai had brought a gift to show proper gratitude: an alabaster jar of spikenard, worth a year's wages.

There was a blast of trumpets. Pilate's uniformed soldiers emerged from a door at the rear of the platform below which Zachai stood.

No one else was present. Zachai had not been invited to bring any guests—even his Nubian bodyguards had not been allowed entry into the plaza—but the publican had hoped some Roman officials might be on hand to witness his triumph.

Pilate strode out onto the dais, followed by a pair of men wearing the purple-striped toga praetexta of Roman officialdom, then the governor's secretary. The governor approached his X-shaped chair of office but did not seat himself.

While Zachai drew himself to attention, eager to hear the words of praise that would fall from the governor's lips, Pilate waved a negligent hand at his secretary and turned his back on Jericho's chief tax collector.

"Be it known to all by these present . . . ," the secretary intoned.

"And I told my wife," Pilate said loudly to his Roman guests, "everything's quiet just now. No Zealot activity. So we'll not stay one minute longer in Jerusalem than absolutely necessary. Back to Caesarea as quickly . . ."

". . . reported favorably that Kazai of Jericho . . ."

"*Zachai*," the publican murmured almost inaudibly.

"For my taste it's Crete for this time of year," sniffed one of the guests. "The sand is warm, but not too hot, and the wine is tolerable."

". . . to that effect, an endorsement being added to the governor's . . ."

"I get so infernally sick of lamb," Pilate complained. "With all this seacoast you'd think they'd at least have decent fish. But no! All salted and dried."

". . . . to which the governor is pleased to add his signature."

There was another flourish of trumpets and the audience was over. The official party moved toward the back of the stage.

In stunned silence Zachai almost forgot the gift. "Excellency," he called loudly, "I brought . . . I wish to express . . ."

The pair of guards barred Zachai's way forward with a clash of spears. As he stumbled back, the alabaster jar slipped from his fingers and smashed on the stones.

But the sneer of disdain that played across the governor's features as he departed felt even worse.

The am ha aretz *hate me*, Zachai thought. *The Romans tolerate me but despise me. I am treated like a latrine . . . necessary, but still a stench in everyone's nostrils.* Then Zachai of Jericho consoled himself: *But Tiberius Caesar will hear of me . . . or, at least, one of his treasurers will.*

The Zealot camp in the Judean hills was dusty and desolate. While prone to flash floods during the rainy season, it was bone-dry the rest of the year. Besides the complete lack of any comfort, it was so difficult to reach that new recruits had to be led there; no directions or map would suffice.

Such obscurity suited bar Abba perfectly. Near enough to the Jericho Road to make banditry possible, it was an extraordinary refuge. Lookouts posted on nearby hills made it invulnerable to surprise attack. Even if an enemy managed to arrive in force, unseen, they would still have to climb an almost sheer cliff to reach the narrow slot leading to the site.

Every time a Zealot climbed up or down the narrow draw, he showered rocks and sand on his fellows waiting below. There was no avoiding the hail of gravel either, since below the narrow ledge was a sheer drop of another eighty feet. The bones of a spy lay bleaching on the boulders there . . . a warning to would-be traitors.

In the camp a stolen sheep had just finished roasting on a spit. A score of hungry men, each with a price on his head, eagerly eyed the mutton, awaiting their share. There had been no fresh meat for over a week. By bar Abba's orders the band had carried out no recent attacks . . . not on wealthy merchants, nor on small detachments of Roman soldiers, nor on collaborators like publicans. The bandit chief wanted no attention paid by the authorities to his presence in the Jericho area. In fact, he hoped the patrols would be so convinced the Zealots had left the region that troops would be sent away to track someone else.

Part patriot and part thief and wholly ruthless, bar Abba had planned something more elaborate than a smash-and-grab raid, and he was anxious for its success. The only reason he relented to the point of one stolen sheep was to increase the strength and morale of his men for what lay ahead.

Grease dripping from chin and fingers, Lamech now stuffed his jaws with sliced mutton. Shifting a mouthful the size of an apple to the other cheek, he managed to say, "Good! Very good! Wish we'd stolen some fresh bread too."

Bar Abba cuffed him across the back of the head. "Quit griping! Another week and we'll be over the border in Nabatea with enough money to buy food and decent weapons both."

After the men assuaged the worst of their hunger, bar Abba began to talk again of his plan, reminding them of who played what role. Some were part of an elaborate diversion. Some were to intercept any caravan guards who thought to be heroic, while bar Abba, Lamech, and two others were to conduct the actual kidnapping.

"And are you certain they'll pay to get him back?" Lamech wondered aloud, after taking care to be on the other side of the cook fire from bar Abba's fist. "What makes a publican like Zachai worth anything to anyone? Everyone hates him, even his Roman masters."

"Because," bar Abba explained yet again, "he's fabulously wealthy and he knows things! If we tickle his ribs with a knife point, he'll sing like a bird about what Roman decurion has been taking bribes to look the other way at the border . . . and what governor's secretary has a private income from smuggled myrrh . . . things like that. They'll pay to get him back before he lands all of them in the governor's prison."

"But what if they don't?" Lamech persisted, wiping his greasy hands in his beard.

"Then he'll order his own steward to pay up."

"And what if the steward steals the money and won't pay up?"

Bar Abba shrugged. "Then there'll be one less publican in the world. We'll skin Zachai and nail him to the gates of Jericho as a message to other collaborators."

The two daughters of Elijah the Vintner, ages ten and fourteen, trailed their mother as she hurriedly stuffed the family dishes into crates and straw-lined barrels, then went out to direct the loading of a cart. "But why, Mother?" the younger girl demanded over and over. "Why must we leave our home? I don't want to live with Uncle Reuven. Why?"

"Hush, child," Elijah's wife insisted. In a shawl tied around her neck was slung the youngest of the family, a baby boy just six months of age.

A squad of four Roman auxiliary soldiers lounged insolently outside the fence. At the appearance of the teenager there were whistles and comments. The girl, a shy, easily embarrassed child, blushed furiously and fled back inside.

The soldiers laughed and called after her.

Hands on hips, her sister frowned and shook her fist at them, making them laugh all the louder.

Elijah the Vintner stood between the cart poles. The wagon was designed to be pulled by an animal, but all the beasts had been sold, along with the house and the vineyard. It was the only way to avoid debtors' prison.

After retrieving the older girl from the now empty house and veiling their faces, mother and daughter reemerged. Turning a last time toward what had been their home, the mother took each girl by the hand and said, "Why, you ask, child? Better to ask who! Zachai of Jericho, that's who. As short as he is, his soul is more shriveled than his body. And may he never know a moment's peace from this time on, but live in fear of his life." Raising her face heavenward, she intoned, "Hear me, O Lord God, King of the Universe . . . not a moment's peace for Zachai!" Then she led her children after her husband, who was already trudging down the road, dragging what was left of their lives in one oxcart.

Salmon the Great was chief of Zachai's bodyguards. He was an enormous bull of a man, with arms and shoulders muscled like an ox. Black, searching eyes were set like onyx stones in a face filigreed with tattoos. Rumor in Zachai's slave quarters was that Salmon had been a prince among the Nubian tribes. He had been betrayed and sold into slavery by his brother. Scars on his body bore testimony to a harsh life before he came into the House of Zachai. His skill with a sword confirmed that he had undergone some gladiatorial training, which added to his enormous price.

Salmon never relaxed his vigilance when he accompanied Zachai to the Customs House. His teeth were filed to sharp points. He frequently lifted his lip as if to snarl a silent warning that he was capable of using his teeth to bite off noses and ears and to tear out the throat of any who threatened his master.

But off duty, Salmon was a pleasant fellow who often smiled when he was with his wife and three small children. He spoke broken Aramaic with a quiet, gentle voice. Zachai liked him. Salmon was tutored with the children, and now he could write his name and figure sums. This seemed important for a man who had once been a prince in Nubia.

Today, as Zachai's Nephilim gathered before the gates and waited for their master to appear, Salmon's eyes were red-rimmed. He blinked back tears. Tattooed lips trembled with unspoken emotion as his three comrades consoled him.

Zachai's aged servant, Olabi, stood before the quartet and lectured sternly. "Salmon, listen! I had a dream. She must be carried to him and then she will ride upon your shoulders in joy again." He raised his gnarled finger to instruct the Nubian. "But you must take her now." The Old Man suddenly turned on his heel, leaving them to argue in the courtyard.

Salmon whispered, "How can I take her anywhere? The master cannot do without us all."

His comrades counseled, "Salmon, but you must! A dream, the Old Man said! A good omen. Master Zachai may allow you this favor if you but ask."

"You must speak. Ask him, Salmon, my brother."

"She will die if you do not. Is there anything to lose?"

"Only a few days' journey, Salmon. Ask the master. He will let you take her."

Zachai heard their urgent whispers as he emerged into the bright morning light. His keen eyes took in everything at once. Something had happened. The normally stoic Salmon trembled slightly. He wiped his cheeks with the back of his hand and wagged his massive head like a sorrowing child. Salmon shifted his weight from one leg to the other. The group under his command all spoke to him at the same time.

"What, then?" Zachai planted his hands on his hips and scowled up at his giants.

"A small thing, master." Salmon's fingers intertwined in the gesture of a supplicant.

Zachai looked from man to man. "A small thing is not small when it causes one as large as you to quake. What is it, Salmon? Why are you sad?"

"My child. The middle one. Marisha. She is dying."

Marisha was a pretty little thing. Quick and happy in school even at five years old. "Dying? Your Marisha? The bright one? What? When? Why wasn't I informed about such a thing? She is the property of the House of Zachai. Speak up!"

Salmon stammered, "For some time now she has been unwell. Two months she has declined. Her mother has tried everything. Marisha's belly swells. She bleeds at the nose. She cannot eat. She has gone very weak and given up. She cannot walk. Last night she will not sip broth."

Zachai stormed, "We must fetch the doctor."

Salmon wrung his hands. "The steward has done so. Last week. Something grows inside her, eating her flesh, he says. Hopeless, he says."

"Then what is to be done?" Zachai sat down hard on the stone bench beside the fig tree. "What?"

Salmon looked to his troop for support. "Master, we have one hope. A dream. One in your household dreamed that I carried my child over Jordan and into the camp of Yeshua the Nazarene. In the dream I brought Marisha to Yeshua. In the dream, Master, I carried her on a brief journey. When I returned home she came riding upon my shoulders."

Zachai frowned. "You are a good fellow, Salmon. You know they say this Yeshua only heals the sheep in Israel's flock. You know well that unrest in Judea grows because of him. I have been cut off from the flock of Israel. And you . . . are of my house."

"I have heard these things. But, my lord, we have no other hope.

No choice but to approach him. If he truly is the King, will he not grant grace to all people who come to him? I must beg him to touch her and give my child back to us."

Crossing Jordan for a valuable slave like Salmon could well end in his disappearance and loss. His request to travel to the camp of Yeshua took him far beyond the jurisdiction of Judea.

A tear coursed through the carved flesh of Salmon's face. "She is worth nothing. So little. No value to you, master. We know this. She is a small thing. Worth nothing if you sell her. If she dies, we will make other children for you. But, Master Zachai, my child, little Marisha . . . there is only one of herself in all the world. She is greatly beloved by her mother . . . by myself. All of us."

Zachai nodded. Though he would not say it aloud, his slaves were the only family he had. In all the world no man considered him worth wasting a kind word on. Zachai had the power to let Salmon cross the river and possibly escape in his attempt to make the child well. Zachai had the right to keep him here and let his child die. Salmon was worth much more than the child. Suppose she died on the way and he never returned?

Zachai tucked his chin and stared at the enormous feet of Salmon—feet created to gobble up Roman miles in long strides. "Take her, then," Zachai said. "But know that this miracle worker Yeshua hates men like me. He only helps the sons of Avraham. His sheep are not black. His sheep are not slaves. His sheep are not . . . publicans . . . or the slaves of publicans."

Behind them in the portico Olabi said quietly, "It is right that Salmon go across the river. We who remain shall pray to the God who does not hear us. We shall pray to The One who will not listen. We will ask him to guide so that Salmon may find Yeshua and that Yeshua will take the child and work his magic upon her."

The boy approached the garden through the sukomore grove, moving furtively from the trunk of one tree, peering out, then scuttling on to the next. His progress was slow and noisy. Shimona heard him long before he came into view. On her hands and knees, pulling weeds, she glanced up when the crunch of his footsteps stalled for several minutes. Her presence had blocked his forward movement.

Raising up and wiping her hands on her apron, she addressed him. "I know you're there. You might as well come out."

He peered around the trunk, then ducked back as she stood up.

"Come out," she instructed. "I won't hurt you."

A quavering treble voice called, "You're . . . the one they call Shimona? . . . the Leper?"

"What are you doing in my fig grove?" she demanded.

"F-Father sent me. . . ."

"Step out in the sunlight. I won't hurt you. Does your father want to buy cakes of figs?"

A lad of about nine years old stepped into the dappled light. "You're . . . the leper . . . the . . . woman."

"Why did your father send you to my grove?" Shimona observed that the boy was a peasant. His clothes were ragged and dirty. The sack in his hand appeared almost empty, yet he carried it cautiously, as though it contained something fragile.

"What's in your sack? A treasure?"

"No."

"I see you have something in there."

"My father . . . he didn't . . . send me. . . . I mean . . ."

"What are you doing here?"

"Shortcut."

"Yes?"

"He sent me to . . . your creek."

"My creek?"

"To drown these kittens. The kittens in this sack. Drown them in your stream. On the other side of the grove. I didn't want to take the long way round so I . . ."

"Drown? Kittens?"

The boy nodded as if saddened by his task. "I didn't want to. Then I thought . . . I mean, we all know Shimona the Leper. You live here alone, and I thought . . ." He held the bag up, as if offering it to Shimona. Something in the bottom stirred. "So here I was, taking the shortcut through your trees to drown these kittens like my father told me. And then I thought, *What would it hurt, if maybe kittens could live in the sukomore grove of the leper?*"

Shimona smiled but did not come closer, lest the child bolt and take the kittens with him. "Tell me. . . ."

His eyes brightened. The story gushed from the boy. "Three of them, there are. I can't tell boy kittens from girls. Can you? It's hard to tell with kittens, I think. One is black-and-white. One is gray-striped with fine black feet. And then a white one. Well, it's cream-colored, with black ears and tail."

He paused and opened the sack to peer in. "Shalom, little ones," he said gently. Then to Shimona, "My father says they all must have different fathers because the colors are so different. You see? They're very nice. But Father says so many cats will take over the world if we let them live. Like all the cats in Yerushalayim. Take over the whole world, Father says. So drown them in the creek on the far side of the leper's sukomore grove, he says."

The boy sighed deeply. "But I found them, see? In the stump. Almost weaned. The mother is a fine mouser in the barn. She disappeared a few weeks ago . . . and we only just found her with them in a stump."

As if to confirm the story a tiny mewing emanated from the bag.

"So. You thought you'd turn them loose?"

A hawk screamed far above the treetops. The boy looked up at the great bird, then back at Shimona. "At first I thought so. But then . . . the hawk, there. It's circling."

"Yes. He's a fine mouser too. But a danger to little kittens, I fear. Until they're grown."

"Then I can't turn them loose. He'll eat them."

"I'm afraid so. Good mousers, you say? Maybe I could use them here?" Shimona stretched out her hand. "Let them live here with me. Instead of drowning?"

"Sure. My father won't mind . . . if he doesn't know. I didn't want to drown them. Very fine kittens and . . . they'll have a chance with you, eh? Even if you are a leper."

The boy stepped nearer, thought better of it, and halted. Warily, he extended the sack of kittens the full length of his arm. He set it gently on the ground. "So then . . . I'll just go now. Take them. I have to go." He studied her with narrowed eyes for some sign of leprosy. "I have to go now." He backed away, then turned and ran all the way to the highway.

Cradled in Shimona's arms like a baby, the sack of kittens wriggled and mewed as she hurried back to her cottage. The hawk circled high above the treetops.

"O Lord, Almighty God, you always hear my prayers. I asked you to send one cat to fight the Philistines. But you have brought me not one cat but *three*. Three kittens doomed to be drowned! Now you have brought them to me!"

Her breath came fast as she entered her house, closed the door, and placed the sack on the earthen floor. She knew kittens found in a tree stump would be feral—wild, unused to any human contact. Resisting the urge to dump them out, Shimona sat on the three-legged stool to watch and wait until her tiny guests emerged. The soiled linen cloth stirred. Shimona clasped her trembling hands together. "Come on, little friends," she crooned. "I've been waiting so long for you."

Cautiously the kittens moved toward the mouth of the bag. The pink nose of a black-and-white kitten poked out and wriggled, testing the air for danger. Shimona knew at a glance it was a little girl. Delicate yet courageous. She sighed with joy and love for the tiny creature. The head emerged. The kitten greeted the world with a tentative mew. Her ears were black, and a single white blaze ran up the center of her face.

Shimona chuckled. "Oh! More than I imagined. I'll call you Rose, because you are beautiful but have a thorny courage which makes you stronger than your siblings. Come out, Rose!"

As if on command, Rose came out and peered around the room. She was no bigger than a double handful, but seemed very self-assured. Ears were small and pert. Her chest and front feet were white. Her back from the shoulder to tail was cloaked in black, with a patch of white on each hip.

Shimona could almost hear the furry tribe of Philistine mice shriek and run for their holes at the sight of the enemy. "Oh, Rose! You are most welcome here."

Rose replied with a loud mewing. She toddled directly to Shimona's bare toes. Loud purring erupted with an affectionate rub against Shimona's ankle.

Shimona scooped her up and nuzzled Rose beneath her chin. "Blessed are you, O Lord, who heard me. You didn't forget the longings and needs of my heart!"

The second kitten followed. He was larger than the first and gray-and-black striped. Shimona knew at once he was a boy kitten. He leapt from the bag, stumbled on the corner of the fleece, and cried for his sister. Rose called to him. He looked up and bounded across the floor. Shimona gathered him up in her apron, where he wrestled with Rose. "And you . . . brave and clumsy boy. You are Gideon, who fought the great army with only three hundred soldiers."

Gideon was undaunted by Shimona or the new surroundings.

"Blessed are you, O Lord, who guided the boy through my grove. Blessed are you who kept these kittens from being drowned!"

Shimona stroked the two purring babies and watched for the third to come out from hiding. But the last kitten did not move.

Was it ill? Or perhaps dead?

Shimona resisted the urge to look in. "O Lord, would you send me a dead kitten with the live ones? Would you temper my joy with any sorrow when you know how very much I need the bread of joy to feed my starving heart?"

She closed her eyes. "I will not fear a bad report. I will trust the Lord, who hears my prayers always." She began to sing the song she had learned in the Valley of Mak'ob:

> "Give ear to my words,
> O Lord, consider my sighing.
> Listen to my cry for help,
> my King and my God, for to You I pray. . . ."[14]

The bottom of the bag moved at the sound of her voice.

> "In the morning, O Lord, You hear my voice!
> In the morning I lay my requests before You
> and wait in expectation!"[15]

Slowly the bump beneath the linen cloth inched toward the light. Rose and Gideon mewed.

The third kitten replied in a soft, muffled, questing cry. Minutes passed before a tiny face, half the size of either of the other two, peeked out. Bright blue eyes searched for Rose and Gideon. At Rose's call a white kitten with gray tail, ears, and mask left her hiding place. She hesitated, trembling on the verge of the cloth, unwilling to walk on the earthen floor of Shimona's cottage.

Shimona leaned close and, stroking the kitten's head with a finger, whispered, "Don't be afraid, little one. I will call you Lily, after my dear friend Lily. Here is the story: Lily was a leper, doomed to die with us all in the Valley of Mak'ob. We all had come to die in Mak'ob, as surely as if someone had drowned us. One night, a healthy baby was born in that place . . . and Lily went forth into the world to carry the baby out from us lepers and save his life."

She smiled down at Lily. "Just like you and Rose and Gideon save my life from despair and loneliness. You see, it's been a long time since I've had anyone to talk to . . . but back to the story, eh? So my friend went out from the Valley, out into the world from among us.

Lily wandered far in the outside world until she thought she was lost. But she was never lost. God always knew where she was. Then Lily was found by Yeshua's mother, who cared for her. And the baby was saved. You see? Although Lily was afraid, she did the right thing. Good things followed her."

Stroking the kitten again thoughtfully, Shimona continued, "Then Yeshua came to our Valley searching for us . . . like a shepherd looks for his lost sheep. We, the lost sheep of Israel, injured and dying. Alone and forgotten. Fit only for drowning. But Yeshua knew where we were all along. He knew how lonely we were, and he came to us. And so all the lost sheep in the Valley of Sorrows were saved. So, little one, you are named Lily. Though you were afraid to come out into the light, you were courageous. The God who always hears my prayers has answered me with a triple blessing. You were not drowned today. Instead you are loved. It's a good day, and good things will follow."

Shimona gathered Lily into her palm, kissed her head, and reunited her with Gideon and Rose. The trio licked one another with relief and settled in.

The hawk cried outside as he pounced on a Philistine. Shimona covered the kittens protectively beneath her hand. They slept in a warm, tangled heap on her lap as she sang softly.

10

It was morning. The donkey was packed with provisions and Salmon dressed and ready to carry Marisha in search of Yeshua of Nazareth. All the families, the servants of the House of Zachai, gathered in the courtyard to say farewell. Salmon's diminutive wife, toddler on her hip, her oldest child at her side, wept inconsolably.

From a distance Zachai and Olabi watched the scene. "It looks as though they are parting forever," Zachai said, expressing his doubts to the Old Man.

"And perhaps they are. If the child dies along the way, Salmon's wife will never see her again."

Zachai frowned. "I wonder if Salmon will return either way. Or if he values his freedom so much that he will keep walking."

"You hold his family hostage here, Lord Zachai." The Old Man rubbed the white stubble on his face.

"*Hostage*. It is a word used in warfare, not in a home or a household."

"Love is a great weapon, controlling families and nations. *Hostage* is the right word. Salmon's family. Or his freedom. I think love will bring him back."

"And if I let them go with him?"

The Old Man almost smiled. "I cannot say, Lord Zachai. The world being what it is, and men loving to be their own lords. I cannot say if Salmon takes all he loves with him that he would return to your service. But he is a man of honor, and I think he might."

"A wager?"

"I have nothing to wager."

"Your freedom. If Salmon takes his family today and yet returns to my house and my service, then I will believe there is an honorable man in the world. And, Old Man, I will grant you your freedom."

The Old Man smiled broadly. "Then my freedom will stand as hostage for the return of Salmon's family."

"But you must not tell them of our wager. Go . . . tell them Lord Zachai says they should all go now, this hour, together as a family. Seek and find Yeshua of Nazareth. Bring back news if Yeshua is Israel's true deliverer. And give them this—" Zachai produced a leather pouch with money enough to set a free man up in a shop in Damascus—"to meet their needs on their search."

Zachai stood on the roof with the Old Man. Master and servant watched as Salmon, his sick child, his wife, and two other little ones on the donkey hurried down the highway toward the ford of the Jordan.

"An interesting wager." Zachai stared at the broad back of Salmon as they went.

The Old Man said, "One I think I have lost already. Lord Zachai, you have let them all go free, and you know this. Wager or no wager, even if you give me my freedom, you know I will never leave the House of Zachai. You gave him money. . . ."

"A year's wages."

"Salmon has no reason to return to your household if his child lives or dies," the Old Man argued.

"He gave me his word. I have known few men in my lifetime that keep a promise even when it hurts. *Integrity* is almost a foreign word to me."

"In all languages, *integrity* is most often foreign."

"In my business dealings truth is irrelevant. I have reveled in winning every contest at all costs. Integrity has not entered into my considerations." Zachai spoke without remorse.

"You have tempted him more than any man could withstand. A sack of money. This contest to prove to me there is no honest man in all the world has already cost you much."

"I want to lose, Old Man. You have no idea how badly I want to lose."

"You made it impossible for him to return," Olabi protested.

"He is my last hope. He is a large man, but my hope is small." Zachai shaded his eyes from the bright light of the rising sun. The dying child was cradled in her father's massive arms. "And besides, if the little one dies, the mother should be there to bury her."

"And if they find the miracle worker? If the child lives? You believe they will keep walking? return to their home?"

"He was a prince of his people, I have heard." Zachai sighed. "He has served me well and I wish him well. I hope they find the one they are looking for. I hope the miracle worker can help their child live."

"Salmon's wife . . . she was a good servant. It is likely you have lost a whole family of valuable slaves."

"And if they don't return, you have lost a chance to be a free man."

"Free or slave, you know I will gladly be your servant 'til I die. If he comes back . . ."

"Then you'll win the wager, and I will know I have two good servants. One will be free—old and free. And I will be certain my good servant Salmon is faithful. I will know the secrets of my house could not have been bought from him for a denarius, for a sack of money, or even for his freedom."

Given the time of day and Salmon's height, the chief bodyguard's shadow reached Bartimaeus even before the flap of Salmon's sandals.

"Greetings, Salmon," Bartimaeus called out. "The size of your feet must match the length of your frame. Perhaps you are truly one of the ancient race of giants, eh? And I hear you are carrying a burden. Also, someone goes with you."

"Good day to you, Bartimaeus," Salmon returned without his usual cheerful banter. The bodyguard tossed a coin onto the outspread cloak.

"Here is a penny for you, but I cannot stop long to talk. My daughter Marisha is very ill. My wife and I go to seek help for her."

"In Jericho?" the beggar replied. "Why not in Yerushalayim? There are many fine physicians there, if one has the money for them."

"She is beyond their help even."

To the passersby Salmon's words registered the agony of grief anticipated.

"Then where?"

"I came this way to ask if you have news of Yeshua of Nazareth. He is a great Healer, they say."

"The man from the Galil? What makes you think—?" Bartimaeus stopped short of mocking Salmon's last hope. "Yes, they do say that. I met two of his talmidim when they came this way to buy provisions. I do not know where he might be found now, but I have heard he is over Jordan, near where Yochanan the Baptizer preached before Antipas cut off his head."

"May your God bless you. Please pray for us."

"And may your gods do the same," Bartimaeus replied. "And if you locate him tell him . . . tell him I wish he would do your daughter this service. Tell him from me that you always have a kind word for a blind beggar."

"Shalom, then, Bartimaeus. And don't forget to pray we find the Healer soon."

It was Sabbath morning. The last stars began to fade. The colors of earth blended into a monochrome palette of grays and blues. The dull light of approaching dawn ascended above the mountains of Moab. Soon the congregation of the Jericho synagogue would gather for worship. Husbands, wives, children, young and old of Israel, bound by common heritage and common affliction, would make their petitions known to their God.

Zachai, though forbidden to pray, knew their prayers by heart.

"The needs of your people are many and they are unable to express their wants. May it be your will, O Adonai, our God and the God of our fathers, to give each and every one his daily sustenance and to everyone whatever he lacks."

Zachai had everything yet lacked everything he wanted. He could not pray. Excommunicated, cut off from Israel because of his role as a publican, he would not be heard. Even so, he prayed in his heart, *God of Israel, who cannot hear a sinner's prayer, forgive me for speaking to you. How I wish I could be like one of them.*

He paced the length of his rooftop garden and stared toward the east, beyond Judea, where the great Healer had made His camp outside the reach of Herod Antipas or High Priest Caiaphas.

The bird awakened in the fig tree and began to sing. Did the notes of her music contain some hidden prayer? Did she, whose nest was filled with blue speckled eggs, praise the God of Heaven for her life and the lives of her young?

"So. Even birds are happier than I am," Zachai said to no one. "The slaves of my household are happier than the master they serve."

Though Zachai could purchase a woman for his pleasure at any time, he took no pleasure in a woman bought for money. He wanted a wife—a true Jewish wife descended from Abraham and able to bear him children.

A wife like Barucha, the woman he'd chosen long ago, from his perch above the synagogue. Barucha meant "Praise." She was eighteen and the third daughter of the Chazzan, who was renowned as a righteous poor man. Her betrothed husband had died last year, so she remained unpledged. But Zachai did not dare hire a matchmaker to approach the girl's father with a proposition of marriage. His request for a Jewish bride would be refused, no matter how much money he offered in the contract. The daughter of a man of integrity could not be purchased. And Zachai did not desire the daughter of any other variety of Jew.

"Barucha! God of Israel who cannot hear me, I remember the third daughter of the Chazzan today. Such a wife she would make! Such a mother! Dress her in silks and plait her dark hair with golden ribbon, and she would rival any princess."

Could a man as hated as Zachai truly love one woman from across such a wide gulf?

Perhaps it was not love, he consoled himself. Perhaps it was only the lust of a man to possess what he could never have. He had never spoken to her. Her father openly despised Zachai and had spat at Zachai's feet after paying his taxes. When the Chazzan passed the gates of Zachai's estates, he made the sign against the evil eye and shielded his eyes from looking. Barucha's father hated Zachai with a tangible hatred. It was a problem.

But even so, Zachai climbed to the roof each Sabbath morning and waited to see Barucha approach with her family. For weeks and months Zachai had smiled from above as she, unaware of his admiration, nodded and spoke to other women. Last week Zachai had been pleased with her kindness when she stooped to embrace a child who had stumbled. He did not turn away when she entered the building through the women's door. He listened to the singing of psalms and imagined he could pick out her voice from among them all.

Zachai had anxiously awaited this morning to see her again. He sighed and urged dawn to hurry. He stared down into the synagogue courtyard and rehearsed what he would say to her if only he could.

"Barucha, I have loved you from afar for a very long time. We will be very happy together. Even if I cannot enter the congregation and worship as other sons of Avraham, I am still a man and I love you."

The sky grew brighter. Olabi brought a bowl of warm water and shaved him. "Shall I bring your breakfast now, master?"

"After services," Zachai replied curtly as though he were attending. "Any word from Salmon about his child?"

"No, sir. It has only been three days. It is a wilderness place where Yeshua of Nazareth teaches. And how long will it take Salmon to present his child to the Healer? Salmon is, after all, no Jew. The Galilean has said he comes first to seek the lost sheep of the flock of Israel. Good Shepherd of Israel, the common folk are calling him now."

"Israel only." Zachai dried his face and ran a hand over his smooth skin. "I am shut out of synagogue. Worse than an infidel. It's good I have no desire to make a request of this Yeshua."

"Yeshua has the power to raise even the dead. He is the most hated and feared of all men by the high priest, the Herodians, the Romans, and the Sanhedrin. He has unified old enemies in a common cause. The high priest has secretly put a price on his head. So is the rumor."

"The Nazarene? Most hated?" Zachai smiled bitterly. "I am most hated. So. We have much in common. The people who love him hate me. The people who value me, for my services to the treasury of Herod and Rome, hate him. Perhaps there's a connection between us after all."

"Salmon is a black sheep and not a Jew, but he will be received by Yeshua. I saw it in a dream."

"So it was you, Old Man, who dreamed the dream for Salmon's child?"

"Yes, Lord Zachai. I saw in my dream the child running. Saw her riding high on the shoulders of her father and smiling as they crossed the Jordan coming home."

"May your dream be true prophecy. What would you ask this Rabbi? this Yeshua? If you could ask for anything?"

"Health for Salmon's child." The Old Man tucked his head as though embarrassed somehow by his master's personal question.

"A worthy petition."

"I am an old man, Lord Zachai. In your father's service and now in your service I live better than most beyond these gates. All my needs are met. As I have been servant to your father and now to you."

"Can you guess what I would want?"

"If you could take a wife from among your own people . . . that would be a good thing, my lord. Each Sabbath you wait for her to come."

"Yes. She is a good wish. Impossible. So, if only one attainable thing?" Zachai frowned and squinted down into the empty courtyard.

"Well then. If only one thing . . . and if it is not a wife? I cannot guess." The Old Man smiled and rubbed the white bristles on his chin.

"My freedom," Zachai replied.

"You are no man's slave, my lord Zachai."

Zachai turned away. "My freedom," he muttered and silently prayed, *God of Israel who does not hear the prayers of a sinner like me, I am so alone. Is there freedom in death?*

Even Zachai's slave could openly cross the Jordan and seek Yeshua with a petition. Zachai was a prisoner within the walls of his own home. The mansion he had built was a beautiful cage, but it was an empty, lonely cage all the same.

It was Sabbath afternoon.

Zadok's sons, Avel, Emet, and Ha-or Tov, splashed and sailed leaf boats in a watering trough.

Yeshua rested on the stone wall enclosing the nearby well. After sunset they were going to resume their journey. Seated at Yeshua's feet, Peniel hearkened back to the discussion about how hard it was for the rich to enter the Kingdom of Heaven. It brought a familiar question to his mind: What was the Kingdom of Heaven like?

It was not a new query. Yeshua had addressed it on many previous occasions, but each time Yeshua responded, Peniel learned something new, some new facet he'd never considered before. Listening to Yeshua was like having a chest of valuables: No matter how well you thought you knew the contents of the chest, each time it was opened new treasures were revealed.

Today was no exception. What was the Kingdom of Heaven like?

Yeshua looked around at the travel-worn apparel and weather-beaten features of his friends and smiled at them. "The Kingdom of Heaven," He began, "is like a master of a house who went out early in the morning to hire laborers for his vineyard."

On the hillside across the way there was a vineyard. New growth of bright green leaves gleamed in the afternoon sun. The image of casual laborers hanging around the market early in the morning, hoping for work, was familiar. The talmidim nodded with contentment and settled back to listen.

"After agreeing with the laborers for a denarius a day, he sent them into his vineyard."

A denarius was a reasonable day's wage. So far there was nothing unusual in what Yeshua suggested. The very commonplace nature of the tale heightened Peniel's expectation that some surprise was coming.

"And going out about the third hour, he saw others standing idle in the marketplace, and to them he said, 'You go into the vineyard too, and whatever is right I will give you.' So they went."

This was nothing abnormal either. A good-sized vineyard always needed tending: pruning, pulling weeds, routing out pests, tying up the vines to keep them from trailing on the ground. By midmorning some latecomers, unemployed by other growers, would be anxious to find work, and there would still be more effort required.

"Going out again at the sixth hour and the ninth hour, he did the same. And about the eleventh hour he went out and found others standing. And he said to them, 'Why do you stand here idle all day?' They said to him, 'Because no one has hired us.' He said to them, 'You go into the vineyard too.'"

Peniel thought this had gotten interesting. The vineyard owner had added more workers at noon and at midafternoon, but the eleventh hour was near the end of the workday. No one worked after dark.

Where was this tale leading?

"And when evening came, the owner of the vineyard said to his foreman, 'Call the laborers and pay them their wages, beginning with the last, up to the first.' And when those who were hired about the eleventh hour came, each of them received a denarius."

Judas snorted. Peniel knew it was the group's treasurer, even without turning to look. No one else could express disapproval without even speaking as Judas could.

Still, when Yeshua paused in His story, Peniel heard others of the talmidim whispering too. Those who had worked only one hour received a full day's wages? What would those who had sweated all day in the heat get?

Was this parable about unexpected rewards? Was this how Yeshua amplified His promise to Shim'on Peter about how rewarding their service would be?

Yeshua squelched this notion by resuming: "Now when those hired first came, they thought they would receive more, but each of them also received a denarius. And on receiving it they grumbled at the master of the house, saying, 'These last worked only one hour, and you have made them equal to us who have borne the burden of the day and the scorching heat.'"

Now Peniel was confused. Was this story about workers demanding justice? Was the vineyard owner crazy?

But the question had been about the Kingdom of Heaven.

"The master of the house replied to one of them, 'Friend, I am doing you no wrong. Did you not agree with me for a denarius? Take what belongs to you and go. I choose to give to this last worker as I give to you. Am I not allowed to do what I choose with what belongs to me? Or do you begrudge my generosity?' So the last will be first, and the first last."[16]

Peniel thought he understood. This story was like another Yeshua had told about whether a servant got extraordinary praise for doing what he had been hired to do. The answer, of course, was no.[17]

In this latest anecdote the first workers received proper compensation, but because of envy they resented the others, whom they saw as getting off easy.

The issue was not that they had been cheated; it was about having an attitude of resentment born out of spite.

As often happened when Yeshua stopped speaking, the talmidim broke into small groups to review and discuss what they'd heard. Peniel was grateful to join Zadok and El'azar and not have to listen to Judas gripe about how unrealistic and foolish it all sounded.

Peniel spoke first. "Yeshua's saying, 'Serve God because you love him, and don't envy those you think are getting better treatment than you.'"

Zadok nodded. "Aye, lad. You've pegged it, sure."

"Envy is a much bigger problem than many believe," El'azar suggested gravely. "It's because of envy that Lord Caiaphas and Herod would kill Yeshua . . . and us."

"Nor is that new," Zadok rumbled. At his feet his dog looked up attentively, then lay back down. "Even shepherds envy those whose pastures are greener . . . whose lambs are fatter . . . who live closer to market . . . or are less plagued by jackals. Famous shepherds, some of 'em. Famous jackals, too, come to that."

"Go on, please," Peniel urged.

Zadok coughed and lowered his voice. The old shepherd loved to tell stories but never wanted to "put on airs," as he called it, especially in front of an educated man like El'azar. "Now mind, this is just a rumination born of long nights in the fields, but if you're certain . . ."

Both Peniel and El'azar encouraged him to continue.

"Take the first ever murder, eh? Cain killed his brother, Abel—who was a shepherd, mind—because why? Because of envy, that's why."

Peniel saw El'azar nodding. Abel had offered the sacrifice of a lamb to God, while Cain had tried to please God by making up his own approach. When Abel was approved by God and Cain was not, brother had killed brother.[18]

"Say more, Zadok. You're on to something," El'azar said.

"And take our forefather Isra'el and the trouble he had with his brother, Esau.[19] Envy again, eh? And the same with Joseph the Dreamer, envied by his brothers because they saw him get special treatment from their father, Isra'el. Envy got Joseph almost killed and did get him carted off t' Egypt when his own brothers sold him as a slave."[20]

"Envy is a great poison," El'azar agreed. "Even King David was envied by his brothers. After all, the prophet Samu'el anointed him king and not them, even though he was the youngest.[21] No place for envy in the Kingdom of Heaven . . . or in the service of the Good Shepherd."

Zadok adjusted his eyepatch and patted his dog on the head. "Amen t' that, I say. But if Abel had Cain, and Isra'el faced Esau, may God keep jackals like Caiaphas and Herod far away from us!"

To her sparse furnishings Shimona added a low box of sand in the corner for the kittens' needs, one wooden bowl of curds from the goat's milk, and one for water. It would be a while before these tiny creatures could go outside.

The hawk took up residence near the cottage. He perched on the low branch of a tree just outside in the yard. This evening Shimona could see him clearly through the barred window. He kept the Philistines far from her door, but would he not devour her kittens too?

The thought made her shudder. She loved the hawk, but now she had reason to be wary of him.

Rose and Lily and Gideon wrestled on the floor at Shimona's feet. Their squeaks and peeps and rumbling purrs seemed to draw the great raptor ever closer to the house as if it were a cage with bait inside.

Shimona picked up each kitten in turn, laying her cheek against each face. She prayed a blessing over each one: "Blessed are you, O Lord, who has given these little ones to me for my company and for their care and nurturing. Blessed are you . . . O Lord! You know I fear the day that one may slip out the door or jump onto the window ledge and . . ."

Shimona shuddered as she glanced out beyond the barred window and spotted the hawk on his perch, watching, watching. . . . "Natural enemies . . . hawks and cats. O Lord, who hears all my prayers, I don't hold it against Hawk for wanting to have a taste of kitten for his supper, but speak to him, Lord . . . if you please. Tell him, please, there are still mice enough for him to eat for the rest of his life without eating Rose or Lily or Gideon."

Lily gamboled up to attack Shimona's toes. Coming from this smallest of the trio, it was a toothless attack and ineffectual. While Rose and Gideon were getting teeth, Lily seemed far behind them. Such a tiny thing would have no defense at all against the sharp claws of any predator.

Shimona gathered Lily into her apron and placed her hands protectively over her as she envisioned the worst thing . . . the very worst thing that could happen.

Gideon, the strongest, seemed intent on escaping through the window. Shimona could see his little thoughts leaping up and slipping through the bars to the outside.

"Little ones," Shimona explained to the kittens, "you can't go outside for a very long time. Until you're grown up. And even then you'll have to be careful. I know you may feel I'm holding you back from a life you want to experience for yourself . . . but you could get hurt . . . it's possible, you know."

Shimona's mind went blank for a moment. A different thought crowded in and took over. It wasn't a thought about kittens and hawks but about her own life.

She heard a whisper . . . not her own voice, but another's. *Just so you understand. You mustn't leave for a very long time. Be careful. You're lonely . . . yes. I understand. I know you feel I'm holding you back from life, but you could get hurt. Herod . . . Caiaphas . . . they're afraid of The One who healed you. They fear you now too because you're a witness to Yeshua's power. You could get hurt. . . . It's possible, you know.*

Shimona cried, "Oh, Lord! Is that you? Is that you?"

There was no reply. But here was God's lesson lying in her hands.

The kittens, oblivious to danger, hummed and rumbled beneath the protective warmth of her touch.

Shimona prayed, "Lord who always hears my prayers, I think I understand. I think I know what you're saying. I'm so worried about these little ones. What difference would their lives make in the big story? No one would know or care if the boy had thrown them into the water. Or if the hawk . . . ?" She could not speak the fear that leapt to her imagination. "Lord! Who would care? But *I* care. Rose and Lily and Gideon. Their lives matter to me . . . Lord!" Suddenly the meaning of her solitary confinement became clear. "What difference did my life make? A leper in Mak'ob. Easy to forget. No one would remember my name. Or my life. Then Yeshua came. Until now . . ."

Shimona stared through the window as daylight faded. Herod. Caiaphas. The others. Suddenly healed, a leper emerging from the Valley of Mak'ob mattered to the world. Clear evidence of the miraculous power of Yeshua of Nazareth, Shimona could no longer be forgotten or ignored.

"I am their enemy. Thank you, Lord, for keeping me hidden all these months. Safe. I didn't understand. Rome . . . the wolf. Herod Antipas and the Temple leaders . . . jackals. All of them."

PART II

This is what the Sovereign LORD says to them: See, I Myself will judge between the fat sheep and the lean sheep. Because you shove with flank and shoulder, butting all the weak sheep with your horns until you have driven them away, I will save My flock, and they will no longer be plundered. I will judge between one sheep and another.

EZEKIEL 34:20-22

labi's smile was that of a man who knew the way to a woman's heart. He confided to Zachai, "When wooing a woman, it is important to know her secret desires."

"How can any man know what a woman wants most in all the world?"

"That is simple. They all desire the same thing." Olabi shrugged.

"Love? Kindness?"

Olabi laughed large, rocking back on the garden bench. "No!" he cried. "What every woman wants most in all the world is her own will!"

Zachai smiled tentatively as Olabi burst into gales of laughter again. "Do you not see, master? Under your own roof? Among your people? In our quarters? We men are not the final word on any matter. Oh no! It is the will of the women who rule among the men who guard the great House of Zachai!"

Zachai directed his gaze to the two birds who perched on the edge of their nest. The plain, small female was clearly the dominant of the species. "I have never spoken to the daughter of the Chazzan."

"But we have seen you look at her."

"She doesn't like to look at me."

"It would not be proper while you are looking at her for her to look at you. You look away and then she looks."

"But how does she look? Is it a kindly glance?"

"You are very rich. You have no wife. This must interest her."

"I am cut off from Israel."

"Bad men also interest women. You might reform."

"But how can I woo her? You know how I'm regarded by her father."

"True. But you must know details about her to begin."

"How can I do that?"

The Old Man winked. "My wife."

"Your wife?"

"Women love plotting when plots lead to love."

"Your wife? How can she help?"

"She knows the servant who serves the daughters of the Chazzan. Servants know everything. Sometimes, for a price, they will tell everything they know."

"The servant of Barucha?"

"The same. There is only one servant in the House of the Chazzan. She and my wife speak to one another in the souk. They speak to one another when they draw water at the well. The young woman is a *Shabbes goy*—a Gentile the Chazzan keeps to do all the work on the Sabbath. On Sabbath evening during the services she could meet with you. Tell you what she knows. The Chazzan will never guess she left the house."

"For a price servants will tell . . . everything?"

Olabi placed his hand upon his barrel chest in an unspoken oath. "Not all servants can be bribed, Lord Zachai. Not your servants. But, you know, silly women . . . the girl who serves the Chazzan. I think she would talk without a bribe. But a bribe may make her talk quicker."

"She must not know it is I who speaks to her about her household."

"Disguise. A dark street. Sabbath evening. Street of the Shoemakers. She will not know, my lord. We will say you are . . . a Jewish shoe merchant from Alexandria who made a delivery of Roman sandals at the House of Zachai. That you wish to inquire about the daughter of the Chazzan for noble purpose."

"A large sum?"

Olabi held up one finger. "With this girl? For one denarius a river of details." He added another. "For two, you will sail upon a great sea."

The grass beneath the trees was green and fragrant. A pleasant breeze from the west stirred the silvery olive leaves with a gentle rustle. The village of Lebonah was famous for its olive groves. Both sides of the route along which Yeshua and His talmidim had been hiking were lined with them.

Trudging down the road made everyone drowsy by midafternoon. The band had broken their journey for a meal of bread and dried fish, shared out of their store of provisions by Marta and the mother of John and Ya'acov bar Zebedee. After the midday meal, it was not uncommon for many of the talmidim to seek a shady spot and a nap before resuming the journey.

Which is how Peniel found himself tucked into the bole formed when a gnarled olive tree branched multiple times near the ground. It had created a mossy depression perfect for use by a slender young man for sleep.

He had not meant to eavesdrop. In fact, it was the sound of voices that woke him. He recognized Yeshua's words at once. Peniel recalled that the Master had taken His group of twelve special ambassadors apart just as the rest were settling down to rest.

The polite thing would have been for Peniel to announce his presence, so far unnoticed, at once. He knew this was the right thing to do, but he refrained. Judas would smirk at him, and Shim'on Peter would bluster and scold and threaten to send him away.

Besides, the conversation was of great interest.

Yeshua said, "See—soon we are going up to Yerushalayim. And the Son of Man will be delivered over to the chief priests and scribes."

There was silence, then angry muttering from the apostles. This was exactly the situation many of them had predicted would happen when Yeshua first announced His intention of returning to the Holy City.

Yeshua continued, "They will condemn him to death and deliver him over to the Gentiles to be mocked and flogged and crucified."

"No!" erupted from Philip.

"Not unless they account for me first!" This from John.

"It's not too late to return to Caesarea Philippi . . . or even take ship for Alexandria," suggested Peter's younger brother, Andrew.

Then Yeshua added something that must have electrified the Twelve. It raised the hair on the back of Peniel's neck. It certainly silenced the others. "And he will be raised on the third day."[22]

Raised? From the dead? Raised like El'azar was restored to life? But in El'azar's case, it had been Yeshua who did the raising. Who would attempt such a thing for Yeshua?

And why? If He could come back to life, could He not avoid the mocking and the flogging and the crucifixion?

Peniel's stomach churned. The worst thing he had yet forced into his newly minted eyes was the sight of a mangled body still hanging from a Roman cross. It could not happen to Yeshua! It must not!

This was not the first time Yeshua had tried to mention the subject of His death to His followers. Way back north, back near Caesarea Philippi, Yeshua had also broached the subject. Shim'on Peter had protested the very idea and received a sharp rebuke from the Master.[23]

The notion that Yeshua was willingly going to His death upset everyone. There would be turmoil in the camp for at least a day. Next, everyone would pretend He did not mean it. After that they'd all act as if He'd never said it . . . at least, not the way it sounded.

Judas probably believed it was another test of their faithfulness, another effort by Yeshua to weed out the true followers from the hangers-on.

The rest probably regarded it as some parable they still did not understand, but which Yeshua would explain in time. Peniel hoped this view was correct, but in his heart he felt differently. In Yeshua's voice was the sad resignation that even among His closest friends He could find no one to share this burden.

They just did not choose to believe Him.

Wrapped in his father's old cloak, his features concealed by darkness, Zachai was certain the Chazzan's servant woman would never guess who he was.

She put out her hand. "A denarius, the girl promised me in the souk. A denarius, she said, just to tell you what's what in my master's house. A coin first, then I'll tell you what I know about my master's household, though it ain't much, and I don't know why anyone is in'trested in the household of a Chazzan. Soooo?"

Zachai firmly placed a coin into the young woman's palm. Fingers snapped around it like a trap.

"All right, then. Your mistress Barucha," he began.

"Barucha? Her? Why, she's a shrew if ever there was one. Beats me regular if I don't move fast enough. I swear that fellow she was betrothed to died because he saw no other way to get out of a life of misery tied to the likes of Barucha."

This was more than Zachai had bargained for. "What I mean is, what I wanted to ask . . . has she any suitors? Anyone else come round the house, speaking to the Chazzan about his daughter?"

She snorted. "Barucha? Suitors? Lovely to look at but poison, that one. Poison! Trouble. Trouble. All in the congregation of Israel who know her give the warnin' to others. Once a month she's like a wild donkey. Brayin' and kickin'. Oh, her father'd love to get that one out of the house. Pure misery. Only a pure fool would wed that one."

Zachai cleared his throat. Were they speaking of the same Barucha? The tall, lovely, elegant creature who followed her father to the synagogue every Sabbath? "I'm asking about . . . the third daughter of the Chazzan. Is this . . . can she be the same girl you are describing?"

"The same. The very same. If ever she weds, pity the poor fool who's caught in her web. Spin him round, roll him up tight, hang him upside down for a while, then suck the blood right out of him, she will."

Zachai stared at her in stunned silence for a long moment. "She has no prospects, then?"

The servant laughed. "Prospects? Damaged goods, she is. Her father'd give her away to a passin' camel drover in the caravansary as long the camel drover was a Jew. It'll take a camel drover to handle that one. And I'll wager he would bring her back and drop her off next time through Jericho."

"I'm glad I asked."

"You're a stranger in these parts or you would know. Everyone who doesn't live in a tree knows. They're all spiders except the one. Poor thing. But the eldest sister . . . Shimona is her name. Thirty-two years old. No one had seen her or had word of her for a dozen or so years. A widow come home again after a long illness is the story. Husband died. This and that. She shows up on the threshold of the Chazzan's house one night. The sight of her face nearly killed the wife. Didn't let her come in the house, though. Looks fine and well enough to me, but her father won't have her in his home. Don't know why. Rumor is she come from the Valley of Mak'ob."

Zachai replied, "No one ever comes *from* Mak'ob. Not ever."

"Maybe so. But I hear the whole Valley of Lepers is deserted now. All healed . . . all sent home. Yeshua, the miracle worker, they say."

"Lepers healed? Never. All dead more likely."

"Dead. Hmm. Yes. So says the high priest too. Dead, they say. Even so . . . Shimona, my master's daughter, returned about a year ago. Well enough from what I could see. Destitute and barren as a stone. Her father's charity case. Now *there's* a sweet calf, but the Chazzan can't get rid of her either."

She pursed her lips at the thought of her master's dilemma. "Lives nearby in the little house in the old sukomore grove, which my master the Chazzan rents from that devil Zachai. Shimona tends the fig trees since the caretaker died and . . . once a week my husband picks up the harvest at the grove and sets off provisions for her. She'll be there in isolation 'til she dies to hear the Chazzan and the rabbi talk about her. They'll never let her out though she's as healthy as a horse from what I hear."

She tossed her head. "Well, no man nor any children in her future, if you know what I mean. Each month she sends her father a request for a cat . . . a simple request. A cat to keep the mice down. A cat for company. But her father pays no attention. Poor girl. There's a rumor she's become one of those followers of Yeshua who teaches now over Jordan for fear of Herod. If you ask me, that's the real reason her father won't have her in the house. Suppose she really was healed of leprosy? What's that say about Yeshua, who we all know the leaders in Yerushalayim hate? Maybe they're afraid she's proof Yeshua really is . . . someone . . . and that Shimona'll bring down the wrath of Caiaphas. Or Antipas. Or the Romans."

"Shimona, you say? I didn't know about this," Zachai remarked.

"Not many do. Like I said, she tends the orchard. Poor Chazzan's got his hands full of unmarried daughters. Is that what you wanted to know about? Daughters? Ask me anything."

Zachai believed the servant would have told him all she knew for free. But he held up a second coin. "Your master's finances . . ."

"Worry, worry, worry all the time. Never enough. Poor fellow. A few small fields and renting the fig grove of that devil publican—Zachai, I mean—plenty to worry about there. Then serving as the Chazzan . . . well, what do you expect? And so many mouths to feed. He keeps me on because Barucha needs someone to beat and lord it over. I suppose if ever she marries, I'll be sent along with her to the household of the poor fellow. There'll be some comfort for whatever fool marries her. He'll be getting me as a faithful servant right along with the mistress. And my husband? What's that mean if Barucha marries? My man is the one who fetches and carries for the Chazzan. He knows a lot. The Chazzan will separate us for certain."

Zachai nodded once and flipped the coin to the woman. She caught it, laughed, and said conspiratorially, "And . . . here's something you didn't have to pay for: The Chazzan doesn't pay all that's due on his rent to Zachai. Very clever in his accounts, he is. Hides the true income from the fig orchard and the weaving. So, anything else you'd like to know?"

Zachai smiled behind the fold of material shielding his face. "Zachai's sukomore orchard, you say?"

"The old grove. A fine stand of trees it is since Shimona became caretaker. Like I said, rented from the House of Zachai. Sukomore figs. My husband thinks they've put poor Shimona out there under pretense that she's a suspected leper so no one will ever enter the grove or ask questions about the harvest. Warning signs posted and everything. Clever fellows. My husband says Shimona's no more a leper than you or me. She never complains. A hard worker. Once a week my husband tells her the news of the world. She keeps her distance like a timid deer and asks about her family. They don't care about her, it's plain, except what she can do for them. My master gets a sum for the figs his daughter harvests and dries and prepares; then he pays off Zachai's steward, who collects the rents for that scum of a publican."

"Ah. Then the Chazzan is indeed a clever fellow. And Zachai's steward is . . . you say he's in charge of collecting the Chazzan's revenue? Is it Haman?"

"Aye. That's it. Haman is his name. Steward of Zachai. Like dirty old Haman in the book of Esther. He'll be as rich as his master Zachai one of these days. The Chazzan says Haman cheats the cheater. No harm in that. No one in all the territory deserves to be cheated out of revenue like Zachai does. Swine. Someone will string him up to that grand old sukomore in his courtyard, and we'll all be glad to spit upon his dead body."

Zachai drew himself up, quite finished with the interview. It was money well spent for information he did not have. So Haman, his trusted steward, cheated the cheater. Zachai's heart was pounding with anger at Haman and relief that he had not approached the Chazzan for the hand of Barucha. He was sweating under the cloak.

"I thank you . . . for your help." He stepped back in an attempt to disengage.

The servant rattled on without thought of further remuneration. "Anything else? If you're lookin' for a bride, I know everything about the unwed women round about—I've thought of assisting the matchmaker a time or two—but we'll never get Barucha married off unless the groom is deaf and dumb. As long as he's rich, I don't think my master would mind if it was Zachai the Publican himself! Serve him right to marry the likes of Barucha!"

It had taken less than a full night and a day for Zachai to hatch a plan. Dealing with both his steward and the Chazzan would be swift . . . and sweet. Action quickly followed decision, hard on the heels of enlightenment.

Shaved and dressed in his finest Roman tunic of black and gold, Zachai felt tall and almost handsome on his horse. The spirited black gelding, named for the Norse god Thor, was a reward from Herod Antipas for exceeding last year's expected revenues. Zachai was an excellent rider and a good judge of horseflesh. He had bet and won a fortune on last year's chariot races after spending only two mornings watching the teams train in the Jerusalem Hippodrome.

Haman the Steward was not an equestrian. Nor did he like horses. Unaware his neck was in a noose, Haman rode beside Zachai on the back of a plump, docile mare. Zachai wanted to make sure his maladroit steward would not attempt an escape when it came to light that "cheating the cheater" did not pay. Three bodyguards accompanied them. This was to be a short and decisive tour of Zachai's personal estates.

"We will begin with the fig orchard," Zachai announced. "The orchard rented by the Chazzan of the synagogue."

"A small holding." Haman coughed as they rode out the Jordan Road.

"But of great sentimental value to the House of Zachai. My grandfather planted the sukomore fig trees from cuttings taken from the old tree—the tree of the prophet Amos that grows in my garden, where it was planted by the prophet eight hundred years ago. As a young man, my grandfather planted the saplings with his own hands. Did you know I held this orchard in sentimental regard, Haman?"

"No . . . no, my lord Zachai."

"My grandfather's fig trees bore seven crops of fruit every summer when I was a boy. I pierced the fruit with my own hand and plucked it when it was ripe. It was my first holding. Did you know this, Haman?"

"No . . . no, my lord Zachai."

"My first profit and my first understanding of business were earned when I managed the orchard. It was a fruitful orchard before the Chazzan became tenant."

"Perhaps it will be fruitful again. . . ." Haman shifted uneasily in his saddle. The mare had a stiff-legged, jolting gait, sure to jar the bones of her rider.

Zachai glanced at the steward from the corner of his eye and refrained from smiling. The steward's stubby legs stuck out at an awkward angle from the mare's rotund belly. Haman seemed pale. "Does the stride of the mare not suit you, Haman?"

"She is . . . a lovely creature. White and . . . better than a donkey, my lord Zachai."

"But not as smooth as riding in the chariot of the House of Zachai, eh, Haman?"

"Well, no . . . but a fine animal."

"Glad you think so. I was wondering what gift I might give my faithful steward as a reward for overseeing my personal estates." He pressed the sides of Thor with his calves, urging the gelding into a smooth, easy lope.

Haman's smile faltered as the mare followed after in a pounding trot. The steward grasped the mare's stiff mane in an effort to stay mounted.

Zachai was pleased to note the ludicrous appearance of his steward. What a justifiable humiliation was imposed on the disingenuous lickspittle! Zachai smiled as the words rang in his thoughts: *Cheat the cheater!* He continued the conversation. "It must be the lack of care of my orchard, eh, Haman?"

The steward's reply came in breathless spurts as hooves smashed down on the hard-packed road. "Some . . . relative . . . of the Chazzan . . . some . . . destitute . . . a strange case . . ." He did not finish the thought.

Zachai nodded in mock sympathy. "So it often turns out. A man gives someone a position out of sympathy. Trusts the fellow to work loyally . . . and then . . ."

Haman's face contorted in pain as the mare's forefeet came down forcefully. He did not seem to hear the parable of his own life in Zachai's words. "Yes . . . yes." He grimaced. "But . . . may we not . . . slow down?"

Zachai reined his mount to a walk. Haman followed suit with a sigh of relief. The orchard was just ahead. Trees with broad, leathery leaves glistened in the sunlight. Great clumps of fruit ripened on the thick trunks of thirty-six healthy sukomore fig trees. Around the bottom of each tree a damp berm of earth indicated that they had been individually watered.

The signs warning of the quarantine were prominently displayed. Haman pointed them out. "My lord, I remember now. The woman who tends the orchard . . . she was . . . she is . . ."

Zachai replied calmly, "I heard she was once a leper, healed by Yeshua of Nazareth. Her father has hidden her here. That's the rumor."

"But what if she is . . . ?" Clearly Haman had been counting on the signs to keep Zachai from entering the grove.

"I heard the suggestion that she is still ill is meant to discredit the Healer."

"But if she is still a leper, we . . . we'll be defiled!"

"Good enough," Zachai commented, turning aside toward the caretaker's stone cottage in the center of the grove after posting his guards at the boundary. "Am I not a publican . . . and defiled already? But perhaps there's been a change in . . . conditions."

The pained expression on Haman's face was no longer from the pace of his horse.

The door of the one-room dwelling was ajar. Women's clothing hung drying on a line in front. Vegetables grew in neat, perfect rows in a small garden beside the house. A shed for harvested fruit was surrounded by lavender to keep the insects away.

Zachai growled, "So! Where is this lazy, worthless caretaker?"

Behind him, a woman's gentle voice replied, "I am the keeper of this orchard."

He turned in his saddle as a woman bearing a yoke supporting goatskin water bags emerged from the stand of trees. Her brown hair was tied back with a yellow scarf. Sun-browned face dripped with perspiration. Brown eyes squinted in the glare. She was tall and big-boned. Her feet were bare, covered with mud, and her sleeves rolled up. She carefully set the yoke on the rim of the well. With hands on her hips she demanded, "So? You're off the road. What do you want?"

Zachai replied, "Whose orchard is it?"

"It belongs to the House of Zachai the Publican. He is a powerful man. You may have heard of him? Zachai is landlord. The trees are his. The fruit is his. The house and the land are his. My father, who is the respected Chazzan of the synagogue, is tenant of it now and I tend the trees. Who wants to know?"

"I am Zachai." Zachai did not dismount. "Who are you again?"

Her mouth worked silently a moment as she seemed to consider her appearance and her challenge. She rolled down her sleeves. "I am Shimona . . . eldest . . . daughter . . . of the Chazzan," she stammered. She looked from Zachai to Haman, then back at Zachai.

He let his gaze linger disdainfully on her muddy feet. No trace of leprosy.

She blushed, turned, and darted into the house.

After a moment Zachai said, "That went well."

Haman sniffed. "Perhaps, since the orchard seems to have recovered . . . perhaps we should come back some other day?"

"Do you think she's coming out again?" Zachai licked his lips and wished for a drink as he wiped sweat from his brow.

"A waste of time." Haman turned his horse as if to ride back the way they had come.

Zachai did not budge. Thor pawed the ground and reached for a stray blade of grass.

Shimona appeared framed in the doorway with a tray of cups—one for Zachai and one for Haman. "Good sirs . . . for your thirst."

Gracious but still barefoot, she served each man on his horse and did not ask them to dismount and find a shady place to rest.

It was apple juice. Zachai drank it all in one long draught and wiped his lips with the back of his hand. "My thanks." He gave her the empty cup. "You know my steward, Haman?"

She glanced toward Haman. "No, sir. There have never been visitors. Not in the year since I came here to live. I am alone here almost always except when my father sends the cart with supplies and to pick up the figs each week."

Zachai shifted in the saddle and feigned surprise. "Each week?"

"Yes, sir. It's a fine grove. Very good fruit. Seven crops each summer. I wound the fruit to ripen it, so it will be perfect for sale in the souks of Yerushalayim." She lifted an iron nail dangling from a leather thong about her neck, then let it drop.

"You sell . . . my figs . . . in Yerushalayim? Does my steward know this?"

She seemed flustered by his questioning. "He must know it, sir. He—" she bowed slightly to Haman—"I have never seen the man before now. My father deals directly with him and all matters of the harvest. It is, as you know, a fruitful orchard." She finished with enthusiasm. "I love it here."

Haman looked everywhere but at Zachai. His expression was too innocent not to be guilty. He smiled sheepishly. "She seems to . . . care for the trees . . ."

Zachai feigned deep thought and puzzlement. Perhaps too much puzzlement not to betray that he knew exactly what had been going on. At last he spoke. "Cheat the cheater."

Haman blanched. His eyes widened as his very words were repeated back to him. "My lord Zachai . . ."

"The information cost me two denarii. It has cost you everything, Haman."

The steward began to weep.

The daughter of the Chazzan looked from one man to the other. What had just happened? "My lord? Is it the sun?"

Zachai snapped, "It's nothing. He is nothing. Your father is nothing."

She fell back a step with each phrase. "The trees. My work. Lord Zachai . . . has my work displeased you?"

Zachai swept an angry gaze around the lovely garden, the neat little house, the perfectly cultivated sukomore fig trees. "But you," he said gruffly to Shimona, "you have done well. Faithful. Yes. I would say that to you. . . . You have done well. . . . It's evident." He paused, letting his brusque praise penetrate her consciousness. "You are innocent in all this . . . collusion. My displeasure doesn't concern you. I'm sorry to trouble you. Thank you for the drink. You will hear from me at a later time."

He whirled Thor around violently, charging toward the white mare, who skittered out of the way. Zachai brought his whip down on the shoulders of his steward, then on his mount. The panicked little mare darted off to the highway and galloped all the way home to Jericho.

The Chazzan of the Jericho synagogue stood trembling before Zachai's desk. This was the first time in a lifetime that the Chazzan had ever entered the home of his landlord.

"'Steal from the thief'?" Zachai asked quietly. "Is that the phrase? Or was it 'Cheat the cheater'? And using the excuse of your daughter's illness to keep everyone away . . ." He shook his head.

The Chazzan blinked down at the heap of scrolls beside Zachai's lamp. He could not reply. His mouth had dried up. "Lord Zachai," he muttered, spreading his hands out in the gesture of a supplicant.

"You know the fate of my steward? Of Haman, your accomplice?"

"It was . . . he approached me with the scheme."

"I do not doubt it. A clever fellow, Haman. To think, all the while you've rented my orchard the balance sheet shows no profit."

"Lord Zachai, it was not profitable until . . . until . . . my daughter . . ."

"Yes. Your daughter. We'll speak about what is to become of her later."

"She had nothing to do with it. The guilt is . . . Haman's."

"And yours. Do you know where Haman is now?"

The Chazzan shook his head miserably. "No . . . no, I . . . cannot think."

"I'll tell you. He's on his way to debtors' prison. A bleak place. I may have him sold to pay for what he's stolen. Only I doubt he's worth a fraction of what he's stolen if everyone in Jericho is involved in defrauding me."

There was an instant when resentment flashed in the Chazzan's eyes. Zachai mentally conceded that it was an absurd situation. Zachai himself had, through his authority, taken more than was owed from nearly every household in the territory. And now, to find that those he stole from had, in turn, stolen from him . . . it was a strange economy, built on deception and fraud.

Zachai continued, "Debtors' prison, Chazzan. Think of it."

The Chazzan dropped to his knees with a wail and lifted his hands, begging, pleading, "Oh no! My family! My daughters. My wife. They will all starve if I am sent away."

Zachai recognized that this was the moment he could have demanded Barucha as a wife, had he not been warned she was a shrew.

"What about the one who tends my orchard?"

"Shimona? What? I've told you she didn't know! Please, sir, I am begging."

"What about her? Why do you hide her away? Why isn't she home with you?"

"She takes pleasure in her work. It pleases her to tend the old suko-more trees."

"That's not what I'm talking about. Dolt! Speak up! What's her story? Where did she return from? Why do you hide her away and make her work like a slave? Why is she never with the congregation on Sabbath? Who is she? I want to hear the truth from your own lips."

The Chazzan wiped his tears. "Mercy, Lord Zachai. I know you are a powerful man. I know what I have done offends you. But . . . as for my daughter. I am the Chazzan of the synagogue. . . ."

"The very synagogue my grandfather built and from which you have made me an excommunicate. But your daughter . . ."

"She is . . . was . . . unclean, you see."

"Unclean? Like a tax collector? Like a prostitute?"

"A leper." The Chazzan dropped his voice to a whisper.

Zachai drew back at the word. "What are you saying, man? She's a leper? Living in the stone house? Harvesting the fruit of my fig orchard?"

"She was . . . was . . . you see."

"I don't see. Once a leper, there's no returning from that."

"But she did . . . she did return to us. Just as you see her now. Without any sign of it. Not a spot."

Zachai snorted. "Impossible. Either she was or she wasn't. She is or she isn't."

"She was, but she isn't."

"Impossible."

"So say we. So say the high priest and all the Sanhedrin. But Yeshua of Nazareth—"

"The Healer, then . . . him?"

"Then *he* came to the Valley of Mak'ob. And first he spoke to them. All of them. Six hundred and twelve. All of them in the Valley. What he did or how, she can't say. But she says he touched them all . . . every unclean creature who crept across that cursed Valley to him. He healed them all."

Zachai frowned at the information. "And she came home to you. To her family."

"We had gone on with our lives. Many years had passed. We did not know if she had died. And then, like a dream, she was at the door and crying, 'Father! Mother!' And we saw her whole again. But I said in my heart, *What if the leprosy returns? What if she infects us all with it and we simply don't know? How can we know?*"

"And so you made up some story about her. You put her away . . . out of sight."

"Yes. Yes! Call it what you like. And out of danger. Danger to her. Danger to us. You know the edict against Yeshua. Against all who follow him. Those who have been healed by him."

"Where's the proof he's healed anyone?"

"My daughter is evidence he has some power. Whether of God or Satan—who can say?"

Zachai cradled one fist inside the other. "I see what you mean. Danger."

"No one can know the truth of it. She left so long ago. And now she seems well enough . . . yes, well . . . and yet . . . if she's a leper, she will die. If she's healed, her very life is in peril."

"Your life is in my hands, Chazzan. You are quite the hypocrite."

The Chazzan nodded. "Is there one who is not?"

"First you cheat me, and now you beg me to keep this information from those in authority whom I serve. You expect me to put my own position at risk over your little secret?"

Again the hands raised in supplication. The Chazzan began to weep piteously. "What do you want, Lord Zachai? Tell me what I must do."

Zachai felt no pity for the man. He rocked back in his chair. His lip curled with disdain. "I will tell you when I decide. Just so long as you understand . . . I own you, Chazzan. I, the most hated man in Judea, own you."

Clasping his hands behind his back, Zachai paced the length of his private courtyard. Beneath the enormous fig tree he paused to consider the woman who tended the trees that had grown from cuttings taken from the tree fifty years before. Clearly she was not responsible for the dishonesty of her father and Haman. And yet she must be questioned about the accounts. He marched back again along the high wall that separated him from the common folk of Jericho. Were all the citizens of the town complicit in Haman's embezzling? Had the steward of the great House of Zachai made deals with every tenant and taxpayer in Judea? Were they all laughing behind their backs at Zachai? No wonder he encountered such disrespect when he passed through the souk. No wonder he was despised.

The Old Man emerged from the house, bowed slightly, and announced, "The woman. Shimona, daughter of the Chazzan. She is here, Lord Zachai."

"A moment, then admit her. I'll receive her here. Prepare refreshment." Zachai remained standing, staring at the portico. His jaw twitched with anger. He rocked back on his heels.

Shimona emerged from the shadowed portico, scanning the garden for Zachai.

He stepped away from the tree. "I am here."

"Am I to meet with you alone?"

"It is best."

"I prefer witnesses. For my reputation, sir."

"For the reputation of your father, the Chazzan, it is better if we speak together of this matter without witnesses."

Averting her eyes from his fierce gaze, she curtsied and waited for his instruction.

She was dressed in tan homespun, the clothes of a poor woman. Her thick hair was clean and plaited.

"You are wearing shoes today," Zachai noted.

"Today I am not watering the sukomore grove of the great Zachai. Why have you called me here? I am forbidden to leave the grove, yet you summoned me. Why?"

"You don't know?"

"No, my lord."

"To discuss my fig trees."

"Has my care of the orchard displeased you?"

"Come closer."

She hung back, unwilling to cross the twenty paces to where he stood. "I . . . it is cool here. Where is my father? I was told this meeting was about the orchard my father let from you."

"Your father is not coming. I must speak to you about my grove before I discuss the matter with him."

"He doesn't know I'm here?"

"No." Zachai noted the flush of her cheeks. "My servant will bring us refreshment."

As if on cue the Old Man appeared with a tray of sweet wine mixed with spring water and offered her a cup. Shimona thanked him and seemed relieved that they were not alone.

Zachai took the cup. "Wait just there," he instructed the Old Man. "In case the lady should need her cup refilled."

The Old Man bowed and backed out of sight.

Zachai said, "The Old Man will not be far. If you need anything, you may call and he will come." Then he instructed, "Come closer, Shimona. Beneath this tree."

She raised her eyes to the twisted white trunk and enormous branches that were supported by thick planks driven into the ground. "When I was a little girl, I saw the top of this ancient tree above the high walls of your garden."

"Ten men holding their arms out couldn't encircle this tree." Zachai plucked a large, leathery leaf.

"It must be . . . beloved by God." She walked slowly toward him.

"My grandfather said the prophet Amos planted this tree hundreds of years ago. He told me this when I was a boy. Maybe it's true. I don't know. But he believed it."

"The fruit." She kicked a rotted fig on the ground. "Who tends the tree?"

"It's mine. It is father to the thirty-six trees in the orchard your father rented from my personal estate. And the fig trees along the highway to Yerushalayim? They were planted so the poor may have shade and free figs. They also came from this one old sukomore."

She smiled and relaxed, sipping her wine. "Who wounds the fruit to help it ripen?"

"I do. Myself. It's my tree."

"A man can own such a tree only for a short time in its life. For a while I suppose it can belong to you. But there's something about these trees. They live to be so very old, and trees have no memory of the men who sat beneath them or ate their fruit. It will live on after you are gone."

"Yes. But meanwhile it's mine. And the orchard you care for and the fruit you harvest and half the profit from the fruit . . . that is mine."

She touched the bark of the tree as if it were an old friend. "Yes. Seven crops of figs each summer. I love the grove."

Zachai indicated she should sit on the stone bench beneath the gnarled sukomore. "Sit."

"No. But thank you." She remained standing. She was taller than Zachai by several inches and probably as strong as a man. Perhaps she knew her height made him self-conscious. On his horse, towering over her, his small stature had not been an issue. He did not like it that she looked down on him.

"We were speaking of my orchard."

"We were speaking of living things that outlive men."

"You say the harvests have been plentiful?"

"You should know."

"Yes. I should know."

"Then you can answer your own question."

"I can't answer with any certainty. That is the point."

Her brow creased as she considered the implication of his words. "But the profits. My father and—"

"My steward. Yes. And your father, the Chazzan. It seems the accounts of the grove you tend show no profit. All your work, I am told, yields nothing for the landowner."

She blanched. "Sir! But it can't be! Every week the cart comes and takes away . . ."

"How much each week? An estimate."

She stared into the cup an instant. "Half a bushel basket filled for each fig tree. Eighteen bushels each week. That's easily . . ."

"A handsome profit in the souks of Yerushalayim." Zachai inhaled deeply. His eyes hardened. "Did you know of the fraud of my steward and your father?"

The cup dropped from her hands. Wine splashed the hem of Zachai's white tunic. She cried, "Not my father! No, he wouldn't—"

"He has done. And he is done for."

Shimona dropped to her knees, imploring, "No! Sir, please. I am mistaken. The grove is . . . it's barren. The trees haven't borne fruit. I meant . . . the fruit from . . . from my garden! Please, sir!"

Zachai turned away from her. He regretted the red stains on his robe. "You're lying."

She began to cry. "Please. My father is Chazzan. He must be innocent of the charges. He's an honorable man! Respected in the synagogue."

"There are no honorable men, Shimona. Have you lived alone so long that you haven't learned that? No man can be trusted. Especially not a man who disguises himself in his religion like a cloak."

"Not my father . . . you're mistaken."

"Your daughterly love causes hallucinations. You see what you want to see. Meanwhile I'm told my fig trees have borne no fruit and you're a failure and all your labor has been in vain. Get up. Stand up. I may let your father live. Or I may send him to debtors' prison, where my steward now resides. Your father's life may be spared if you tell me the truth. We may yet strike a bargain."

"Yes. Truth! Please, Lord Zachai! Ask. Ask me anything. . . . I'll tell you."

"The orchard. It is profitable?"

"Yes." Defeated by his authority, she stood slowly.

"A half bushel from each tree every week of the summer?"

Shimona nodded and fixed her gaze on a clump of figs hanging on the trunk of the prophet's ancient sukomore.

Zachai continued, "Touching on another matter . . . on the honor of my family. Did you know money from the treasuries of the House of Zachai built the synagogue in which your father is honored?"

"Yes."

"Good. You know that. You know the building is there because of the House of Zachai's generosity. And do you also know I am . . . anathema? Cut off from Israel? I was cast out, forbidden to enter the synagogue, by order of the council on which your father serves."

Now she almost smiled. "No, I didn't know."

"Why are you smiling? You think this is a joke?"

"No. Truth. It's not a joke. No, Lord Zachai."

He snapped, "Then why smile when I tell you I am forbidden to enter and pray? My sacrifices are refused. My charity is forbidden. It's men like your father who prevent me."

She did not reply for a long moment, then raised her eyes in a challenge. "The truth. Can you admit that the theft of your harvest by my father—his sin against you—pleases you?"

"Pleases? Why should it please me?"

"Truth. My father's hypocrisy justifies every commandment you have broken. There must be some pleasure in that for a man who had made his fortune stealing the harvest of other men."

"You're walking on dangerous ground."

"So are you. What will you do? Take back the orchard?"

"Do I have a choice? Your father has violated our contract. He's a thief even if he is the Chazzan."

"Will you throw me into prison too?"

"You're innocent in this affair . . . aren't you?"

"Are you? Innocent, I mean?" she asked.

"I don't pretend to be anything I am not. I'm a publican. I work for the good of Judea and am by extension an agent for Rome."

"And my father is also a thief, a liar, and a hypocrite."

"It gives me pleasure to hear you admit the truth."

"I've known my father all my life. And in spite of what I know, I love him. Love is my truth. I love my father, the hypocrite, the thief, and the liar."

"Your love is wasted on such a man."

"Love? Wasted? Do you speak from experience? Is that what they say about Zachai? Someone has wasted love on you, perhaps?"

"I'm the most hated man in Judea."

"So I've heard. And with good reason."

"I don't pretend. I live out every expectation the people have about the chief tax collector of Judea."

"So now, Publican, tell me: What tax have you assessed on my father's sin?"

"Revenge."

"Has his hatred of your guilt pierced you so deeply?"

"Not his hatred of my guilt. Rather his pretense that he is guiltless."

"Revenge is a price beyond calculation. How will you know when the debt is paid?"

"When your father is stung with humiliation as he has stung me."

"Well then, here's a proposition: I offer myself in payment of his debt. The daughter of the Chazzan of Jericho . . . as a slave in the household of Zachai the Publican."

"Such payment has potential."

"I'm strong. Healthy. I proved my worth in your orchard, though the harvest was stolen. I worked hard because I loved the work. I suppose I'll still love the trees, though you'll own me and call my love an obligation."

"I was impressed with your management."

"Then we agree. A slave with my skill should be ransom enough to pay my father's debt to you. Is it possible . . . my father could be saved from debtors' prison?"

Zachai cherished this moment of power over the Chazzan. "I'll consider it. So. Go home. I'll let you know if and when. I'll consider the factors and decide if your proposition is enough to cancel his debt."

"Home. I have a home?"

"Better in my sukomore grove than in the house of your father. Never speak to him the terms you presented to settle his debt. Go on. Back to your cottage. Say nothing of our meeting to anyone."

"Who would I tell?"

"If word of this meeting gets out, understand me: All bargains are off. Continue your work. If I decide favorably? If I accept your offer? I'll send terms to keep your father out of prison. A contract of settlement."

It was a triumph, Zachai thought, as he listened to the distant voice of the Chazzan in the synagogue next door. He rested on his couch beneath the spreading limbs of the old tree that Amos had planted so long ago. The jumbled morning prayers of the congregation drifted through the open windows and over the wall of Zachai's compound. Discordant psalms settled in the thick branches of the giant sukomore like squabbling crows.

Zachai waited until the early service, then sent the Old Man with a note to wait at the door of the synagogue for the Chazzan to emerge.

Silence fell. Zachai smiled and flexed his ankle, as if dancing in celebration.

Minutes passed before the Old Man entered Zachai's private garden from the house. "Lord Zachai." The Old Man bowed formally.

"What is it?" Zachai answered calmly, as though he had forgotten why he sent the Old Man to snag the Chazzan in front of the synagogue.

"Lord Zachai, the Chazzan of the Jericho synagogue has come as you have summoned him."

Zachai rubbed a hand over the stubble on his chin. "I need a shave, Old Man. After I see to this unpleasantness with the Chazzan, I would like a shave."

"Yes, my lord." Another deep bow. "He is waiting."

"Waiting? The Chazzan? Waiting for me to call him into my garden? He who was always too good to walk on the same side of the street as my house? He is waiting?" Zachai knew the Chazzan could hear every word.

"Yes, my lord. You summoned him after morning service, and now he waits to hear your will in the matter of the stolen figs."

Zachai and the Old Man played out an unrehearsed script to strike terror into the heart of the religious leader. "Since his sin has been discovered and he confessed, I have been considering what I might do with him."

"Any conclusions?"

"There is always prison. He might still like to join his partner in the crime. Haman would like company. Debtors' prison. Hmmm. Perhaps that is best. . . ."

Inside the house a wail erupted. "No! Lord Zachai!" The Chazzan burst from inside and flung himself onto the ground before Zachai's couch.

Zachai wondered if the members of the synagogue who lingered in the courtyard outside could hear the cries of their friend. He sighed deeply and continued the play. "So, Chazzan, what am I to do with you, eh? What shall I do with you?"

The man held his hands up, imploring, "Not prison. Oh, Lord Zachai, not prison! My wife. My daughters. Think! Think and have mercy!"

Zachai cleared his throat and feigned surprise and disgust at the synagogue ruler's display. "Yes. Your family. You should have thought of them. But we've been through all that. I told you I would come to a suitable . . . appropriate way for you to pay your debt to me."

"Anything! Anything, Lord Zachai!"

Zachai enjoyed watching him grovel. "Well, there is your daughter Barucha."

The eyes of the Chazzan brightened. "Yes! My daughter! Marriageable. A lovely girl! Sweet-tempered and . . . suitable for the wife of a rich man."

"Don't lie to me, Chazzan."

"Lie?"

"Word is, Barucha is bitter and cruel. Beautiful, yes. But a hot-tempered viper. Neither suitable for any man's wife nor trained as any sort of a servant. It is said she could be neither a courtesan nor the maid of a courtesan. Worthless."

The Chazzan's eyes widened. He grew pale. "Courtesan?"

Zachai waved away his fear. "As I said . . . not worth the price of one night at a good brothel."

"But . . . she . . . my daughter Barucha . . . surely worth something toward my debt."

Zachai laughed. So the righteous fellow was willing to sell his own child as a harlot to keep out of prison. "No. She will not do."

"I have a servant girl. . . ."

"She will not do."

"But what? How?" Copious tears flowed onto the Chazzan's beard. "Oh, please, sir! Not prison! It was the idea of your steward. Haman is the one who conceived the idea."

Zachai lifted his chin in a sort of regal gesture. "The older daughter, Shimona . . . the one you say may still be a leper."

"Yes! Shimona!"

"A hard worker from all I saw at the sukomore grove."

"Yes! Shimona! A hard worker, she—"

"Perhaps since she already tends the figs. Why should I hire a caretaker since she is there? Why should I buy another slave when I might take her into servitude to pay at least a portion of her father's debt?"

The Chazzan wiped his face eagerly and nodded and nodded again. He seemed speechless at the thought that anyone would want to own Shimona the Leper. "Oh, merciful Zachai! Merciful . . ." He moved forward on his knees and kissed the hem of Zachai's tunic.

"It pleases me. The thought of owning this woman who seems so . . . contented in her work. When did you last see her?"

"Nearly a year, my lord. We do not dare venture in—" he caught himself—"I mean, there is no sign of the disease . . . so I have heard from the fellow who takes the provisions."

"A year." Zachai found himself hating this groveling worm. "Your own daughter. A year since she came home and—"

The eyes of the Chazzan glinted in a moment of unguarded resentment. "She was a leper . . . by all accounts."

"But she is no more a leper . . . so I saw with my own eyes."

The Chazzan fell silent.

Zachai clapped his hands, summoning the Old Man with the parchment contract he had prepared beforehand. "I knew you would sell your own flesh and blood to save your skin." Zachai put his signature to the paper, then gave the quill to the Chazzan.

The Chazzan signed. "There. She's yours."

"Yes. And as you see, if she proves to be defective, I return her, and you, Chazzan, are doomed to debtors' prison."

14 CHAPTER

S ukkot—the town's name meant "Booths"—was an ancient city east of Jordan. It was said to have received its designation from being the location where the patriarch Isra'el dwelt for a time in tents on his way back from his uncle Laban's home.[24]

At the moment Peniel was not as interested in Sukkot's history as he was in its present fame: It was a center of metalworking. During the course of Yeshua's itinerant ministry the band's cook pots and utensils had all but worn out. Peniel had been dispatched into Sukkot to purchase replacements.

Unfortunately he had arrived on a market day. Since Sukkot was the only village of consequence in the area just north of the Jabbok River, it was crowded with sellers and shoppers.

Peniel had located a merchant offering what was needed at reasonable rates, but so had a horde of other bargain seekers. The youth maintained his composure outwardly, but inside he was eager to get back to camp.

When Peniel was finally third in line from the counter, a well-dressed man bustled in with an entourage of servants and went straight to the front of the queue. "How long must I be kept waiting?" he demanded after thirty seconds. "Don't you know who I am?"

The shopkeeper shook his head.

The pushy newcomer thrust out his chest. "Bera ben Dives, private secretary to Lord Caiaphas, the high priest. I need information."

"How can I help?" the merchant responded.

Peniel shrunk back. The exit out the only door was blocked by men in armor. Obvious flight would only make matters worse.

He waited and prayed.

"It is said that the Galilean rebel, Yeshua of Nazareth, is preaching near here. Do you know where?" ben Dives demanded.

The shop owner shrugged. "I do not."

Without seeming to pause for breath, ben Dives raised his finger to the nostrils of the first customer. "You?"

Another negative response.

"You?" This applied to the woman just in front of Peniel.

"I-I heard . . . ," the shopper stammered.

"Yes? Be quick."

"East? Yes, I think . . . east, up toward the mountains."

For an instant ben Dives studied Peniel. The high priest's secretary started to demand Peniel's opinion, curled his lip scornfully, twitched his robe aside, and stalked out of the shop.

Moments later, Peniel departed Sukkot toward Yeshua's location . . . west of the town.

Marcus Longinus, Roman centurion and commander of the garrison of Jerusalem, was troubled about many things. In his chambers in the Antonia, adjacent to the Temple of the One God of the Jews, he pondered troop dispositions and discipline.

Soon Jewish pilgrims would begin arriving from all over the world in order to celebrate their Passover holy day. The population of the city would double, and with the influx would come all manner of associated evils. Thieves, pickpockets, and sicarii bent on murdering Romans and collaborators would all sneak inside the city by mingling with the pilgrims.

One year ago there had been a Passover riot that had killed scores and stained Governor Pilate's reputation; overzealous troopers had clubbed innocent bystanders. Pilate, maliciously grinning at the charge he laid on Marcus, had demanded that this year his centurion keep the peace. Then the governor departed for the Gentile security and calm of Caesarea Maritima on the seacoast.

While Marcus nominally had half a legion under his command, the truth was, the force present for duty was only a fraction of that number. A hundred were out securing the caravan routes. Another hundred were accompanying Governor Pilate. Still another century of men had been detached to help quell a disturbance along the border with Parthia.

Marcus scratched his head. It was considerably grayer than when he had first arrived at this posting several years earlier.

The other difficulty Marcus pondered was the nature of the auxiliary legionaries: None of them were Jews. By a wisdom inscrutable to all but the province's army headquarters in Syria, the troops assigned to this post were all Syrians, Samaritans, and Idumeans. Jewish troopers patrolled Cyprus, Sicily, and North Africa . . . but not Judea.

Hereditary enemies of the Jews, the Roman mercenaries from the bordering nations were as likely to savage the sheep they were supposed to be protecting as save them. It was a fulfillment of the Roman philosophy for ruling conquered peoples: Hating or fearing Rome did not matter as long as they obeyed.

Marcus sighed and bellowed for Quintus, his guard sergeant, to bring more wine and be quick about it.

In one respect only was Marcus pleased: Yeshua of Nazareth was safely out of harm's way, preaching in obscure villages in the hill country.

Marcus had known Yeshua for years, had heard His teaching, had personally witnessed miracles. Most recently Marcus had been present when Yeshua raised El'azar of Bethany to life. It was no trick, no ploy to gain fame. El'azar had been dead . . . and then he was not just alive again but perfectly strong and well.

Yeshua was . . . Marcus was not entirely sure how to regard Him. Since Marcus was not himself a Jew, he could not very well claim Yeshua as his Messiah.

Yet the centurion knew the man from Galilee was more than any mere man. The Teacher had referred to Himself as the Son of God. But what did that mean? Since Tiberius Caesar was the adopted son of

Augustus Caesar, who was worshipped as a god, Tiberius himself could claim he was the "son of god" too.

Marcus snorted. If rumors were true, Tiberius certainly behaved like one of the gods of legend: lecherous, gluttonous, petulant. . . .

The door smacked into the wall as Quintus kicked it to enter with the wine. "You don't need wine; you need fresh air."

"Awfully free with your advice, aren't you? Or were you seeking a transfer to guard duty in the tin mines?"

Quintus, who had served with Marcus for over fifteen years and in campaigns too many for counting, was not deterred. "You need exercise. You need air. So does Pavor. Good horse bit the groom yesterday . . . man may lose his arm. He's barn sour—the horse, not the groom—and so are you."

Marcus slapped the flat of his hand on the charts. "Guard Sergeant Quintus, you're exactly right! You will accompany me."

"Aye, sir. Full troop as well?"

Shrugging, Marcus demurred. "Four young recruits for an honor guard. Make certain they ride well. This will be for exercise, not dress parade."

"Destination, sir?"

"Jericho. I warned their captain about a surprise inspection that was coming. It's time I made good on the threat."

Bar Abba stood beside the well inside the customs compound. His hair was pulled back from his face and secured with a headband, but the tail of his keffiyeh concealed his features. Bending over, he unwound the head scarf and casually dipped the end in the water trough, then mopped his face.

All the while bar Abba scanned the compound, the guards, and his own men. A quick nod to the east gate, another to the west, confirmed all was in readiness. Across the compound Lamech waited with a rolled-up rug slung across his shoulder.

Straightening up, bar Abba strolled toward Lamech . . . just another laborer waiting for some tradesman to need a day's work.

Under his cloak, on the left side, bar Abba patted the hilt of a short

Roman sword, taken from a dead trooper. When he smoothed the right seam of his robe, it was to adjust the dagger hidden there.

All that remained to do was wait. If Zachai continued to be a man of predictable habits—unwary because of the protection of his Nubian sentries—then bar Abba's plan could not fail.

And even if today's routine changed, there was always tomorrow. Sword, dagger, and rug would all keep.

One scowling Nubian stalking in front and two more pacing slightly behind, one on either side, accompanied the chief publican of the Jericho district. Today was the day for compiling a month's worth of tax reports. Import taxes, export duties, land fees, and Caesar's special assessment on luxury items like incense and balsam. It was also time for the quarterly payment of license fees owed by caravan promoters. Today would see a huge influx of payments from those who had waited until the last moment to pay what was owed.

Ordinarily this day would be nerve-racking for Zachai. So much money in one place was bound to tempt legions of robbers. In the normal course of events, today would keep Zachai looking over his shoulders until evening closed the tax office. Once that was done, Zachai would take the account books home while the receipts were turned over to the Roman soldiers to guard. Tomorrow the cash boxes would go off to Jerusalem, but Zachai's responsibility would end tonight.

Instead of his usual nervousness, Zachai smiled and hummed to himself as he walked down the hill on the path from New Jericho to the Customs Office. Despite having only three bodyguards instead of four, he felt remarkably secure. The usual amount of banditry in the hills had fallen off of late. Jericho was too well garrisoned and Jerusalem's reinforcements too near, it seemed. Apparently the raiders had taken the hint and moved their operations elsewhere.

Today's threat was only from the black looks and muttered curses that greeted him . . . and those were everywhere. All the same, nothing would darken Zachai's mood today.

He gave Bartimaeus twice the usual amount of copper coins and received profound thanks and blessings in response. "You'd better spend some of that on a new cloak," Zachai warned. "There are so many holes in the old one you'll lose more money than you take in."

"Yes, sir! Thank you, sir. Very kind of you to take an interest!" announced the blind man.

Passersby raised scornful eyebrows.

Grandly Zachai passed on to his office, secure in the day's good fortune.

CHAPTER 15

Eight miles east of the Jordan and five miles farther east than Sukkot lay the town of Penuel. Judas Iscariot paced up and down impatiently behind the village's only inn.

Near sunset Bera ben Dives appeared, accompanied by a lean man and a pudgy woman.

"I told you I can't help you now," Judas protested.

"You don't have a choice," ben Dives said menacingly. "I won't traipse all over Perea any longer. Where is he?"

"This morning I could have said, but now, tonight, who knows? I'll have to hunt for him myself."

"Why can't you take us with you and . . . introduce us?"

Judas studied the two innocuous-looking companions with suspicion. He shook his head. "It's impossible. Yeshua . . . knows things. I mean, he trusts me, but he'd see through you in an instant. Besides, the other eleven are constantly with him. So is El'azar of Bethany. You'd never be able to seize Yeshua and get away with him."

The unintroduced man and woman exchanged a knowing glance but no commentary.

"Send word of the next large village you approach and leave the rest to me," ben Dives urged.

"No! The others are already curious about my absences. Don't try to contact me again. He'll go back to Yerushalayim, where things'll be easier; I'm sure of it."

"For your sake, I hope so," ben Dives concluded.

Two hours had passed since Amos bar Abba watched Zachai and his bodyguards enter the Customs House. The bandit chief could not help smiling to himself. Things were better than he had hoped. The publican was accompanied by only three guards today instead of four. That meant one less to dispose of when the action began.

If the morning went true to form, it would not be long now. Rising from his tables groaning with extorted money, Zachai would soon appear at the door of his office, on his way to the necessary.

One of the guards would see that no one else occupied the little house. Once it was clear, the Nephilim would post themselves around it until their master reemerged.

Only today, he would not reemerge . . . at least, not in the same condition as he entered.

To provide ventilation, the back wall of the privy did not reach to the roofline. The gap was wide enough for even a man as bulky as bar Abba to lever himself through. He knew because he had practiced the move on several moonless nights when the customs compound stood empty.

Of course Zachai would yell for help, but by then the diversion would be in full swing.

Overpowering the little man would not be difficult. Then the real genius of bar Abba's plan would unfold.

Zachai was pleased with himself. Revenues were running 20 percent ahead of last term—a fact certain to bring additional recognition from Governor Pilate, as well as monetary remuneration. The district of Jericho was already the most lucrative in Judea. What would a promotion bring? A posting to Caesarea Maritima, perhaps? The position of customs officer for the port city was an Imperial appointment.

Did Zachai's ambition stretch that far?

In addition to dreaming of the future, Zachai was pleased because he was secretly proud of his revenge on the embezzlers. What an exquisite trap he had sprung, and what a glorious catch! The daughter of the Chazzan was employed as a servant by the House of Zachai. The Chazzan had been foremost in reviling the publican and demanding his expulsion from the synagogue. What would the congregation of the synagogue think now? The Chazzan could scarcely admit that he cut a deal to save himself from being exposed as a thief.

But how could he ever explain that he'd willingly sent his daughter to serve the most defiled . . . the most traitorous man in the land?

Zachai rubbed his hands together with glee. Instead of having a daughter of the Chazzan as his wife, making one his field hand was even better!

Rising from his desk, he excused himself to the two bookkeepers slaving away at side tables. The lone bodyguard who had remained inside the office accompanied Zachai. The other two, who had been guarding the door, likewise marched alongside as the publican crossed the compound to the latrine set against the far north wall.

The lead bodyguard was cousin to Salmon. Young of face and lean of body, the warrior carried himself proudly. At his side he toted a short stabbing spear with a leaf-shaped blade. Eager to demonstrate his capabilities as Salmon's substitute, the Nubian trotted ahead into the privy. Moments later he hustled a protesting Parthian camel drover out and pronounced the location secure.

"You may go in now, master. We will keep watch here."

The three men posted themselves across the doorway to see that Zachai was not disturbed.

Bar Abba heard Lamech's whistle. It was the signal! Emerging from where he had crouched behind the wall at the back of the privy, bar Abba waved his hands above his head.

Let the diversions begin!

The timing could not have been better. In the northern compound an inbound caravan had only just repacked and reloaded their camels after the customs inspection. The merchants were eager to get into

Jerusalem before sundown. The smack of the drovers' sticks roused the beasts. Those at the back were already milling about. Exclamations of "Hut, hut, hut!" from the riders urged the camels into motion, stirring up clouds of dust.

Bar Abba had just a moment to witness his men plunging into the mix. Wielding crooked, finger-length blades shaped like miniature sickles, the brigands slashed at the cinches holding the packsaddles and reaped a harvest of confusion.

In the billowing grit no one noticed for an instant. Then camels began to bellow and drovers to curse. Carefully loaded silk became hapless heaps of cloth. A crashing note of destruction increased the chaos as incense and unguents were transformed into perfumed mud amid shattered alabaster jars.

Bar Abba could not see it, but he was confident a similar scene was being played out at the opposite gate as well.

The tumult was perfect; the time was now.

Dagger between his teeth, bar Abba vaulted for and caught the latrine wall's ledge. In a flash he rolled through the opening and landed on his feet on the inside . . . face-to-face with a startled Zachai.

Bar Abba brandished the point of the dagger toward the publican's face as a demand for silence. Zachai choked back a scream, and his eyes widened with terror, as if holding in the cry for help would burst him.

Then bar Abba reversed the dagger and swung the brass-and-oak hilt against Zachai's head. The publican crumpled to his knees, emitting a cry of pain stifled by bar Abba's other palm across his mouth.

Another tap of the heavy handle behind Zachai's ear ensured that the tax collector would remain unconscious all the way back to the wilderness hideout. Now to dump the little man over the wall, where Lamech waited with the rug. Once Zachai was rolled up inside the carpet, no one would be the wiser as they trudged away with the chief publican as a hostage for ransom!

16 CHAPTER

Marcus caught sight of the milling chaos as he and his companions emerged from New Jericho at the top of the hill above the customs compound. From a distance, with the scene shrouded in roiling dust and obscured by colliding camels, the centurion could not tell if it was a robbery or a riot, but his response was the same. "Charge!"

A Roman officer, especially one as experienced as Marcus, knew that nothing was gained by hesitation. The sooner order was reestablished, the better; the sorting out would follow after.

Nothing imposed order on chaos faster than a troop of Roman cavalry brandishing short swords. The fact that the several hundred drovers and animals caught up in the melee were opposed by only six troopers bothered Marcus not at all.

"Rival caravans fighting . . . or Zealots?" bellowed Quintus.

"Doesn't matter" was the return shout. "Take two men and ride to the opposite gate. No one gets in or out 'til we get this sorted. Club them apart, but no unnecessary killing, understand? Don't make things worse!"

"Aye! Come on, lads! Follow me!"

Everything was going perfectly! Bar Abba heard Zachai hit the ground outside the privy building with a thud. This was followed by a groan. The shouting of enraged merchants and the screams of terrified pilgrims mingled with the bugling of angry camels. He knew the guards were trained to retreat to the Customs House in order to protect the tax money. In the upheaval, no one would even notice the little scene being played out with two men carrying an extra-heavy carpet.

The tail of bar Abba's cloak caught on the ledge as he vaulted through. It pulled him sideways as it unwound, landing him toward the wall instead of outward. "Let's go, Lamech," he ordered as he spun around. "Did you get him rolled—?"

The question was never completed, since bar Abba was not facing his accomplice but Zachai's young bodyguard. The publican was unconscious on the ground . . . and so was Lamech.

"You will drop your dagger and lay upon the ground," the bodyguard intoned, brandishing the stabbing spear at bar Abba's midsection. Dropping the dagger as ordered, bar Abba raised both hands in token of submission. As he did so he stepped closer to the Nubian, his posture that of a beaten foe.

Seeing the brigand surrender, the bodyguard relaxed slightly and the spearhead swung away from bar Abba.

It was all the opening bar Abba needed. He did not try to draw his concealed sword; he simply shoved down hard on the hilt, swinging the tip upward from under his cloak. One hand grasping the hilt, with the other the bandit chief grasped the guard's shoulder and yanked the man toward him.

The Roman blade entered under the bodyguard's ribs and angled upwards into his heart. His mouth worked soundlessly as his spear dropped from nerveless fingers.

Bar Abba contemptuously kicked him backwards off the weapon. Bright red blood spurted all over the recumbent Zachai, soaking his cloak.

No one else had appeared. The other bodyguards were nowhere to be seen. The way was still open.

Without a single glance at Lamech, who would be left to fend for himself, bar Abba calculated that he could still get away with Zachai. No time for the rug ploy; bar Abba would act as if he were helping a friend wounded in the tumult.

Closely followed by two young troopers who were suddenly getting more exercise than they bargained for, Marcus spurred Pavor through the gate of the compound. The force of his rush knocked over two of bar Abba's men who were trying to escape in the confusion. As soon as Marcus saw them with weapons in their hands, he shouted, "Seize them!" then galloped straight on to the Customs House.

The decurion, the captain of the ten-man detachment guarding the tax receipts, was under the portico of the veranda and recognized the centurion. "A robbery?" Marcus demanded without dismounting. Pavor pranced in a tight circle, snorting at the feel of battle.

"No, sir, unless they were frightened off. Mischief only."

"Mischief?"

"Aye, sir. Pack cinches cut! Loads spilled all over. Fists are flying, but no one's seriously hurt."

"Keep your men watching all sides of this building. Let no one in without my express permission."

"Aye, sir."

"And the chief publican?"

"Gone to the latrine, sir. Two of his bodyguards ran back to help us when this melee started, but the other one and Zachai haven't returned."

A sudden suspicion seized Marcus, and he dug his heels into Pavor's flanks. The horse leapt forward instantly, clearing a pair of men wrestling on the ground and darting around a snarled string of donkeys.

Approaching the wall of the compound, Marcus did not slow but galloped directly toward the barricade. At the last second he planted his spurs and lifted the reins. Pavor soared over.

Marcus reined up. Behind the privy two bodies lay prostrate and unmoving.

A short distance away a thickset man ran with something slung over his shoulder. "You there! Stop!" Marcus commanded.

Bar Abba cast a look over his shoulder at the Roman. He snarled something and continued running.

Marcus recognized bar Abba and, in the same moment, saw that the burden being toted was the publican. Pavor's hooves churned as Marcus set him to a parade canter. Then the centurion jumped from the horse's back onto bar Abba's shoulders, bowling all three men over in the dirt.

Zachai sprawled like a sack of figs.

Bar Abba rolled free of Marcus and came up with sword in hand.

Marcus closed with the brigand and steel rang against steel as the short swords clashed together.

The two men were much a match in size and strength. Marcus was the better trained, but bar Abba fought with desperation.

Bar Abba feinted toward Marcus' face with the point of his weapon, then hacked downward, aiming for the centurion's sword hand.

Marcus batted the blow aside, but the dodge allowed bar Abba to grab a handful of dust, which he flung into the Roman's eyes.

Blinded, Marcus gave back a step, then parried a two-handed swing aimed at his head. Lunging low, Marcus scored a gash on bar Abba's thigh, then narrowly avoided a return cut that whistled past his shoulder.

The sound of approaching hooves indicated more combatants were arriving. But whose men? Marcus' or bar Abba's?

"Hold! Enough!" It was Quintus. "I'll spit you like a goose!"

The bandit chief danced away from another blow, then retreated to stand over Zachai. Both hands gripping the hilt, he placed the point of his sword in the hollow of Zachai's throat.

"Call your men off!" he snarled. "Or I'll kill him."

Marcus straightened up, wiping his eyes with the back of one hand. "Kill him and I'll crucify you today on the wall of the Customs House."

"I swear it! I'll kill him!"

Marcus gave a slight shrug. "Kill him, then. He's nothing but a publican. Or let him live and you might have a trial. Your choice."

After studying Marcus' impassive face and the ring of troopers surrounding him, bar Abba cast the sword away and fell to his knees.

Back now in his Jericho office, Zachai sat alone in the gloom. Tax rolls were open on his desk. He stared down at the figures with unseeing eyes. A tray of food brought hours earlier remained untouched.

He had not allowed his cloak to be taken away and washed. It was thrown across the chair with the splattered blood of his bodyguard upon it.

Zachai gingerly touched the knots on his aching head.

The keening of women and cries of small children in the slave quarters echoed in the courtyard. The agonized lament flowed over the windowsills into the house like a polluted tide on a white sand beach.

"My people do not mourn quietly. How loudly would they wail if I had died and not him?" Zachai whispered. "God, you who do not hear my prayers. God of my fathers, not God of myself. God of Avraham, Yitz'chak, and Isra'el, you hate me though you made me. Your people, who are also my people, hate me though I am kin to them. They hate me enough to transgress your commandment not to kill. Cheat the cheater. They would kill because I have transgressed your command-ment not to steal. God of Israel, who does not hear my prayers, why didn't I die today? Why didn't you allow the knife to plunge deep into my sin-filled and lonely heart? Why plunge the dagger into the heart of a man with a wife and children?"

Zachai's throat constricted as he tried to hold back his sorrow. He began to weep, though no tears flowed from his eyes. Covering his face with his hands, he tried to blot out the image of faces looking on during the attack. The people had hoped Zachai would fall. They had all been cheering for the assassin. How they howled and scattered when Marcus the centurion waded into the fray, as if wishing Zachai were dead had made them somehow guilty of the attack.

Zachai's shoulders shook as though he were laughing. He raised his gaze to the cloak. He grew quiet and stared at the blood of an innocent man who had fought and died to save him.

The room grew darker as the sun set. The wailing of Nubian grief did not slacken. Zachai replayed the events of the day again and again. Was there anything he could have done to change the outcome?

"Freedom. God who does not hear the prayer of sinners, I would die and sleep forever gladly to be free from such hatred. Why wasn't it me?" He fingered the hilt of his razor-sharp dagger and contemplated how quickly he would bleed out if he slit his wrists.

A glimmer of light seeped in around the door. A soft rapping sounded.

The voice of the Old Man called gently, "Master Zachai?"

Zachai withdrew his hand from the weapon, clasped his hands before him, and straightened himself in the dark. "Enter."

A beam of light flooded in with Olabi, blinding Zachai. He shielded his eyes. "What do you want?"

The Old Man took in the scene with a glance. His gaze rested on the blade of the dagger. "You will not need that now. Two Roman soldiers stand guard outside the gates, lest there be a riot. They have hauled the other assassins away to Yerushalayim. Bar Abba. A Zealot. A big criminal who has these years set his face in rebellion against Rome. They say you will be given a reward by Pilate, the Roman governor, for your part in his capture." The Old Man looked at the bloody garment. "A reward from Rome. Enough to replace the . . . slave . . . you have lost this day."

The high shriek of a woman's anguish pierced the night.

Zachai inhaled deeply, pretending he was unshaken by the sound.

"Ignorant people." Olabi raised his chin.

Zachai wondered whom the Old Man was referring to. "Ignorant? Who?"

"All. The Romans who rule. The religious leaders who condemn. The people who rebel. The assassins who kill. The servants who die. The women who grieve . . ."

"And . . . me?"

The Old Man did not pause. "And all those who by greed and oppression are the nexus of human misery." His eyes lingered on Zachai's dagger. "Is the blood of the innocent the only river flowing to freedom? Perhaps." He shrugged.

"I am now truly a prisoner here."

"Yes. You have many others in your service who will collect the taxes and bring the money to you here."

"Here. Only here. What good is it to me? If I own half the world and can't see it?"

Olabi's lips curved in a half smile. "The beginning of wisdom."

"What do you mean?"

"You are a son of Abraham, circumcised on the eighth day, yet you dress like a Roman. You cut your hair and shave your beard like a Greek in Alexandria."

"I am . . . not one of them."

"They have said so. Yet they hate you because you are one of them and deny what you are."

"I am a prisoner. Confined in this . . . my own jail. There is no freedom for me. I am not just a prisoner. I am a corpse living in an elegant tomb like a dead pharaoh roaming through his pyramid."

"You are a Jew. Why do you not grow your beard like a Jew? Become what you are born to be. Send others out to transact your business. Hide awhile inside these walls. For a few weeks become a voice behind this door. Your private garden is there. You will have sunlight. You will have books to study. We will say Lord Zachai is . . . recovering from a slight illness. The shock, you know. Such a thing leads a man to spend time in meditation."

"I am not known to be a contemplative man."

Olabi raised his finger. "Or this: Say the Romans advise you stay out of sight in case there are more assassins on the loose. Yes. Who will deny the sense of that?"

"My business."

"Those agents who serve the business dealings of Lord Zachai can speak to Lord Zachai through me and you to them."

"You know what they'll say if I don't show myself."

"They will all say Zachai the Publican is in hiding in terror after such an event. No one will blame you for hiding after today. Does it matter what they say? Does it matter if they now believe you are afraid?"

"I am afraid," Zachai admitted.

The warm eyes of the Old Man smiled at him. "This is a moment when truth is essential. And a small deception as to your identity."

"Even with a beard I will still resemble . . . myself. They'll see my face and know I look like me."

"You will be . . . your cousin. And when you leave from this house as cousin of Zachai . . . a true son of Abraham . . . dressed in your father's clothes, with beard and hair flowing, the *am ha aretz* will not know it is rich Zachai the Publican, traitor to Abraham, servant of Rome and the Herodians. Then you, a Jew like any other, will go out among them for a day and listen. You will hear their words. See how they survive and what they long for."

Zachai nodded once in agreement . . . carefully so as not to jar his splitting head. "My beard grows fast," he admitted.

The plan seemed good.

PART III

As for you, My flock, this is what the Sovereign LORD says: I will judge between one sheep and another, and between rams and goats. Is it not enough for you to feed on good pasture? Must you also trample the rest of the pasture with your feet?

EZEKIEL 34:17-18

17

Spring had come to Perea. The sky was a rain-washed blue. The hills were vibrant green, alive with what appeared to be moving shoals of wildflowers.

Peniel sighed and stopped walking behind Yeshua long enough to take it all in. The colorful flowing display was in reality knots of pilgrims seeking the Master: family groups, clumps of friends, sometimes the populations of whole villages.

All coalescing around the source of Living Water.

There seemed to be no prearranged meeting sites. In the morning Yeshua led His talmidim out into the countryside for teaching and prayers.

The others came seeking Him, wherever He might be found. And when the two groups met, Yeshua had them all sit down, like now, in this mulberry grove.

The roots of a mulberry tree had wrapped around a boulder. It was on this natural bema that Yeshua sat, in the shade of the tree.

Then He taught them about the Kingdom of God: "Pay attention and always be on your guard, looking out for one another. If your brother sins and misses the mark, solemnly tell him so and reprove him. And if he repents, forgive him.

"And even if he sins against you seven times in a day, and turns to you seven times and says, 'I am sorry,' you must forgive him. You must give up resentment and consider the offense as recalled and annulled."[25]

Shim'on Peter looked at Yeshua and said loudly, "Increase our faith!"[26] Then, in an aside to John and John's brother Ya'acov, Peter said, "This may be the toughest thing he has demanded so far!"

Yeshua patted the tree trunk with one hand while pinching thumb and forefinger together on the other. "Faith, Peter! It's all about faith. If you had faith even like a grain of mustard seed, you could say to this mulberry, 'Be pulled up by the roots and be planted in the sea,' and it would obey you."[27]

Peniel thought about that. Closing his eyes, he pictured the silver-barked, broad-girthed tree towering forty feet over Yeshua's head. In Peniel's vision he saw an invisible hand wrench the mulberry out by the roots, then fling it in a high arc, ending with a visible splash in a distant sea!

If faith as small as the tiniest seed was all that was required, then how did one achieve it? Was it a matter of the head . . . or of the heart?

With his eyes still closed, Peniel heard voices other than the Master's, whispering, but insistent:

Will he have time for me? a woman's voice worried.

If he asks me about my faith, what will I say? came the anxious murmur of a young man.

Uproot a tree? Why not cast Herod and Pilate and all the Romans into the sea? was the angry, hostile cry of another.

Peniel's eyes popped open. Gazing around the crowd, he saw no one's lips moving; no one but Yeshua was speaking.

In a flicker of understanding, like the brief glimpses of azure heavens seen through the fluttering mulberry leaves, Peniel understood. Once more Yeshua was allowing him to hear the thoughts of the throng. Some of the pilgrims were curiosity seekers, moved to see this man of whom they had heard so much. Some in the audience were eager to determine if Yeshua would be *their* sort of Messiah: proclaim Himself king, drive out the Romans, and restore Israel to earthly grandeur and power.

Some in the crowd pretended to be in one of the first two groups but actually came with deeper longings . . . comprised of loneliness, fear, or depression. Peniel shut his eyes again and listened.

My husband was supposed to be back from Damascus two weeks ago. Is he dead? Am I a widow? How will I live?

Others were present because of immediate, concrete needs.

I've lost all the strength in my hands. The only trade I know is tinsmithing. Can he heal me? Will he heal me?

Is he real? Can he make these headaches stop? Or am I dying?

Then another voice, stronger and more anguished than all the rest: *She is dying! I know it! We've come so far, and now, will he heal her? Will he even see her? Will no one let us through?*

Involuntarily Peniel opened his eyes. The love and pain mingled in that last expression of longing must surely be evident on the face of the sufferer!

The man born blind turned inward again and listened . . . and now heard angry thoughts:

Who do they think they are?

Black as night! Foreigners! And just look at that tattooed face. Probably heathens!

He'll send them packing, right enough. This is our messiah. Our healer. He's not for the likes of them!

At the edge of the audience the crowd stood six or eight or ten deep to see Yeshua. Part of the circle was in jostling, shoving activity. The commotion seemed to center around a man who loomed head and shoulders above the rest . . . a black man.

As Peniel watched, the man raised the limp form of a slightly built girl child to shoulder height, to keep her above the crush of the throng. That was the source of the conflict Peniel heard in his thoughts. A black man—not a Jew but a Gentile—was bringing a sick child to Yeshua.

The harsh thoughts increased in volume:

What nerve!

A true messiah will send him packing back to his own kind.

Jewish healer for Jewish children!

Elbows dug into the tall man's ribs as he politely asked for room to pass. Faces were averted but shoulders pressed together in impenetrable ranks—a briary thicket of prejudiced hostility. The man, his daughter, his wife and other children . . . none were welcome here.

Peniel left the side of Levi, where he had been sitting, and made his way through the crowd. Some made room for him because he was known to be one of Yeshua's talmidim. A few recognized him as the man born blind whom Yeshua had healed.

He'll set them straight, the thoughts continued. *Send them packing!*

The pleading in the tall man's eyes was almost unbearable to Peniel. *This is our last hope*, his thoughts implored. *If the healer cannot . . . if he will not help us, Marisha is doomed. And my heart will break.*

Three paces from the black family Peniel almost collided with Judas Iscariot. "I'll take care of this," Judas said with authority. To the black man he waved as if shooing away flies. "Go away, you. The Master has no time for you. Be gone."

Peniel's hand reached between two sets of clashing elbows to grab the father by the wrist.

At the same moment everyone heard Yeshua proclaim, "Allow the little children to come to me, and don't hinder them! To such as these belongs the Kingdom of God."[28]

Judas turned about sharply and his movement left a space through which Peniel tugged the man and his silent burden. Clinging to the hem of his robe, his wife and other children also passed through the momentary opening.

Yeshua's voice rang above the muttering and complaining: "Truly, I say to you, whoever does not accept and receive and welcome the Kingdom of God like a little child shall not enter it at all!"[29]

As soon as Peniel grasped the man by the arm, the disharmony of resentment receded, but the strain of terrified emotions intensified. No longer merely hearing the man's longings, Peniel actually shared them. He not only knew what anguish the loss of the child would bring; he felt it.

It was to gain some relief from the powerful sensation that Peniel studied the little family. The mother clung to the back of her husband's tunic. She balanced one child on her hip while another's fingers were twined in the cords of her belt. Her face was full of alarm at the hatred around them.

It was not so with the man. He carried himself with dignity and without fear, masking the ache except where it leaked out through his eyes. Gazing past the tattooed swirls glazing his cheeks that spoke of heathen customs in distant lands, Peniel looked into the man's soul. The father would accept any cost, bear any ridicule or scorn, offer any sacrifice, if it would lead to the healing of his daughter.

The child was limp in her father's grasp. Her head hung down over one of his arms; sticklike legs, bent at the knees, lay across the other. Beneath the blanket with which she was covered, her belly protruded, in stark contrast to the half-starved, dead-sparrow appearance of the rest of her. One arm wagged listlessly with each of her father's strides.

Because the Master had called for them, a way miraculously opened, but their passage was not without muttered comments.

"See how he's dressed? Servant to a government official, likely. Maybe even slave to a Roman officer."

"No! Don't you know who 'e is? I recognize 'im. Salmon, his name is. Waits on that blasted publican Zachai, 'e does. What's lower than a publican, eh? A publican's 'eathen slave, is what!"

Peniel wanted to reassure the man: *Yeshua will heal her. He gave me my eyes. He raised El'azar from the grave. He can heal your daughter!*

But what if it did not happen this time?

What if the mulberry tree remained firmly planted in the rocky soil of unbelief?

Peniel hoped Salmon could not overhear his thoughts. Now was no time for doubt.

The walk from the edge of the throng to Yeshua's side seemed to take forever, even after Yeshua rose from His seat on the boulder and approached them.

Still paces away from the Master, Salmon knelt on one knee. With bowed head he extended the body of his daughter on uplifted hands, like a sacrifice before the altar of the Lord. "My daughter is . . . something devours Marisha from within. You alone can help us."

Peniel held his breath.

Gravely, Yeshua accepted the sagging form of the child and cradled her close to His chest. His head bowed in prayer. He whispered something in her ear, then kissed her.

Peniel stood close enough to see her eyelids flutter at the touch of the Master on her cheek.

And then several things happened at once. The girl stirred in Yeshua's arms. The mother gave a small cry and quickly stifled it. The protruding lump of Marisha's belly receded. Her eyes opened, fixed on Yeshua, and she smiled.

He smiled back at her.

Salmon raised his gaze, tears streaming down his face.

Yeshua placed Marisha back in Salmon's outstretched arms. "Take her and feed her. All of you need to eat. Peniel, will you help them with that?"

A shock wave spread outward through the multitude, like an earthquake with Yeshua at its center. Exclamations of wonder and surprise.

"The Kingdom of God," Yeshua said, waving toward the mulberry tree yet again, "is like a great tree in which *all* the birds of heaven may roost and find refuge."[30]

Salmon, though Marisha was hugging him tightly around the neck, still had not risen from his knee. "Master," he said. "Command me. I will follow you to the ends of the earth. I will lay down my life for you. Whatever you ask, I will do."

Stretching out His right hand, Yeshua laid His palm on Salmon's head. "Your service is this: Remain with us for a time. Regain your strength and let your family rest. Soon I will need you as a messenger for me, and you will keep your vow. Then you shall return as my witness where and when it is most needed."

Peniel wondered what oath Yeshua was referring to. Salmon had not mentioned any vow . . . at least, not out loud.

The question did not distress Peniel at all.

The evening shadows grew long inside Zachai's garden. Pale golden light outlined the leaves of the sukomore under which he sat. The air was still. Atop the wall a lone dove called mournfully.

Zachai, sitting beneath the sukomore, fingered the growth of beard on his cheeks. Not long enough yet. The bristles and an untrimmed mop of hair made a scruffy change from his normal, clean appearance but were not even close to being a disguise yet.

The publican's right hand crept upward to the twin lumps on his head, left over from the assault by bar Abba. If Zachai sat perfectly still, his head no longer ached as it had. But let him stand up suddenly, or bend over, and the roaring in his ears returned with a sound like the Jordan in flood.

Zachai stared into the distance, his other hand plucking idly at his tunic. There were no bloodstains on this garment, but the recollection seemed to exist just below the surface of his thoughts, all the time.

On one of the topmost branches of the Amos tree there appeared another bird; a common blackbird as far as Zachai could tell. It cocked its head and watched a plover fly past. Zachai, propping his chin gingerly in his palm, watched.

The plover emitted a staccato call that sounded like "*too-ooo-eee.*"

The next instant the blackbird copied the plover's song, complete with perfect pitch and rhythm.

"Well done, bird." Zachai applauded. "Excellent. In the dark no one could tell you from a plover."

The blackbird acknowledged the compliment by mimicking the dove, which abruptly flew away.

"Need more practice on that one," Zachai noted. "Just like I could fool people now who don't really know me . . . but not many. And hear me, bird: While you're learning to fool others, don't forget who you really are, eh?"

The blackbird, chastened, likewise left the tax collector alone.

"Don't forget who you are," Zachai repeated to the empty branch, with a sense of regret at the bird's departure. "A good lesson. Even when I'm not recognizable, it won't change who I am, will it?"

He transferred his attention to another branch. This one was as thick as his waist where it branched from the trunk. From its origin close to the ground, the limb ran upward at a forty-five-degree angle before flattening out to parallel the top of the fence from above.

"It would be easy to climb up to that spot over the wall," Zachai mused. Then: "How many in Judea are sorry at the news that I survived this attack? How many hope some other Zealot will try again soon . . . and, this time, succeed?"

Zachai's ponderings grew as dark as the shadows pooling around him. There was just enough light in the west to silhouette the tree limb against the sky.

If Zachai were gone, would anyone miss him? Would anyone remark that he left an empty space, or would some newly appointed tax collector suddenly succeed to the title of most hated man? Would anyone spare him even as much sorrow as he felt when a bird flew away?

"God who doesn't hear me," Zachai said, "under this tree of the prophet, whose name even I remember after hundreds of years . . . would anyone recall my name a year after my death, except with satisfaction that I was gone?"

Unbidden, a half-forgotten bit of Amos' prophecy flashed into his thoughts:

Because you trample on the poor
and you exact taxes of grain from him,
you have built houses of hewn stone,
but you shall not dwell in them . . .
you who afflict the righteous,
who take a bribe.[31]

Zachai studied the branch. "It'd be easy to climb," he said to the tree. "And plenty strong enough to hold me all the way out to that open space just inside the wall, where the smaller branches thin out. I wonder if there's any rope in the garden shed."

He shook his head, and something felt like it rattled within his skull. "Not tonight," he told himself aloud. "I won't go see about the rope just yet. Not tonight, anyway."

Yeshua was teaching in the hills north of Bethel. It was truly, Peniel thought, one of the best examples of a land "flowing with milk and honey" that he'd ever seen. Not that he'd seen much of the world since receiving his sight, but this was truly a fertile paradise. The uplands sparkled with wildflowers amid which honeybees droned. Downslope, toward the Jordan, date palms flourished, producing juicy, sweet fruit that literally oozed milky white syrup at each bite.

Peniel, too eager to hear Yeshua, too excited about each new day to ever sleep late, was often the first one of the talmidim to awaken. This morning was no exception. Knowing how annoyed Shim'on Peter and the others got when he interrupted their rest, Peniel had hiked to the top of the hill above their camp.

Turning slowly about in place, he surveyed the pale blue distances. Northward were the hills of Samaria and the mountains of blessing and cursing: Gerizim and Ebal. Eastward lay the river valley, steeped in shadow. West was the slate-colored canvas where sea and sky were indistinguishable.

And south?

Peniel was startled to realize that the square bulk and fingerlike projections on the southern horizon could be nothing other than the walls and towers of . . . "Yerushalayim," he breathed aloud. "So near? No wonder Peter urges Yeshua to move the camp every night. I had no idea we were still so close to his enemies!"

Peniel jumped when a nearby voice seemed to comment on his very thoughts: "Only a dozen miles as the crow flies. Fifteen at the outside. Too many ravines to cross in a single day, but no great distance at that."

Judas.

Peniel did his best to like the man but struggled just the same. The youth knew Yeshua trusted Judas with the money pouch and had appointed him to oversee doling out charitable assistance to the needy, but Peniel found his attitude superior and condescending.

"Afraid?" Judas questioned. "You've probably no need to be, you know. It's not like you were an important person, like El'azar or someone. Who remembers the name of a blind beggar, even if he does get healed?"

The morning was too beautiful for Peniel to allow Judas' tweaking to spoil his mood. "I'm not worried for myself. If you remember, I was there when the Master raised El'azar from the dead. Why should I be afraid if I stay close to him?"

"Why indeed?" Judas drawled, as if he knew something Peniel did not. But then, he always acted that way with everyone. Right on cue, Judas expressed it: "I don't suppose you've heard this . . . no reason the Master would take you into his confidence, is there? But we're going back to Yerushalayim."

"What? Why?"

Judas shrugged. "For Passover, of course. He wants to be in Bethany by the Sabbath before the feast."

"But we haven't been away long enough for it to be safe."

"But there, you see? That's the rest you don't know. Passover . . . pilgrims . . . big crowds from the Galil." Peniel must have looked blank, for Judas commented, "You really are stupid, aren't you? It's time. Yeshua will let the crowd acclaim him as king. The moment when he takes his rightful place as the heir of David has come at last."

"Are you sure that's what he said?" Peniel asked doubtfully.

"He said he's setting his face toward Yerushalayim. What else can it mean? All this talk about going to his death is nonsense. It's just designed to weed out the faint hearts. Yeshua has to know who he can trust when he appoints his governors and stewards and the royal treasurer."

Judas swelled visibly as he uttered the last title. There was no doubt in Peniel's mind which position Judas had chosen for himself. "Come on. Yeshua sent me to fetch you. He said you'd be up here."

Dressed in the clothes of a commoner and a cloak of the tribe of Levi, Zachai stood for Olabi's inspection.

"Tell me what you think. I will pass?" Zachai ran his fingers through his short beard.

"But for the fact your beard is short . . ."

"They'll think I shaved it for a vow. It's only now growing back."

"Then . . . I would not know you as my master."

Zachai clapped his hands in delight. "Well then, I'm ready to go out among the *am ha aretz.*"

The Old Man's brow furrowed. "You must test your disguise here among your servants."

"Surely my own will know me."

"If they do, then you must not leave this haven. It is not safe, Lord Zachai. "

Zachai nodded. "It will be good to hear what they really think . . . my own servants, I mean."

The Old Man stiffened at the possible danger to the servants. "You must make a vow indeed that no matter what they say, no matter what anyone says, you will not take revenge upon them for—"

"For hating me?"

Olabi's head bobbed only once. "Yes. You will not like what you hear. What the people think and say behind their hands as you pass by."

"Will I be angry?"

"Not if you are wise."

"How am I to react to insults?"

"What man ever has the chance to truly know what others think about him?"

The stubble of his beard and the clothes of a peasant might protect him from physical harm, but how would he react to the true thoughts of those who fawned over the great Zachai, yet despised him when he turned his back? "They wish me dead." His gaze scaled the high garden walls and the limbs of the ancient tree. "At times I also think it would be better not to live on."

"Even an evil man is praised when he is dead."

"It is the praise of the living I long for."

"You will not find it in Jericho," Olabi said.

"Or Judea?"

"Or Jerusalem."

Zachai frowned. "Or in my own house? Among my own servants?"

The Old Man bowed deeply. "No, my lord. Not even among those who love you. They will speak the truth when you are not present."

Zachai winced. "Who in my household should I test with the disguise?"

"Whom do you respect?"

"Your wife. Aphrodite. She is a fierce bear with her cub when she speaks to me. I fear the honesty of your wife, Old Man. Yet I think she always loved me when I was a child."

"Aphrodite will tell you the truth about yourself even if you came to her as yourself and asked."

"I know. She disciplined me when I was a boy." He stared up at the sunlight breaking through the branches of the sukomore tree. "She used to warn me what I would become if I didn't repent. *Teshuvah*, turn around. That was the word she used."

"*Teshuvah*." Olabi smiled faintly. "A Hebrew word."

"Strange this word came from the mouth of a Cyrenian slave raised in Greece."

"She knows Lord Zachai is a Hebrew . . . a true son of Abraham who has lost his way and so must turn around."

"All right, then. How do we test this?" Zachai swept a hand across his clothing.

"You are . . . the new gardener, eh? I will put a broom in your hand and you will work outside the kitchen until she notices you."

The Old Man's wife had skin like a dried fig. Her upper lip sported a sparse white mustache. She had been lithe and lovely once . . . long ago. Her name was Aphrodite, like the goddess. Owned in her youth by a Greek diplomat in Alexandria, she had been purchased by Zachai's father as a cook thirty years ago and brought home to Jericho. She was married off to the head slave, but Aphrodite could not give him children. She was barren, bitter, and had a heart like a stone. Since then she had doubled and quadrupled in size.

Aphrodite hated Jericho and had little good to say about the House of Zachai. This made her the perfect test for Zachai's disguise.

He swept the courtyard as she executed three chickens for supper.

At last, sitting down opposite her as if to rest from a long day's chores, he said, "I'm the new gardener."

Plucking feathers from a scalded hen, the broad-faced servant glanced up and scowled at something over Zachai's shoulder.

He turned to see what she was staring at. "What?"

"Nothing. My cat." She returned to her task, plucking with enthusiasm.

"Do you ever look at people? Or only dead chickens and cats?"

At the accusation, she paused, stared directly into his face, then, arching her brows in irritation at his demand, shrugged and returned to plucking.

Did he catch a flicker of recognition in the old woman's expression? "What is it?" he asked.

"You're something like . . . except the beard."

"Like who?" He leaned forward, eager to know.

"You look like—" she lowered her voice conspiratorially—"the sukophanteo."

He sounded out the epithet. "So, *suko* . . . fig. And *phanteo* . . . informer? A Greek word. Fig informer?"

"When I was a young girl in Greece, it used to be illegal to export figs . . . the sukomore . . ."

"Sukomore figs from Greece?"

"Yes. I worked for a Greek diplomat once. Those were the days. But now I work for this sukophanteo . . . sychophant."

"You mean Zachai?" He surmised she did not recognize him.

She continued, "You know Greek?"

"A little."

"A little," she scoffed. "Like everyone in this stinking place. A little. So, a sukophanteo is someone who works for the authorities, the government, informing about who shipped figs illegally. Extortion. Bribes. Informs on his own people."

"Who are you talking about?"

"Don't pretend. You know who I mean." She gestured at the limbs of the giant sukomore fig tree. "They call him Zachai because of this." She jerked her thumb at the towering branches of the sukomore in Zachai's private courtyard. "There. The sukomore tree of Zachai . . . sukomore figs. His grandfather got the sukomore grove from Herod the Great, Butcher King. A reward, they say. Murdered the rightful owner and gave the grove of sukomore figs to Zachai's grandfather."

She snapped her fingers. "Now three generations of the House of Zachai have worked for Herodians. The House of Zachai is all fig informers. Sukophanteo. Look at his signet ring if you don't believe. Sukomore fig trees are upon the gold signet of the House of Zachai. The perfect seal upon the signet of the most hated man in Judea."

"Sukomore tree. Sukophanteo. Sycophant."

"Ha! Greek wordplays! You'll make pleasant company if only you learn to speak Greek. A lovely language. You catch on quick."

"You're saying his sukomore trees were an honor won by a sycophant for betraying the people of Judea."

"Yes. The sukomore trees. Zachai collects a percentage from the harvest of all sukomore figs in Jericho . . . and everything else! There is a saying about him here: 'The little man Zachai is like Adam in Paradise, who sold his soul to taste a fig on the great sukomore tree in Gan Eden' . . . a fig informer who grovels at the feet of the Roman devils."

"A terrible thing to call a son of Avraham."

"All the same, there are few who would be sorry to see this son of Abraham strung up like this stewing chicken from the giant sukomore tree in his courtyard." She fixed her gaze on some distant vision. "Greek wordplays. So descriptive, don't you think?" She cocked her head to one side and said wistfully, "I miss the sound of Greek in my ear."

"Who are . . . they . . . who hate him so much?"

She shrugged and yanked free a fistful of feathers. "Everyone."

"You?"

"Everyone. Except me and my old fool of a husband." She spat. "Even the Romans, the very masters he serves, hate him. So do the Herodians . . . hate and ridicule him.

"I hear from their servants when they come. Servants know everything. All equally detest this sukophanteo who owns the sukomore trees. And the citizens of Judea? Zachai collects their taxes by false accusation, threats, and extortion, so they wish him dead. They were all very disappointed bar Abba failed."

Zachai rubbed his hands together. His palms were blistered from the handle of the broom. "Servants know everything. Yes, I've heard this," he muttered. "So, where is our master? I haven't seen him."

Aphrodite jerked her thumb toward the towering wall that enclosed the giant sukomore fig tree. She whispered, "He's brooding behind that wall. Brooding under the great sukomore tree. Hiding. Perhaps trying to disguise himself by sewing . . . disguise, eh?"

Zachai started, then realized it was still part of her tale.

She continued, "Sewing the sukomore fig leaves together, eh? But disguise will do him no good. His sin is too great to hide. He is scared to come out because everyone on this side of the wall wishes him dead."

"Not . . . everyone?"

"Well, not I myself. I pity him. So alone he is. Too rich to know he is so unhappy. And perhaps not my husband. The Old Man does not hate his master. He is head servant. Since he could not give me children . . . my husband has tenderness for little Zachai. But my husband is very old and a fool. His very soul belongs to the House of Zachai."

"No one else cares if Zachai lives or dies?"

She paused. Her eyes narrowed in thought. "They all care very much . . . hoping he will die, strongly desiring he will not live."

"Does he—Zachai—know?" Zachai blinked in shock at the truth. He rubbed the scruff of his beard, not certain he would wish to go outside and hear more of this from the citizens of Jericho.

Aphrodite waved a half-naked chicken in the air. "The little man had four bodyguards. He must know he needs protection, eh? He treated them well. Even so, one named Salmon has run off with his wife and children to Yeshua the Galilean prophet, never to return. And now another bodyguard is dead. There are only two left. Perhaps they wish to keep the master alive because they don't want to be out of a job. Or perhaps they will all run away when next the attack comes."

"Are they not loyal men?"

She snorted and wiped sweat from her brow with a greasy forearm. "Loyal? Not since they saw the dead body lying before them . . . pitiful and dead. A good man dies for no reason? This changes perspective about what and who is important and why. The blood of their comrade who died, splashed about like an animal sacrifice . . . for what?"

"To save the master?"

"Are they not men? As worthy of life? Perhaps they have more reason to live than Zachai. They all have wives and little ones. Zachai has nothing to live for but his money. Snuggle up to a big sack of shekels!" She puckered her lips and made kissing noises toward the chicken. "Why should men with families give up their lives for little Zachai?"

"They are his slaves."

"Hmmm." She jerked her head downward and pursed her lips. Clearly his comment had soured their pleasant conversation. She frowned. "So this is the way you think, eh? Then *you* are well suited to be a slave. I will confide in you . . . little gardener. New little gardener. There is a saying for the way these men feel about the life of Zachai."

Zachai's mouth was suddenly dry. "What is it?"

"Here is the truth." She paused, snapped her fingers, and laughed. "They do not give a fig!"

19 CHAPTER

Zachai returned the broom to the garden shed. He was lost in his musings. Given the musty darkness, it took some time for both his eyes and his thoughts to adjust to the change in surroundings.

The first thing he noticed was how still it was inside the shed. Bird songs, the noisy conversations of travelers on the highway, the breeze in the sukomore leaves—all this was shut out. The loudest sound was now the sigh of Zachai's breathing.

Likewise, the interior of the shack replaced the fresh, clean garden fragrances of spice and blossoms with the smell of damp loam. It was not unpleasant, but darker and richer, warmer and closer.

And in contrast to the bright light outdoors, even now that Zachai could see within the shed, things remained faint outlines of reality. Brown and gray objects appeared colorless against a black backdrop; darker items disappeared completely.

It was as if all Zachai's senses were muted and he was wrapped in a cocoon that replaced the outside world. Very like a grave, he imagined.

Then his gaze lit on a coil of rope. Neatly spiraled hemp, it was beside the bare rack where the broom belonged. When he replaced the tool his fingers brushed against the cord.

Good, stout cord. As thick as Zachai's thumb. Plenty of it too: fifteen cubits at least. Capable of tying a sapling upright against the strongest gale. Useful for hoisting a hundredweight of grain into a wagon . . . or raising a carcass off the ground.

One of Zachai's hands closed around the coil. His other touched his neck beneath the brush of his beard. Barely bigger around than a sapling. Zachai glanced down at his frame. And he weighed less than a hundredweight.

Would it hurt? he wondered.

With the rope slung over one shoulder, Zachai bustled, blinking, into the sunlight.

Onto the low-lying branch of the sukomore he scrambled, clawing his way upwards against the drag of the cord and the tug of life.

Soon he sat, breathless, but not from exertion, suspended on the limb above the height of the wall.

Which end first? Tree or neck?

Tree, he decided. The rope would have to be checked for length. It would not do for him to misjudge the drop and hit the ground.

Six twists around the branch, a quick knot, and the free end dangled in the air eight feet above the earth.

Now to fashion the noose.

Zachai's view from the Amos tree was extraordinary. Why had he never come up here before? From this perch he could see all the way down the hill to Old Jericho.

In the middle distance a group of pilgrims stood, gathered beside something . . . or someone . . . on the ground. Bartimaeus, most likely.

Once more it came to the publican that while some grief would be felt at the death of a blind beggar, no tears would fall for the most hated man in Judea.

His fingers flew in fashioning a loop with a secure slipknot.

No one would even put so much as a single stone on his grave to commemorate his passing. Who would next own the Amos tree? Or would horror at his use of it require it to be cut down?

Tentatively, Zachai placed the noose on his head. Too small. He lowered it for readjustment until it slipped easily over his head, then almost fell from the limb when a voice called his name.

"Master?" cried Olabi from a back door of the house. "Lord Zachai?"

Now what? Zachai could not launch himself into eternity in front of the Old Man. The shock might kill him.

Neither could he face ridicule for what he was doing.

"Master? Are you in the garden?"

What to say? In another moment he'd be spotted. *How to explain?*

"Here," he managed to croak as he extracted his head from the rope. "Up here." Then before any awkward questions could arise he volunteered, "This branch. I think it needs support. I have found some places where we can tie it up, to help it bear the weight. I'm even thinking like a gardener, you see."

Leaving the rope coiled on the branch and tucked closely against the trunk of the sukomore, Zachai scrambled down. He stood, dusting himself off, before Olabi's incredulous, interrogating stare.

"Your . . . beard . . . is well grown, master," the Old Man observed, clearly baffled for a conversation starter.

Zachai adjusted the collar of his robe up under his chin, wondering belatedly if there were any suspicious marks on his throat. "What do you think?" he energetically demanded. "Is it time? Am I ready to go out among the people?"

Olabi pondered. "What does my Lord Zachai think about himself?" he responded judiciously.

Glad to see the subject of his perch in the tree so easily diverted, Zachai suggested, "Why don't you go ask your wife? We agree she's truthful about all things."

"Truthful? Yes, always that. Wait here a moment, master, until I ask her and return to you."

"Yes. I . . . I'll do that," Zachai replied.

"What says Lord Zachai?" Aphrodite stirred the stew over the cook fire as her husband ate fresh bread and cheese.

"The bird is ready to fly," Olabi replied. "I found him in his courtyard, very high in the branches of the Amos tree, looking over the wall at the people in the street below. He wishes to be like other men, I think."

"Our master has changed his outward plumage, but I fear he is still inwardly a solitary hawk ready to pounce and devour whatever belongs to another."

"If Lord Zachai goes out into the world as a mouse among mice, he'll soon change his mind about being a hawk."

"And when he hears the truth of how everyone . . . *everyone* . . . on the outside hates and fears him?" Aphrodite asked.

"He knows already."

She disagreed. "Perhaps he suspects. But how can he really know what suffering he and his fathers have caused to the *am ha aretz* in the name of Rome? in the name of Herod?"

Olabi broke off another chunk of bread. "We will ask the Great One in the heavens to guide our Lord Zachai to a new heart."

"The Great One cannot hear the likes of a chief tax collector. The Great One is not the god of Zachai. Money is the only god worshipped in this great house."

The Old Man smiled wryly as he considered the purpose of his master's journey. "Perhaps when he sees . . . when he hears . . ."

Aphrodite scowled. "I shall pray he does not return and prey upon those he meets who speak their minds. Revenge is a mighty trait of the House of Zachai. Having served three generations of this accursed family, you know they do not like the truth. You know this is the truth, my husband."

He wiped his mouth and shrugged. "My question to you, my wife, was only this: Will the commoner's disguise of Master Zachai pass? When he goes out among the common folk who wish him dead, will he be discovered and murdered?"

Aphrodite shook her ponderous head as though she doubted the wisdom of the adventure. "They will not know Zachai the Publican in his commoner's disguise, but the undisguised wishes of the commoner folk for Zachai the Publican's death may be a dagger in the heart of our uncommon master."

The Old Man pushed back from the table. "The truth will either cure him or . . . kill him. So, I thank you, Wife. I will go now and tell Master Zachai he has made a fine gardener and fooled even my wise and clever Aphrodite! I will tell him he is ready to venture forth to seek and find Zachai the Publican as others find him."

Yeshua and His talmidim were near an elevated plateau walled on three sides by hills and known locally as David's Throne. It was an omen, Judas said. They were on their way to Jerusalem, where Yeshua would, at long last, acknowledge the desire of the *am ha aretz* and allow Himself to be proclaimed king. Then nothing could stop them. The whole of Judea would rise up in support, followed by the Galil and beyond. The new king would destroy the puppet rulers like Herod and Caiaphas. Rome, knowing it was easier and less costly to make peace quickly, would accept the change and make the new kingdom of Israel a client state.

Judas' dreams had increased in scope. No longer content to be the royal treasurer, he now saw himself as minister of state to treat with the emperor. After all, his reasoning ran, who among the sheepherders and fishermen and beggar-boys could sit down with the Roman Senate and be taken seriously?

Less than a month had passed since Yeshua's words about His coming death in Jerusalem, and any foreboding was erased. Except for chronic skeptics, like Thomas, and those who had seen Herodian treachery up close, like Zadok, the whole band looked forward to the coming Passover holiday with great anticipation.

Nor was Judas the only member of the group with grandiose visions.

Peniel watched as Yeshua soaked His feet in a pond. The stoop of His shoulders revealed His exhaustion.

Just then the Zebedee brothers, urged forward by their mother, approached Him.

He did not look up. This was itself unusual, Peniel thought. Yeshua was always welcoming, eager to chat and answer questions. This reluctance suggested He already knew what was about to happen and found it distasteful.

John, bearlike, heavily bearded, cleared his throat.

Ya'acov wrung his hands but did not speak.

Their mother poked John in the ribs from behind.

"Teacher," John blurted. "Teacher, we want you to do—"

"That is," Ya'acov interjected, "will you . . . do whatever we ask? I mean, we want you to do something for us."

Yeshua waited.

Ya'acov's mother ducked out from behind her boys and knelt beside Yeshua. "We have a request."

Wearily, Yeshua nodded. "What do you want?" Now His searching gaze reached from face to face. Both John and Ya'acov dropped their eyes.

Not so their mother. "Say that these two sons of mine are to sit, one at your right hand and one at your left, in your kingdom."[32]

Yeshua again sat silently, waiting. At length the silence grew so uncomfortable that John and his brother were forced to look up. Then Yeshua asked, "Is this what you want me to do for you?"

"It is," the Zebedee boys confirmed

John repeated, "Since we laid aside our family business to follow you, grant us to sit, one at your right hand and one at your left, in your glory."

Peniel was shocked but not surprised. The ambition that coursed through Judas' veins was infectious, it seemed. That Ya'acov and John spoke without thinking Peniel had witnessed before, like the time they suggested to Yeshua that He should call down fire from heaven and destroy an unwelcoming Samaritan village.[33]

But this naked attempt to grab authority and honor over the top of all the others! Had they heard nothing of what Yeshua had taught lately? The entire journey back to the Holy City had been punctuated with lessons about humility, servanthood, and the expectation of persecution ahead.

"We know you'd never break a promise," John added, as if trying to enlist Yeshua's own character in this quest for aggrandizement. "So before you made up your mind and offered the spots to others, we want to get our claim in first."

"You do not know what you are asking," Yeshua replied.

Peniel shuddered.

"Are you able to drink the cup that I drink, or to be baptized with the baptism with which I am baptized?"

What did that mean? Yeshua posed the questions seriously, but with more sorrow than either eagerness or reproach.

Drink the cup? A toast to the new king in Jerusalem?

A baptism? The ceremonial immersion of a new king before his coronation?

But Yeshua made neither image sound joyful.

John and Ya'acov chose to take the picture that way. "We are," they replied stoutly, as if already standing before the throne of David, accepting Yeshua's anointing to be His prime minister and chief personal counselor.

"The cup that I drink you *will* drink, and with the baptism with which I am baptized, you *will* be baptized."

Did the brothers not hear the prophetic weight of those words?

"But to sit at my right hand or at my left is not mine to grant, but it is for those for whom it has been prepared."[34]

Nodding nervously, the Zebedees backed away from Yeshua as if the rebuke was crushing.

Zadok arrived then behind Peniel, who had been the only one within hearing of the conversation. "What's going on, then?" the old shepherd inquired. "John and his brother look like whipped puppies."

"Oh!" Peniel exclaimed. "They wanted Yeshua to give them the chief places in his new kingdom. Or at least that's what their mother wanted, I think."

"What?" Zadok barked. "Give that pair of fumble-fingered fisher-folk fancy titles? Is that what they asked for?"

Only when Zadok barked this phrase, it boomed around the amphitheater of David's Throne like the formal proclamation of a king's chamberlain.

Instantly the camp buzzed with hostile inquiry.

"They asked what?"

"Gave up their business? Leaky, smelly boats is what!"

"The nerve of those two . . . and their mother!"

Judas was incensed. "Overreaching themselves, clearly! Be lucky if he gives them some backwater village in the Galil to govern. Left and right hands, indeed."

Nor was Shim'on Peter immune. "Besides," he said loudly to his brother, Andrew, "I gave up as much as they did. You too. And anyway, Yeshua already promised that place to me. You heard him: keys of the kingdom, he said.[35] You heard him."

Peniel saw the disappointment in Yeshua's eyes mirrored in those of His mother. Mother and son had the same brown eyes, flecked with gold . . . and both reflected deep distress.

The whole camp was consumed with . . . envy.

Exactly the sin Yeshua had warned against. Exactly the temptation He said would tear them apart like tree roots crack apart stone if allowed to grow.

After Yeshua's warning about torture and death . . . after a powerful lesson about humility and service . . . this was still the result.

And all the challenges of Jerusalem and Passover lay just ahead.

20

Zachai drew himself up proudly as he passed through the crowded streets of his city without even one person recognizing him. He and the oxcart passed the public baths where he had often spent an afternoon playing dice with Roman officials and fellow Herodians. Familiar faces and voices swirled around him. No one gave him a second look.

The oxcart was filled with provisions he would leave for Shimona the Leper when he picked up the harvest of dried figs. He smiled and glanced away quickly as he passed Shimona's father. The Chazzan strode through the crowds as arrogantly as ever. He held himself aloof, careful not to touch anyone among the foreigners.

Look at him, Zachai thought. *I am a commoner today, wearing the cloak of any Jewish laborer, yet still the Chazzan does not look at me. God who does not hear my prayers, you can see that today I am like any other drover in Jericho. If only my disguise fooled you and you heard my prayers just once.*

Zachai asked himself what he would ask God if the prayers of a publican could be heard. But there were so many wishes that he could not choose just one.

An elderly Jewish couple carrying two grandchildren passed close by him. Zachai prayed, *God who cannot hear me, if I could be heard, I would pray that I could be loved . . . and someday like them.*

It was an impossible wish, he knew.

A hidden money pouch was heavy at his waist beneath his tunic. He fumbled for a coin as Bartimaeus, the blind beggar, came into view near the gate, then remembered the extra bundle tied across his back.

Bartimaeus cried, "Alms. Alms for a blind man! Pity on one who has no eyes to see the light!"

Zachai shook his head as he thought, *Am I not also blind as Bartimaeus? Yet who would look at my life and think that rich Zachai lived in darkness in the bright light of day.*

"Have mercy on a blind man!" Bartimaeus begged. As a traveler's coin dropped onto the tattered cloak, Bartimeaus scooped it up and hid it in his pocket.

Zachai drew near. "Blind man!" he called.

Bartimaeus turned his marbled eyes toward Zachai's voice. "Shalom, Lord Zachai!" he called in a loud voice.

Zachai inwardly gasped that a man without eyes still could recognize a voice so easily. "But I'm not—"

"Lord Zachai! It has been so long since you've passed by. Since the day the robbers came. I thought you had forgotten me here at the gates."

Zachai drew up the ox, blocking the blind man's sunlight. "I am only a poor drover. You are mistaken. But my master did order me to give you this." Zachai removed the package from his back and dropped it beside Bartimaeus. "A cloak. He has no further use for it." The garment was washed but still bore the shadowy evidence of bloodstains.

Bartimaeus scowled and wagged his head. "Nothing gets by me, though I am blind. A blind man may not see the light, but he can feel the heat of the sun. You have cast your shadow upon me, Lord Zachai." He fondled the material of the cloak. "I thank you for your gift. Why do you wish to be anonymous?"

Zachai leaned close and whispered urgently, "Please. Silence, please, Bartimaeus. I am not who you think. . . . I am only a simple drover. A common man."

Some comprehension passed across the face of the beggar as he entered into Zachai's charade. "Ah . . . yes? Not who I thought, eh? Forgive me . . . sir. Where are you headed?"

"Out. Beyond the city."

"Why?" He held up his bowl and shook it. Zachai tossed another coin in among the others.

"To take provisions to the woman who tends the fig grove of Zachai."

The beggar grinned broadly. "Shimona, daughter of the Chazzan, eh? I hear she is beautiful."

Zachai nodded. Then, aware the blind man could not see his response, added, "Yes. And no sign of disease on her."

"She would be free to marry if she had not been sold by her father to Zachai the Publican to pay a debt."

"Yes. I heard the same thing. A very hated fellow, this Zachai."

Bartimaeus did not reply. "They say Shimona is one of those healed by Yeshua. He who healed the leper, they say, is the one who is most hated in all the world . . . Yeshua of Nazareth. And that is why Shimona is hidden away."

"Yeshua? Most hated?" Zachai mused. "Who is more hated than a publican?"

The blind man rocked back and forth. "A man who does evil may be hated. But there is a kind of man who is hated even more. That is the one who does good. Who is truly righteous. I hear Yeshua does only good. He may be truly righteous. Therefore, if it is true . . . *if* it is true, he is hated for his goodness more than Zachai the Publican."

"I would like to meet such a fellow."

"And so would I . . . though I doubt the rumors are true. Tell him if you find him on your way that he has left one man unhealed and blind as a stone, remaining in Jericho, will you?"

"Yes. I will tell him. If I find him."

"So. A blessing on you, generous sir. A blessing from one blind man to another . . . as you travel into the wide world. Success on your journey." Bartimaeus unfolded the cloak. Spreading it out on the ground, he sat down on it. With his staff he raised a fold of cloth between his head and the sun.

Zachai departed, pondering the beggar's final words. *"From one blind man to another . . ."* What could he mean? How could he know the darkness that filled Zachai's heart?

Zachai glanced furtively over his shoulder as he urged the oxcart up the road toward the sukomore grove. Wooden wheels slid into grooves worn by a thousand years of travelers between Jericho and the Holy

City. No doubt the feet of prophets and kings and murderers alike had trod upon the stones of the Jericho Road. What prayers did they pray in their own troubled times? Did the God of Israel hear them? Did He care?

In a whisper Zachai began to speak to The One who never heard him: "God of my fathers, God who does not hear me, do my feet walk where my fathers walked as they made a pilgrimage to seek your face in Solomon's day?"

He sighed, wishing he could sing aloud some song of praise for this moment of his freedom. But a man who was accursed did not dare speak the holy words aloud. Someone passing might recognize Zachai the outcast, dressed as a commoner and singing sacred songs. Such an act from the chief tax collector of Judea would be cause enough for Zachai to be arrested, tried, and condemned to death by stoning if it pleased the Sanhedrin. Or, more probably, fined an exorbitant amount for violating Torah. A Jewish tax collector was considered as low as the lowest Gentile to the religious leaders of Herodian Judea. Rome would not protect him in such a case. The Romans left Jewish religious matters to be settled by the Jewish court.

Zachai tapped the ox on its flanks, urging it to hurry.

Why was he drawn to the little stone cottage of Shimona? Just as he thought of her, a flock of doves rose in unison from a field. It was a good omen.

"Shimona is her name," he said to the ox. "I'll speak to Shimona awhile when I load the baskets. She'll never know I am myself. She is a fine-looking woman. Intelligent and truthful. She told me the truth about the fig harvests. Honest, though she knew she might get blamed for her father's theft."

Farmers with crescent-bladed sickles cut the new growth of hay in the broad field between the stone fences. Young boys and peasant women racked the green grass for drying.

This year the harvest seemed especially fine, especially rich. The taxes on revenue were already far above anything Zachai had collected in any year before.

He shook his head, resisting his impulse to consider finances and compute taxes.

The early morning air smelled clean and new, unlike the heavy air of Jericho and Jerusalem.

Zachai tapped the ox on its broad black back. "Everything is so rich this spring because of the Prophet, they say. The people say it's Yeshua the Nazarene who called the rain like Elijah and watered the land by his own will."

The ox shook its massive head in an effort to keep the flies away as the morning warmed. It plodded on, hooves and wheels following the track of the ancients.

"This Yeshua the Nazarene. It is said he will change the whole economy if Rome installs him as king in place of the Herodians. No one will need money. He will give the people everything they need. No bakers because the bread will come like magic when he calls. No shoemakers. It will be like it was when our fathers wandered forty years. . . . Their shoes never wore out. You, ox, will be out of a job. I will also be unemployed."

An elderly farmer in the field paused to lean on his staff as Zachai and the cart approached. Zachai waved at the man, one peasant to another.

The poor man greeted him as he passed. "Shalom!"

"Shalom!" Zachai returned the spontaneous greeting. Astounding event. No ordinary Jew had ever spoken to Zachai. A sense of jubilation welled up inside him.

Then a clear memory crowded out exultation. Zachai, as a tax collector, had seen this very fellow a hundred times at the countinghouse, paying his tribute to Herod and to Caesar one shekel at a time. Elijah the Vintner was his name. The fellow had owned the little vineyard beside the sukomore grove. Zachai had wanted the vines for his own. It was an easy acquisition. The assessment on vines was raised a few shekels. Unable to pay the full amount of taxes due, Elijah's small plot of land and his cottage had been confiscated. Zachai bought the property from the state for what was owed in taxes. A fraction of its worth. The vineyard was now among Zachai's possessions.

Yet today Elijah the Vintner, the very same fellow whom Zachai had dispossessed, did not recognize the chief publican of Jericho!

Zachai perspired as he recalled the venom in the vintner's eyes after he and his wife had been turned out of the little house. He tugged at his collar. "They say it will be hot today!"

"Aye. We'll be finished with this field by noon."

"I'll have to take off my cloak." Zachai held up the frayed hem of his garment as proof that he was just a poor man like any other.

"Aye. A hot day. Where are you going with a cart and such a fine ox?"

"To the sukomore fig grove . . ."

"Aye? And which grove is that?"

". . . tended by Shimona."

"Shimona the Leper?"

"The daughter of the Chazzan."

Instantly Elijah's friendly smile faded. "She was a leper, they say. But somehow healed by Yeshua, the miracle worker who will bring justice again to Israel. He is the Son of David. The One we look for!"

"Justice in Israel? Who has the power to bring that to us?"

"The Prophet."

"You say he healed the leper?"

"Even so, her father the Chazzan won't have her back in his house. She can't come under his roof until he is sure."

"Then it's someone's mitzvah to let a former leper tend the grove, eh?"

The farmer spat and wiped his brow. "Zachai the Publican's grove. The grove beside the vines my father planted." He bit his thumb in a gesture of derision. "A fig for Zachai the Publican. He has a greedy motive for everything he does."

"I don't know Zachai personally. But it seems a kindness he lets the woman live and work in his fig grove."

"Poor Shimona. Poor Shimona." The farmer scowled. "Mind you don't try to sell Zachai the sukophanteo's sukomore figs in the souk of Jericho."

"Because she who tends them was a leper?"

"No! Because he who owns the grove has a leprous soul. It's Zachai the Publican who is unclean. He dwells in the Valley of Sorrows alone. None will enter his house. He may not enter the home of any man of Israel. He may not marry within Israel. His harvest is unclean. His house is as unclean as a leper! A dead man walking the earth alone. None who know him would buy from him."

Zachai's mouth went dry. He stammered, "Cakes of figs—Yerush-alayim bound—I wish you well, sir."

"And I have a wish as well. I wish Zachai the Publican be well bound, and well drowned in his own well."

The sun grew hotter. The cart rumbled past a troop of farmers who glared daggers at Zachai's back. Did they somehow sense that behind the disguise he was Zachai, Zachai the Despised? *Eyes forward. Do not look back. Do not show fear.* He shuddered as he imagined being murdered by the honed blade of a sickle.

Zachai murmured, "God who will not hear me, if only I were free. If only I could live as freely as the poor farmer. How I wish I could be like one of them instead of like myself. What is it like to stand in a field beneath the sun and fear nothing but lack of bread and taxes?"

He raised his eyes to the sky, but heaven was as silent and unyielding as iron.

Zachai passed the vineyard of Elijah. The vines were already overgrown and neglected in the absence of the vintner's care. Perhaps, Zachai thought, he could hire Elijah the Vintner to return to his home and vineyard. Though Elijah no longer owned the house and the land, perhaps it would be profitable if the vintner continued to work what had previously been his own.

Zachai tapped the ox on its left shoulder, turning the beast right onto the narrow lane that cut through the sukomore grove.

He noted with satisfaction that the trees were well cared for. No matter how Shimona the Leper must have hated him, still she lovingly tended the trees of his grove. There were no weeds growing up between the rows. Birds flew up and scattered from the leaves as he passed.

He could hear Shimona singing as she worked in the distance. *"Give thanks to the Lord, for He alone is good! His mercy endures to everlasting. . . ."*[36]

She had a beautiful, clear singing voice. And why not? She was the daughter of the Chazzan.

It was an old song, Zachai knew. It was the very song sung by King Jehoshaphat when the Lord defeated His enemies beyond the hills of Tekoa.[37]

Perhaps Shimona was singing this song in hopes her great enemy, Zachai, would drop dead?

Zachai shuddered at the possibility that a song of praise sung to the God of Israel could be responsible for destroying him.

"God of Israel, God of my fathers but not of myself, if Shimona offers you praise in hopes you will destroy my life, I hope you will not listen. Though I am unworthy of your forgiveness, I . . . regret . . . what I did to Elijah the Vintner."

Zachai cleared his throat uneasily as so many other names and faces of those he had cheated over the years came to mind. He shrugged at the hopelessness of the pit he was in. The thought came, *Ah well, what is one more? More or less.*

Yet Zachai really did regret the old vintner's loss of the vineyard. Elijah's hatred toward Zachai now seemed unquenchable.

"God who is not my God, so many people hate me. Yet I am still breathing. Maybe their hatred is nothing to fear."

The stone cottage of Shimona the Leper came into view. She was sitting beneath an enormous sukomore tree threading figs onto a strand for drying. The fruit was strung up in the low branches like laundry hanging in the sun.

She glanced up at the sound of the plodding ox. Her unlined face seemed at first startled and then beamed with pleasure. Zachai noted once again that there was no sign of illness.

"Shalom!" she cried, setting aside her task and rising to greet him.

"Shalom!" he returned as the animal halted at the watering trough.

"Oh, you've come to pick up the crop? You're two days early. And I have always left the baskets beside the road. But you're not the fellow who usually comes. Where is . . . ?"

"No, I'm new. Do you mind that I've entered the grove?"

"You didn't see the signs? the warning?"

"Yes. But I also heard . . . there's a rumor that you're not a leper. That the village elders put you here out of sight because you were healed by . . . the miracle worker."

Shimona smiled and bowed slightly. "You have a name?"

"Zacchaeus."

"I'm Shimona. Servant of Zachai, who owns this grove. You're also a servant of Zachai?"

"I'm my own man," he declared. "A freedman hired by your master to bring in the fruit from the first harvest and take it to the souk in Yerushalayim."

"Good." She led him to the storage shed and threw back the door, revealing dozens of baskets of fruit. "The season is just beginning." She seemed pleased. "Record harvests this year, they say."

"We can use good fortune."

"In answer to your question about my healing . . . and about the crop. It's because Yeshua the Messiah has come to Israel. The land is blooming because he's here."

Zachai shrugged. "Fortune comes and goes according to the wind and rain. Messiah or no Messiah. That's the way it is."

She studied him with a quizzical smile. Stretching out her hands, each with fingers intact, she seemed to contemplate what she had been and what she was now. She said quietly, "You've never seen him then? Yeshua the Nazarene, I mean?"

"See? I don't go out of my way for anyone. Always something new. A new messiah. A new prophet. A new general. Like . . . bar Abba the assassin, who tried to kill your master." He baited the hook, hoping to catch an insult from her lips. "People said bar Abba the rebel might be the one to take back Yerushalayim and the nation from the Romans. People all stirred up. Some wished he had killed Zachai."

She did not respond to this as Zachai hoped she would. "Yeshua's not a rebel. He's more like . . . a Shepherd. Or . . ." She gestured to the trees. "He's like a gardener, preparing the tree of Israel to bear fruit. It is with people the way it is with trees. It takes a lot of cultivating— digging, pruning, nourishing—to make them bloom. At Yeshua's table even an outcast is welcome."

"An outcast? Like your master, Zachai the Publican?"

"Yeshua welcomed me. I who was once a leper. What's a publican compared to a leper?"

"Some would say they are alike. But you were never . . . ," Zachai argued.

Shimona the Leper tilted her face and smiled. She was pretty. Straight, white teeth; brown eyes; and smooth, sun-browned skin. Zachai tried to imagine this healthy young woman as a leper. Impossible!

She explained, "I lived in the Valley of Sorrows for twelve years. I was among the 612."

"A mistake. It happens. The wrong diagnosis. A fable. This Yeshua— he's not a god. No one cures a leper but a god . . . or Mosheh. And, well, there was some prophet who cured a Syrian. I can't remember. Some old legend."

She shrugged, not attempting to convince him. "You have to see Yeshua for yourself. He's been everywhere . . . done so many signs. I am one of the miracles. Which is why the elders confined me and hid me from the people. True miracles are dangerous. Power and authority never like change. But you haven't gone out with the people to see Yeshua? to hear him teach?"

"Maybe I will see him in Yerushalayim. He'll come to Passover if he's a prophet. They all come to Yerushalayim sooner or later. Maybe he'll buy some figs, eh? Even if they are the figs of Zachai the Tax Collector. The Messiah has to eat sometime."

Shimona nodded, suddenly sober. "Passover. Yes. Maybe he'll come this way. If only I were rich, I would feed Yeshua a banquet." Then she changed the subject. "So, rest awhile in the shade. It's been so long since I've had company here. Someone to talk to. What's the news of the world? I'll fetch something for you to eat. If you're not afraid."

"I'm not afraid."

"Good. There's water to wash and fodder for your ox. A very fine ox."

Unlike the old vinegrower, she did not seem embittered by her servitude. Zachai was certain now that her name, Shimona the Leper, had simply been meant to keep visitors from discovering her father's ongoing theft of a portion of the crop.

21

A s Zachai's oxcart left the grove, the red-tailed hawk shrieked
and followed, circling high above the publican's head as if to
declare that Zachai himself had become prey. Shimona watched
the hawk for a time, following in his flight the progress of Zachai on
his journey to Jerusalem. At last the hawk turned back to the grove.
Swooping down into the yard, he settled on a low tree branch.

The raptor blinked at Shimona as if to ask her if she knew the
secret.

She laughed. "Yes. The eyes of my heart are sharp as a hawk's eyes.
I recognized him too. I knew who he was at once. Behind the beard,
beneath the cloak of a peasant, he is still Zachai, the rich and crooked
publican. Like an elephant trying to be a mouse. So proud. So arrogant.
He justifies every wrong he's ever done. Every lie he's ever told."

Shimona recalled the words of the fifth psalm. *Not a word from their
mouth can be trusted; their heart is filled with destruction.*[38] She raised her
hands in resignation. "Empty through and through. No honor he has
gained at the expense of others truly honors him. It is all stolen, all
acquired by deception. Hollow and empty glory is his who steals what
another has worked for and calls it his own. He is a thief."

Shimona nodded at the patient hawk. "My master, Zachai, is searching . . . hoping to find even one person who truly respects him for himself. But inside he knows that even if he finds one person, the respect is false because respect for him is based on deception."

Shimona returned to her house and closed the door behind her.

Rose, Lily, and Gideon scrambled from the corner to clamber around her feet. "You're hungry, my little ones." She fixed their supper of curds and cream and set the bowl before them. "A very lonely man was just here. He thinks he is important and powerful. But he is unimportant and a weakling."

She was angry as she took her seat on the three-legged stool. Then she pictured the man she hated moving alone and in fear of his life toward an uncertain destination. "I would not trade my kittens for everything he has stolen. Lord God, you who always hear my prayers, I am so sad for that man tonight. Surely you who are love—entirely, completely, you are love—surely you must love Zachai, though you are the only one. Though he has done such terrible wrongs to so many. Wronged me . . . my freedom he took as ransom for my father's freedom. . . ." She began to scroll through all the reasons she had to hate him. Then, as the list grew longer, a sense of pity for Zachai overwhelmed her. She closed her eyes and pictured his desperate, eager face. Dressed in his disguise, pretending to be a simple, humble man, Zachai had longed for her to like him. Like him? Even his humbleness was a lie. How could she like Zachai? He was not his true self in the peasant's clothing. He was still Zachai the liar in a different cloak, pretending, lying. Shimona wondered if she had ever met anyone so alone. So deceived by his own pride.

A time or two in the Valley of Sorrows, when a leper who had once been important arrived, she had witnessed the deception of arrogance. But money could not buy health. Power in the world meant nothing at all when a man became known and feared and despised as a leper. Those who on the outside had been self-important men were only lepers in the Valley of Mak'ob. They soon changed their attitudes and became real and honest . . . or they committed suicide. That was common among the proud and the arrogant who would rather die than repent and change.

Today there was something about Zachai that made Shimona think he was at that same crossroads. His heart was leprous and defiled. He would either change or take his own life. She became more and more certain of it as the evening wore on. The anger she felt toward Zachai turned to dread as she considered his future.

Zachai had stayed too long at the sukomore grove listening as Shimona told about her years in the Valley of Mak'ob. It was late. Soon the sun would set, and Sabbath would begin.

As Zachai walked beside the oxcart filled with baskets of figs, he mused over the story of the wonderful night Yeshua had entered the community of lepers and healed them all.

Of course Zachai could scarcely believe what Shimona had told him. He had heard other rumors . . . fables about the man Yeshua. But she seemed so certain in every detail. Could her version be true?

Zachai did not look back until he had almost reached the shelter of an ancient olive grove that he owned. Zachai knew the place well enough. Behind the trees he could see the broken stone walls of the burned-out estate. The land and the trees and the shell of the old house were reputed to be haunted. It had been cultivated for three years after Zachai's grandfather had taken possession of it. On the third year the house had mysteriously burned, killing the tenant and a number of people who had lived there. After that, workers had refused to enter the grove, and it had remained abandoned as if under a curse.

It was a small grove, of little significance among the vast holdings of the House of Zachai. He watched as the last gleam of daylight lingered in the wild branches, then faded. Perhaps, Zachai thought, the memory of the curse had also faded. Maybe it was time to put the old trees back into production.

Eight hundred years earlier the olive grove had been the site of a bloody battle against Moabite raiders. Oren Pella, captain of a troop of Israel's cavalry, had turned back the enemy and thus had helped win the battle. The land upon which Pella had fought was given to him as a gift from King David. He had planted a tree for each of the mighty men of David.

The olive grove had remained in the family of Pella through plenty and famine, through the exile of the nation, until the time of Herod the Great, when most Jewish estates of value had been confiscated by Herodian tax collectors.

Zachai shuddered when he remembered that it was his grandfather who had been instrumental in assessing the taxes on the Pella Olive Grove and dozens of other properties for old Herod the Butcher King.

The leader of the Pella clan had paid the unjust revenue in full. Then the family of Pella had been accused of treason against Herod and murdered as they sat down for their Shabbat meal.

Zachai's grandfather had been handsomely rewarded for his part in the plot. He had reported the treason, and Herod had given him the Pella Olive Grove for his loyalty. From that time, the locals had spat on the ground and made the sign against the evil eye whenever they passed the olive grove and the family name of Zachai was spoken aloud. It was almost as if the common folk believed Zachai was as bad as the Herodians.

Strange apparitions had been reported walking in the olive grove. For many years none dared enter it alone. Zachai scoffed at the tales.

The sunlight dwindled quickly. Shadows lengthened. Zachai was exhausted from his journey.

Zachai spotted two figures approaching in the distance. They were ragged, rough-looking fellows and appeared to quicken their pace when they saw him.

Robbers? Who else would be out at dusk on Sabbath?

Zachai turned aside and drove the wagon deep into the twilight of his desolate orchard. In the depths of the stand of unkempt trees he stopped, convinced that he was tolerably safe.

He listened for footsteps or some sign he had been followed. The silence all around him was profound, desperately lonely. He sat down with his back to a tree and thought about Shimona, alone night after night in the grove of the sukomore trees. Closing his eyes, a sense of heaviness filled him unlike any he'd felt since the night his mother had died, when he was a child.

"Too tired to move." He sighed, hoping rest would overtake his morbid thoughts.

When he was nearly asleep, he heard a human voice that caused him to open his eyes.

At wide intervals his straining ears detected scraps of conversation in a single male voice. The monologue was hollow and remote. Zachai wondered if he was hearing a real human or perhaps the moaning of the spirits of Pella and his slaughtered family trapped here. The murmur was more eerie than the silence. Was the olive grove truly haunted, as some believed?

It made Zachai shudder to think of spending the night alone in such a place. New energy surged through him. He sprang to his feet and grasped the yoke of his ox. "Lead me out, beast!" he cried.

The ox walked forward but in the darkness lost his way. Linking his fingers in the leather harness, Zachai followed the ox toward the sound of the voice. At last he saw a glimmer of light through the trunks of the olive trees. His animal halted and would not take one more step.

Zachai left the ox and approached the light cautiously, moving from tree to tree. The light and the voice came from the window of a little mud-brick hut. So much for an apparition. This was clearly tangible. Zachai now heard someone clearly reciting what seemed to be the evening prayer for Sabbath . . . but the words were all out of order, jumbled somehow.

For an instant he considered turning around, but light streaming from a window seemed more welcoming than the ghostly depths of the olive grove.

Zachai retreated back toward the ox, tied the animal to a tree, and snuck forward to the window of the hut. Standing on his tiptoes, he surveyed the sparse interior in a single glance. A fire blazed in the center of the hard-packed dirt floor. Smoke rose and escaped through a hole in the center of the woven reed roof.

Seated by the stone fire ring was an aged man. He was large and gaunt. Beard and hair were long and snowy white. Dressed in a long robe made of sheepskins that reached from his shoulder to the top of his bare foot, he lit a lamp. The words he spoke were recognizable but still made no sense. It was like hearing the echoes of voices shouting in a canyon, tumbled all together in a heap.

A grinning skull was propped in the corner on a tall clay wine amphora. Zachai shuddered as he stared into the hollow eye sockets.

As if somehow feeling Zachai's presence, the hermit raised his face but did not look toward the window. "You. I've been expecting you." Standing, the man addressed Zachai. "Shabbat Shalom. Come in. Come in."

Zachai ducked low and scrambled away from the light. His heart thumped wildly. How could anyone be expecting him? Groping in the darkness, he stumbled and fell, unable to find his way back to ox and cart. The olive trees seemed like a fence on every side, hemming him in.

Terrified, Zachai gawked over his shoulder as the hermit drew aside the leather curtain that served as the door to his dwelling. Stooping, the figure emerged in a pool of light and stood sniffing the air, as though he did not need eyes to see Zachai.

"Sojourner! Stranger! You might as well come back." The man chuckled pleasantly. "You'll never find your way through the tangle now."

The image of the grinning skull was burned on Zachai's retinas. It floated before him as if the vision followed him into the blackness. The crunch of the hermit's feet on the orchard floor came nearer. The recluse whispered, "I know you are there."

"What do you want with me?" Zachai cried.

"What is your name?"

"Zacchaeus . . . Zacchaeus . . . merchant of Jericho."

"Ah. Yes. Jericho. It was only a matter of time before someone from Jericho would get lost in the olive grove. Do not be afraid. It is Shabbat. I have been waiting for you. I knew you would come. A sojourner on Shabbat to share my feast. Get up."

Zachai felt a strong hand on the collar of his garment, lifting him up, holding on to him tightly lest he escape.

"But who are you?" Zachai asked as they suddenly came to the hut.

The hermit gave him a gentle shove through the leather curtain and into the room. "There. Water for washing." He pointed to a bowl of water at the base of the amphora. The skull gaped from the corner. It seemed to be watching Zachai.

Zachai hung back. "I'll not wash my feet or hands with that thing grinning down on me."

The hermit shrugged and gathered the skull into his hands. He held it up to his face, nose to nose, and spoke to it. "Ah, now. Never mind. An enemy, you say? He wasn't even born." Then the hermit said to Zachai, "You mustn't mind him. He's not usually so blunt. It's just that he says Zacchaeus of Jericho is an enemy in disguise. He heard your name differently than I heard you speak it."

"Who . . . who is he? A demon?"

"Ah. Yes. I suppose he is. Once he was the true lord of this olive grove," replied the hermit. His shiny black eyes were scuffed with cataracts. "He says he is Lord Pella himself. He keeps me here to do his bidding. Do you not know him?"

Zachai felt dizzy. He sank to the ground and crossed his arms as a pain surged through his heart. "Pella? The fellow who . . . the one Herod the Butcher King . . ."

The hermit chuckled. "Ah! You know the story. Yes. The fellow betrayed to Herod the Great by the grandfather of Zachai of Jericho. Not so long ago. Forty years to the day. Great wealth it meant to the elder of the House of Zachai. The betrayal of the family of Pella. It was the beginning of prosperity for the family of Zachai. It was the end of the family of Pella beyond Jericho."

"But how did you come to possess the skull of . . . such a worthy man? Beheaded by Herod's soldiers."

The hermit sank down cross-legged beside Zachai and cradled the skull on his knee. "Skulls are common. Everyone who ever lived had one."

"But this one? How did you come to possess the head of Pella?"

"Grandfather to grandson . . . to me. Grandfather's been in the family a long time, you might say."

"You? But you are . . ."

The hermit patted his grandfather's skull affectionately. "Grandfather, you mustn't frighten him. I told you he would come. I told you we would have him for supper."

"For supper?" There was no food on the mat. Nothing to eat. Zachai inhaled deeply but could not seem to fill his lungs. "What do you mean you will have me for supper?"

The hermit laughed. "Ah! Not as you think I meant it!"

Zachai frowned. "You are . . . grandson of Pella? The story was that you all, twelve in the family, died."

"Almost." The hermit's voice was singsong—unnaturally cheerful. "I hid beneath the straw when my mother ran to the barn. . . . I saw . . . I saw. Dead. Dead. All of them. Dead. My grandfather's head lying in the courtyard. It was the only one still smiling at me. So I picked him up and he has stayed with me every day and night. Smiling."

"Mad . . . ," Zachai whispered.

"Yes. Since I was ten years old. Mad. Grandfather told me what to do."

"No one enters this grove. They say it is haunted."

"Yes. So it is. Only me. The old house burned down. Only me and Grandfather. The two of us. Plenty to eat. If it were daylight, you would see I keep a little garden. Sometimes stray . . . animals . . . pass through, and then I have a feast."

Zachai drew his foot beneath him as the hermit looked at it in a hungry way. "I'll be going."

"No." The hermit leaned down as though the skull were whispering in his ear. "Oh? Really? Well, Grandfather, if you say so." He looked up fiercely from his conversation. "Grandfather insists. You must stay the night. Stay here with us. You must be entertained. Drink fine wine and share our feast."

Zachai nodded silently as the hermit moved to block his escape.

Shimona lit her Shabbat lamp as the sun sank below the tops of the fig trees. The feline triplets, wide-eyed and solemn, sat together opposite her as she recited the Shabbat blessings, welcoming the day of rest.

Rose mewed and lay down between her brother and her sister. The prayers were going on too long and the black-and-white kitten was growing weary with Shimona's words. Time to eat.

Shimona closed her eyes and waited for the warmth of her prayers to fill her with peace. She said to the kittens, "Someone Eternal wants to join us for supper. The Lord is coming to . . . us. Our house. Yeshua?"

Suddenly a vision filled her mind: Yeshua coming up the road to Jericho. Yeshua surrounded by a great throng, Shimona's mother and father among the faces. And . . . Lord Zachai! Trying to see him. Trying to catch a glimpse of The One who healed her leprosy.

Shimona said aloud, "Yeshua. Jericho. Close by here. Very soon." She smiled wistfully, blessed the bread, and broke it. She passed a morsel of cheese to the little ones. They clambered over one another and gobbled their supper together. Their tails were straight up and quivering with joy.

Shimona watched them eat with pleasure. Kittens. Such small things to give her such enormous joy. "Lord, who knew how lonely I was. Who would think . . ." She sighed. "Lord, I didn't know I was so lonely."

She sang the Shabbat hymns she had learned as a child from her father. The words and melody cheered her in spite of her isolation, as they did every lonely Shabbat night. She imagined her family sitting together even now around the Shabbat table. Did they think of her at all?

Loneliness passed through her like a knife.

And then it came to her—a sort of revelation about Zachai the Tax Collector. They had something in common. "Lonely," Shimona remarked. "He seemed so . . . alone. Don't you think?" she asked her kittens.

After licking lips and cleaning paws, the trio toddled over to Shimona and collapsed, purring, in her lap.

The hermit tossed another stick of wood onto the fire and leaned closer to Zachai. "I will tell you a secret. . . . I am good friends with the Angel of Death. He comes here sometimes, and we fondly remember what Zachai the Elder of Jericho did to my family. And then the Angel of Death tells me and Grandfather what he will do when he catches Zachai the Younger." The hermit shook his head and chortled. He patted the skull and winked. "You see? I told you he would come and we would have him for supper."

Zachai felt his blood run cold. This, the grandson of old Pella, had been waiting forty years to exact revenge for what Zachai's grandfather had done. And somehow, Zachai knew, a demon had whispered into his ear the truth of Zachai's identity.

Oh, if only I was on the highway facing robbers again. I am the prisoner of a demon and his host.

The hermit continued in a low, insistent voice—not his voice, not human. "*I see you know me, Zachai the Younger, publican of Jericho! There's awe and terror in your face!*"

"I am not Zachai. I am a poor man, like you . . . taking figs to Yerushalayim. To market."

"*Liar! You are a liar! I am not poor,*" crowed the demon. "*I am as rich as you. You, Zachai of Jericho. Chief publican. I have only let you borrow all my wealth for a short life span in exchange for your soul. But it is I who own this olive grove, not you! I own this poor, mad grandchild of Pella, who grew aged and more insane as every year passed. He witnessed the beheading of his grandfather at the word of your grandfather, Zachai the Elder. The murder of his mother and father and brothers and sisters. False accusation. A small lie from the lips of your grandfather. And now the memory of your family's sins is played out day by day before his eyes. I, the demon called Mammon, possess him now. I own the soul of your grandfather and father. Ah, the fires! We have them for supper. And soon, Zachai of Jericho, you will hang yourself upon a tree and I will possess your soul as well!*"

Zachai shrieked in terror as the eyes of the hermit reddened and seemed to bore right through him. Leaping to his feet, he pushed past the madman and burst out of the hut. Not caring where he ran, he charged through the brush, slamming past jagged branches and the mire of rotted fruit beneath his feet. The cackle of the madman pierced the night like a hawk ready to pounce on its prey. Zachai did not care where he ran to; he simply ran, stumbled, rose, and charged blindly forward again and again.

Tree branches tore at his clothing and his flesh. The wraithlike cry pursued him. No longer was there any semblance of humanity in the evil voice. "*Soon, Zachai of Jericho. Soon! You will hang yourself, pierced like an unripe fig upon your own tree, and then I will own your soul as well!*"

Zachai cried out, "God of Israel! God who never hears me, hear me now! If only I can live . . . help me! Never mind the ox. Let the creature have it. Let him eat it. God who does not hear my prayers, don't let me die for the sins of my grandfather and father! Take away this curse! Let the demon make himself another garment from the hide of my ox. Let him feast on the ox and eat the figs. God who never answers me, only help me to survive this night!"

It would have been nice to have human company too on such a night, but the kittens . . . well? They made no demands except to be loved, and Shimona had plenty of love to give them. "God who hears my prayers always, I am not ungrateful. I thank you for sending me these three, when I only ever asked for one."

She felt a sudden ache of sorrow for Zachai, as though he were a friend. "And what about him, Lord? What about him? What kind of friends can he have? What is the rest of his life to be? And, Lord, who praises you from the grave? I know you can see Zachai even now. You know my heart and know every word I speak before it is spoken, and I ask you, in spite of how I feel about him, to have mercy on Zachai the Publican. He is a leper inside, just as I was once a leper outside. Lepers have no feeling when their flesh dies. So it is with the heart of a man like Zachai, I think. No feeling for anyone but himself. He steals a vineyard of another and is strangely proud that he has stolen what another man worked his life to build. How false all his accomplishments are. You who are the God of Truth—all truth without a shadow of deception—help this wicked man see himself as he truly is. Then turn him around by the power of your love. Restore life and feeling to his dead heart. Have mercy. Guide him back from the brink of hell to repentance and change."

It was a good prayer, Shimona thought, as she lay down to sleep that night. The Lord of Heaven and Earth loved to hear the righteous ask for mercy for the wicked. The righteous were blessed when they asked for mercy for those who wronged them. Repentance in a great sinner like Zachai would be a blessing to every person he had wronged.

She smiled, knowing something terrible was about to happen to the publican. She wondered what unhappy shipwreck Zachai had caused that God would now show him. What shore of human suffering had Zachai created upon which he would now wash up? What broken man would the Lord send to show Zachai the effect of his terrible pride? How would the publican's leprous heart feel when it was pierced by the truth that his lies were directly responsible for the misery and ruin of so many?

How many had Zachai betrayed over the years? He had forsaken friendship and love all for the sake of power over others. He had sold love for money. Honorable accomplishments had been replaced by his own distorted perception of success. Was there any way back from such a life?

Shimona closed her eyes. "Yes, Lord, it's always good to ask you to show mercy and bring repentance to the hearts of the greatest sinners."

Lily crept up to the side of Shimona's bed and cried to be let up. Rose and Gideon followed. Did the trio sense her sorrow for the lonely little man?

"Shalom, my friends. So glad you're here. I wouldn't have known what I'd missed if you hadn't come into my life. O Lord! Help him. Help Zachai. . . . He is missing so much! Missing *everything*." Rose mewed pitifully. "Yes. I know. No good being lonely, eh?"

Shimona put the purring kittens beside her cheek on the pillow and drifted peacefully off to sleep.

Zachai felt the moist dripping of hot breath on his neck. It was almost morning of Sabbath and he was still alive, lying by the road beneath the nose of his ox.

Zachai moaned. "You. A very fine ox. You and the wagon too."

He raised his head and brushed the grime of his terrible flight from his face and beard. Sitting up slowly, he tested his hands and stretched his arms and legs. Nothing broken, though every exposed scrap of skin was scratched and sore.

Looking back toward Jericho, he could not see the haunted olive grove where the demon-possessed grandson of Pella the Elder dwelt.

How far had Zachai run from him? He could not tell. The memory of the evening before was a terrible nightmare. Whoever first said the olive grove was haunted had been right. There was nothing human about Zachai's encounter with the madman.

Zachai shook off the horror of the night. It was a new day, wasn't it? Last night meant nothing, did it? The world was filled with crazy men who claimed to be friends with the Angel of Death.

Suddenly hungry, Zachai fetched a handful of figs from a basket in the wagon. Raising his eyes briefly heavenward, he prayed, "Thank you, God of Avraham, Yitz'chak, and Isra'el . . . God whom my fathers did not worship. Though you cannot hear the prayer of one as sinful as I am, I thank you this morning, all the same, that I am alive. God who knows everything, don't lay the guilt of my father and grandfather in the matter of the House of Pella on my soul. Poor fellow, poor mad fellow. God who does not hear me, I am sorry for him. Hopeless.

Hopeless. But look not upon the sins of my grandfather against his grandfather. Do not lay that deed upon my tally of sins. I have plenty of my own sins to answer for."

Bera ben Dives consulted with the pair of assassins in their rooms at an inn at Jericho. "It's now certain the Nazarene is returning to Yerushalayim. Discretion must be used near the Holy City. Since I'm known to be in the high priest's employ, I mustn't be connected to his death or Lord Caiaphas might be blamed. It could cause a riot in Yerushalayim."

Ona patted ben Dives' arm. "My methods don't leave connections behind," she affirmed, fingering a glass vial hanging from a cord around her neck.

Her husband grimaced. "I don't know why we don't start picking them off one at a time as soon as they come out of the wilderness. That boy . . . the blind beggar? He's alone, away from the others at times. An easy target."

"Or El'azar of Bethany," Ona suggested. "Stories about a dead man alive again are what keep the crowds coming to see the Galilean."

Ben Dives shook his head. "You really don't understand, do you?" he argued. "Trickery, magic, sorcery—call it what you will. But we have to eliminate Yeshua first. Otherwise, what if he just brings them back to life? His fame will be even greater; things will be worse than ever. No, it must be Yeshua who dies first."

23 CHAPTER

The last mile of the old route into Jerusalem was uneven and rubble-choked. Every turn of the oxcart's wheels landed with a punishing thud. For the last mile Zachai felt each pounding impact like a fist in the kidneys, like a sock on the point of his jaw that jarred his teeth. He got off to walk alongside and sighed with relief when the caravansary outside the walls of the Holy City came into view.

His disguise was holding. Other travelers on the road acknowledged him with "Shalom" or at least agreeable nods. He was accepted as one of the *am ha aretz*. Like nine out of ten people he encountered, Zachai was one of the Jewish residents of Roman-occupied Judea, struggling to get by, hoping to make enough money to pay taxes and meet expenses.

Zachai's adventure had been a success. Now what? When he hit upon the scheme of transporting sukomore figs into Jerusalem, he had not thought through what he would do with them once he arrived. Should he find a fruit merchant and make a deal for the entire load? Or should he try to set up a stall and sell them himself?

Jericho's chief tax collector knew little about either possibility. If he charged too much or too little, people would grow suspicious and challenge him.

Perhaps the best idea was to put ox and cart into the caravansary while he continued into the city. By watching and listening, Zachai would learn what was proper.

As he directed the obediently plodding ox into the stockade opening, Zachai spotted an attendant shuffling toward him. The man's clothes, dirty and ragged, hung from his thin frame as if they had been cut for a much larger man. *Dug from a rubbish bin, no doubt,* Zachai thought, *or received as an act of charity.* The man was a beggar hoping to pick up a bit of coin for menial labor.

Stooped and hobbling, the worker approached. "Water your animal, sir? Perhaps some fodder? Two pennies is all, sir. Is it all right?"

The voice! The man's voice was familiar. His face turned to the side to avoid possible detection, Zachai studied the beggar's gaunt visage.

Rabshak ben Shebna! The caravan owner ruined by Zachai's deception and extortion had been reduced to this! The formerly rich and haughty tradesman was now mucking out stalls and begging for coppers.

Instead of gloating, Zachai felt a sudden stab of fear. What if he was recognized?

"Yes, yes!" Zachai said hurriedly, purposely lowering the range of his voice and coughing behind his hand. "And watch my load for me, eh?"

Ben Shebna eyed the load with practiced judgment. The fellow may have lost wealth, pride, and position, but he had not lost his years' trading experience. Shrewdly he said, "Made it through customs with your load intact? Must have cost you plenty, eh? Publicans and Romans, hand in hand, eh?"

"Just pay the toll and stay out of trouble; that's my motto," Zachai wheezed.

Ben Shebna looked Zachai up and down. "But how, eh? There's those who make trouble for others. Like that Zachai of Jericho."

"Him? Yes, but I mind my own business."

"Ha!" ben Shebna snorted. "Fair enough. But just wait 'til Messiah comes. Then the publicans and the Romans will see trouble! Then *they* will get the business, eh?" Ben Shebna drew an imaginary knife across his throat. "Zachai. I'll point him out to Messiah first thing. Even before Pilate. Even before Herod Antipas. Just wait, brother; you'll see."

"When Messiah comes . . ."

Winking conspiratorially, ben Shebna lowered his voice. "And it may be sooner than they think. You'll see, my friend. Zachai's day is coming! Messiah will hang him from his own sukomore tree!"

"Yes, well, must go. Business calls."

Zachai's breathing did not slow nor his heart rate return to normal until he was several blocks farther away. He mopped his brow, dipping the tail of his scarf in a public water fountain just inside the Gennath Gate. He felt he had experienced a narrow escape. Even beaten down as he was, Rabshak ben Shebna boiled with barely concealed rage.

If Zachai's true identity had been discovered, he might have been murdered right on the spot! Even if he had tried to flee, how many others of Jerusalem's rabble could ben Shebna have called together? Zachai could have been stoned and his death reported as the result of stopping a thief from escaping. Later the truth would be known . . . but precious little good that would do the publican.

Zachai thought about running to the Praetorium and throwing himself on the protection of the commandant of the Roman garrison. But without any identification, how could he prove who he was?

And how would he explain why he was dressed as he was?

Romans, from the emperor himself on down to the lowliest decurion, always saw conspiracies among the subject peoples. What if they chose to regard Zachai as a spy or a Zealot? Even if he escaped crucifixion, the Romans would certainly take away his office and his wealth.

Zachai forced himself to calm down. There was still a valuable load of figs to be sold. Then he could go home to the safety of his walled garden and his bodyguards.

As he walked toward the Street of the Fruit Vendors, Zachai reviewed what ben Shebna had said about Messiah. The Anointed One of the Jews was supposed to set His people free and restore the glory of Israel. Everyone knew that. It was a delightful story to whisper to children around the embers of a dying fire, or to toast with a cup of wine at Passover.

But no one took it seriously . . . did they?

Would-be messiahs were always caught and executed by Rome. No one in his right mind would ever claim to be such a being, unless he really had such a claim.

A drip of sweat ran down between the publican's shoulder blades. Despite the heat of the day, he shivered. Was it true that if, unlikely though it seemed, a messiah did appear . . . was it true that one of his first acts would be to round up and slaughter the publicans?

Zachai knew about sicarii, assassins. He had seen the dead body of an informer after the man was knifed in the streets of Jericho. Protesting that Zachai had only been doing his job would buy no more pardon than such a man had received at the dagger's point. If the whole of Judea rose to follow a messiah against the power of Rome, how little they would be afraid of a handful of bodyguards. Perhaps a messiah candidate would even seek to curry favor with the *am ha aretz* by sanctioning such a murder!

Suddenly the very title of Messiah was evil, terrifying, to Zachai's thinking.

So troubled were the tax collector's thoughts that he failed to notice a crowd of onlookers until he bumped into a spectator's back.

"Your pardon," Zachai offered hastily. Then, "What is happening here?"

The spectator grunted. "Runaway slaves recaptured. No great excitement, except because of that big blond heathen yonder. When he was caught they say he almost killed two guards by smashing their heads together."

It was Torvald, the German slave once owned by Azarel of Emmaus before being sold to satisfy Zachai's greed. Torvald's face had been beaten to a pulp and blood streamed from his hair to his chin, but he was still recognizable. His feet were chained together and his hands were bound to a beam laid across his shoulders.

Zachai hurriedly tugged the ends of his scarf around his chin and low over his eyes. "Will . . . will he be crucified?"

"No," the neighbor replied. "Only because the family that once owned him made a special plea on his behalf. Look there: See the young woman weeping? And that man's her father. They say the yellow-haired giant was just trying to get back to them when he ran. Some trouble with a tax collector or something. Well, that's not news, is it? But instead of death, Rome is being lenient. They're sending the poor brute to the tin mines north of Tarsus. North of Tarsus, I say. . . . Did you hear?"

Zachai did hear, but the words came from behind him as he pushed and shoved his way out of the throng. Every few paces he stopped to check over his shoulder. No one was following him, but he felt eyes on him, felt the prick of dagger points on his spine.

Tomorrow he could send a servant back for the oxcart and the figs, if they had not been stolen.

Tonight Zachai did not care about ox, cart, or figs . . . not one bit. He only wanted to get home as quickly as possible.

His thoughts raced. *Stay away from Jerusalem. Stay away from anyone who might recognize Zachai the Merciless . . . and stay away from an avenging Messiah!*

A patch of golden light shone through the window of Shimona's cottage. She sat on her bed of rushes with her back against the cool stone wall. The kittens lay purring on the pillow next to her. Legs and tails and heads were tangled into a warm and comforting heap.

She stroked Lily's soft, dusky white fur. "Lily, Zachai picked you up. You. He held you in his hands and smiled into your face like a little boy seeing a kitten for the first time. Zacchaeus, he said his name was. But . . . Lily? Did you notice his hands, little one? Did you?" Lifting the kitten to her cheek, Shimona sighed. "His hands. Hmmm? Not the hands of a working man." Shimona smiled and replaced Lily on the pillow. "Do you think anyone else noticed?"

Shimona picked Rose from the pile. "And you, Rose. You notice everything. Did you notice anything unusual about his whiskers? Hmmm? The beard . . . it is not thick enough for a fellow who has been living as a Jew. A few weeks since he has shaved, I would say. Hardly as long as a kitten's whiskers."

At last she retrieved Gideon. "And you, Gideon of the beautiful amber eyes. Did you notice his eyes? Brown. Rich, deep brown, like fertile soil after the rain when it's just been turned by the plow. I caught a glimpse of his turning . . . the turning of a soul in his eyes." She kissed Gideon on his head and set him down. "He had such sad eyes. Sad. Lost. Hoping for something."

Shimona sighed and closed her eyes a moment as she remembered the details of her visitor. "Hands. In Yerushalayim people may notice. He is a rich man. Beard. He has only just begun to let it grow. Eyes. Beautiful and sad. Lonely by his own fault. Hoping someone will see him as he wishes he was. He wishes to be wise and generous and kind

. . . to be loved. That is who he wishes to be, but he is not. In spite of his disguise he wants to be different. Yes, he is . . . hoping."

She whispered as she gazed at the starry vision of The Lion, "Lord who hears my prayers and knows all things, it was Zachai who came to this grove for a reason. You knew it all along, and I thought it might be true . . . now as I think of it . . . put it all together. God of Heaven and Earth who hears all my prayers, help him. He is running from the flattery of men, which he loves. He is addicted to praise, though he does not deserve praise. He is seeking to escape from deceit, which assures him his sin is not really sin. Yet he also is running from the silence of your Truth."

All three kittens appeared to be listening attentively to her prayer. "When will the veil be removed from his broken heart? Poor man. He thinks he is rich. He thinks he owns the trees and the harvest and me, but his soul is owned by all the things he owns. O Lord who visited me when I was dying . . . Lord who restored my diseased flesh! Poor Zachai is no less a leper than I was. Visit him. Heal him, I pray! Poor fellow. Alone. Alone. O God who hears my prayers, come visit Zachai the Publican and heal his leprous heart as you restored my hands and my face. You who are the Great Shepherd, fight for him. Lead him to your pasture. Give him back his life!"

Zachai turned his back on Jerusalem. The great stone towers and Temple walls provided no comfort or hope for him. There was only one person among all whom he had met in his journey who had not shown bitterness and loathing when the name of Zachai the Tax Collector had been mentioned.

"God who has never heard me, God who does not know me—am I not a son of Avraham, as all these are? Yet only Shimona the Leper, my slave, has offered even one word of kindness toward me." Zachai walked on the far side of the highway as he passed his own olive grove and remembered Pella and his demons lurking among the overgrown trees.

High above Zachai's head a red-plumaged hawk circled and soared as if to point the way to Shimona and the stone cottage in the grove.

The dark green foliage of the fig trees stood out clearly against stark landscape. Zachai saluted the bird and, ignoring the signs declaring leprosy and contamination, turned onto the gravel path leading to Shimona's cottage.

There was no one else in all the world Zachai wanted to see but her. No one else had hoped the best for him, spoken well of him. She did not curse him in spite of all the retribution he had exacted against her because of her father's deceit.

Zachai rested his soft, uncalloused hand on a sukomore trunk before trudging forward. "Lord who hates me like all the others, what strange mercy comes from this good woman! I have claimed her life like a piece of property in payment of her father's debt. Yet she is not bitter. It is I who am in debt to her for sharing the treasure of kindness. I am a beggar when it comes to love and friendship. She is rich in her friendship with you, though others have kept her from friendship."

Zachai looked upward at the fruit-laden tree, packed with unripe figs. "What wounding has Shimona felt that has ripened her compassion? My wounds have made me bitter and hard. How can it be that her wounds have made her only more merciful to the wounded? What light has shone in her heart that I, stumbling in the darkness of my heart, cannot see? Oh, Lord God! God who does not hear the prayers of a publican, hear and answer the prayers of my blind heart."

He did not finish his thought as Shimona's singing guided him through the grove to where she worked.

The red-tailed hawk caught an updraft and hovered high above the treetops as if to watch the destinies of Zachai the Publican and Shimona the Leper play out.

PART IV

For this is what the Sovereign LORD *says: I Myself will search for My sheep and look after them. . . . I will rescue them. . . . I will bring them. . . . I will pasture them. . . . I will search for the lost and bring back the strays. I will bind up the injured and strengthen the weak.*

EZEKIEL 34:11-16

24 CHAPTER

Shimona brought Zachai water to wash his feet and a towel. She knelt and placed the washing bowl on a woven mat outside the stone cottage where he sat.

Beyond the first instant she saw him coming up the lane, she had not looked at him. Her gaze wandered everywhere, never pausing to rest on him.

"What is it, Shimona?" he asked gently. "You seem troubled . . . yes, troubled."

"Did you get a fair price for the fruit of this orchard?" She paused and raised her eyes to look him full on in the face. "Lord Zachai?"

He stammered, "But . . . why call me that name? The name of that publican—the sinner Zachai?" He attempted to retreat into the comfort of his disguise again.

She shook her head. "I am your servant, my lord Zachai." She rose and bowed, backing up a step.

"My servant?"

"Yes. Payment for my father's sins; is that not true, my lord Zachai?"

His head suddenly throbbed. So now he had lost even the small hope of her friendship. "Please, don't call me that."

"You are my master, so I will call you by whatever name you choose. Even so, it doesn't change the facts."

"Please sit down."

She obeyed with a formal bow. "What is it you require, my lord?"

"Require?"

"Food. Drink after your long journey. It must be tiring to tend your own ox and sell fruit in the souks like a common peddler."

"Please, Shimona. I didn't mean to . . . deceive."

"Deceive?" On her lips the word clanged like a gong. Denying his deception was itself a great and terrible lie.

"Well, I did. I meant to . . . I *hoped* to find some kind word about myself, my life. Even one friend who would speak well of Zachai of Jericho."

She smiled, knowing. "There is only one time in a man's life when everyone speaks well of him. That is at his funeral."

"Even then—" Zachai sighed—"no one will speak well of the House of Zachai."

"What did you expect? That people you oppress would enjoy the power you wield over their lives?"

"Power. It has its benefits."

"Love is not among them."

"Then it demands its privileges."

Shimona replied quietly, "Gratitude and personal friendship are not among them."

He stared at his blistered palms. "How did you know?"

"I didn't at first. And then . . . your hands."

"My hands?"

"Too soft to be who you pretended to be. You are not a working man."

"What am I?"

"Can't you answer that yourself?"

He paused. "A tyrant, I suppose. A thief."

She changed the subject. "Did you find whatever you were looking for . . . out there?"

"I found myself as others see me."

"And?"

"I did not find any answers. How I might be someone else. Change and become changed. Someone worthy of being . . ." He lifted her chin with his finger. "Worthy of love."

"No." She drew away from him. "There's too much quicksand between you and real love." She raised her gaze as the hawk screeched. "He is a beautiful bird. Catches mice. Keeps the grove free of pests. That's a good sort of power to have. But he is also dangerous. A true danger to my kittens, you see? You understand what I am saying?"

"No. Dangerous?"

"Like you. You can't change on your own. You are a hawk, addicted to wealth and power. You take what someone works for and call it your own. You celebrate the death of his dreams as if you have won some game by destroying him. You pounce on whatever moves. Kill the mice of this world and kill the kittens with the same pleasure."

He lowered his chin and sat in silence for a long moment. "That is the way of all men."

"Not all. Not Yeshua. He teaches a better way. Instead of discouragement, he teaches us how to hold each other up and encourage one another. He taught us that anything not done out of love is not of God. A simple self-test. Actions that are vindictive or envious or destructive are not love. Assuming power and control over the life and calling and God-given talents of another man is not love. You can have all the money in the world, but without love you are eternally destitute."

"What is love, Shimona? I do have everything but I have never known love."

"Yeshua teaches this: Love is kind. And patient. It doesn't envy and steal and claim the talents and possessions of another man. Love keeps its promises even when it hurts. Love does not boast or crow when it is victorious in battle. Love heals the wounded rather than destroys the weak. Love is not motivated by injured pride to destroy the life and work of another. Love builds up. It does not tear down. Love isn't rude or thoughtless in actions or words. Love is not ambitious or self-seeking or addicted to flattery. It does not lie and claim it is somehow serving God. It keeps no record of wrongs or plots ways to take vengeance. Love is not easily angered, yet neither is it silent when confronting evil. It does not accept or delight in the actions of an evil man that hurt the innocent. Love does not defend a lie or accept the persecution of the innocent for the sake of remaining in control. Love rejoices in the truth.

It always protects. Always trusts. Always encourages. Always hopes. Always perseveres. Yeshua teaches us that Love never fails.[39] God's love heals all wounds."

"Do you believe I want to turn my life around? For you . . . for love . . . I think I could."

"For me?" she asked in delight. "I had stopped hoping I could be loved . . . long ago. I put away my expectations and found joy in each day's surprises. You, Zachai, are a surprise I can embrace. I love you, though you are not a safe man to love. What I feel for you frightens me because I know the truth about you."

"I could change if you loved me," he declared.

"Not for love, nor for money, can any man heal the leprosy of his own, inward, hidden life. Sin is a sort of leprosy in a man's heart, you see? And you have the disease, Zachai."

"Shimona, I came here hoping . . . if you could only tell me how . . ."

"If it's truth you're after? I can only point you to The One who never lies. Yeshua of Nazareth will show you the truth! He alone can heal your wounds."

"If only I could meet with him. Speak to him. Ask him so many questions . . ."

She sighed and smiled. "He is the only one I know who can heal all the lepers in Israel, yet you still think he can't heal your heart!"

He clasped her hands in his and kissed her palm. "I want him to, Shimona. God cannot hear my prayers. I know that. I am too black-hearted."

"But he *can* hear you. He *does* hear you! Zachai, if only you could just see him with your own eyes! There is a look in his eyes so deep, so filled with love and compassion. When you see him for yourself, then you will know he loves you and can forgive anyone who asks him."

"I am too lost to be found, Shimona."

Her gaze was steady as a rock. "He is the Great Shepherd of Israel. The one we have all been waiting for. He has come to us, the lost sheep, and he will gather us in his arms, Zachai!"

He reached out to her. "I want to understand."

"Every day of your life you go out, hoping to find yourself. But you're right about one thing: You are truly lost, Zachai of Jericho. Only Yeshua, Son of David, Shepherd of Israel, is The One you have been looking for. And here is the funny thing: When you finally come face-to-face with him, when you look into his eyes, you will know all the truth about yourself. On that day you will not be able to hide what you have been hiding. It is a frightening thing, I think, that there will be no more human disguises when he comes to rule over us. This is the truth: He came here to show you who he meant for you to be from all eternity."

Shimona continued to speak to him quietly about Yeshua. The sky grew dark and stars began to shine. Kittens played around their feet. The hawk cried in the distance as he hunted.

"Go home now, Zachai," Shimona instructed. "I will pray for you. I will. I promise. And I will pray you may soon meet your Shepherd face-to-face one day and be healed as I am healed."

Peniel, roused from slumber by the hooting of an owl in the top of a nearby oak, stirred and looked around. The fire had burned low. What appeared to be heaps of untidy clothing piled about were talmidim sleeping on the ground in every conceivable posture.

Shim'on Peter snored loudly, but everyone was too tired to be bothered by it.

Peniel noted where Yeshua knelt, apart from the group, praying. The boy would not disturb the Teacher.

On the other side of camp, atop a rocky outcropping, a man leaned on a staff. A dog sat by his side. Even in the dark of the moonless night, Peniel recognized Zadok. Slipping out carefully so as not to pull the cloak off Levi, who rested nearby, Peniel joined the old shepherd.

"Are you on guard? expecting trouble?" Peniel asked. "Should I rouse some of the others?"

"No, lad, no trouble. I believe now nothin' can happen before its time, so long as we're by the Master. He keeps t' seasons no one else fully understands, but which no one else can disrupt, neither."

"Then why are you awake?"

Zadok shrugged. "Old habits die hard. Shepherds never sleep the whole night through, but keep watch, turnabout. I've had my four hours. Now I'll stand watch awhile before I snatch a couple more hours before dawn. I'm glad of the company, though."

"Zadok," Peniel inquired, staring into the east where the

constellation of the Scales was rising into view, "remember when you said Yeshua is the Good Shepherd? Tell me more."

"A story, eh? Shepherd tales are homely at best. Not for young scribes in trainin' like yourself t' record."

"Let me be the judge of that," Peniel replied with a laugh.

"So, then. Call t' mind a readin' from the prophet Ezekiel, where the Adonai Elohim tells him t' preach against the false shepherds."

Peniel had heard this passage discussed by other rabbis when he was a beggar at Nicanor Gate. "It's about false religious leaders. But no one spoke it loudly or often, I suppose, for fear of offending the high priests, Caiaphas or Annas, or some other of Annas' family. It sounds like the prophet took aim directly at them."

"Just so," Zadok agreed, then quoted, "*Y' eat the fat, y' clothe yourselves with the wool . . . but y' do not feed the sheep. The weak y' have not strengthened, the sick y' have not healed, the injured y' have not bound up, the strayed y' have not brought back, the lost y' have not sought, and with force and harshness y' have ruled them.*"[40]

"Yeshua does all the things the others were supposed to do but don't," Peniel noted. "He heals sickness; he binds up wounded hearts; he looks everywhere for the lost and the strayed. The others are the false shepherds, and he is the true Shepherd."

"Just so," Zadok agreed. "Y' remember when the Master taught about the evil of envy, and I said it troubled more of our shepherd forefathers than ever did wolves? And they were all true shepherds, after a kind, eh? Abel, Father Avraham, Yitz'chak the Only Son, Isra'el the Wrestler, Joseph the Dreamer, Mosheh the Lawgiver, David the King—every one of them faced envy and strife from those who wanted t' be thought of as good shepherds. The enemies were false-hearted shepherds, every one."

"Seven of them. So Yeshua is the Eighth Shepherd," Peniel mused.

"Aye, and y' know what that means: Eight is one beyond a Sabbath of shepherds. So Yeshua is the fullness of all it is t' be a good shepherd. No, that's still not quite right. He's not *a* good shepherd. He's *the* Good Shepherd."

"And what will happen to the others?"

"The prophet likens them t' bullyin' sheep: *Is it not enough for y' t' feed on good pasture, that y' must tread down with your feet the rest of the pasture? I will strengthen the weak, and the fat and strong I will destroy,* or so says the prophet."[41]

Peniel shivered. "How can they keep acting as they do and not live in terror every moment? How long will the Lord put up with them?"

"Aye, lad, you've struck it. Put up with it 'til he comes t' set it right, eh? For y' know what Ezekiel says about who the Good Shepherd is? *Behold, I, I Myself will search for My sheep and seek them out. . . . I Myself will be the shepherd of My sheep, and I Myself will make them lie down, declares the Lord.*"[42]

"So when Yeshua says he is the Good Shepherd . . ."

Zadok clapped the young man on the shoulder. "Let no one have any doubts on that score. While we may not understand what it means, Yeshua says he is Adonai Elohim come down t' earth t' rescue his human flock from wolves, false shepherds, and the bullyin' of other sheep."

25

Bartimaeus heard Salmon calling his name from a great distance away. The bodyguard's voice rang with elation—uncontained, undiluted joy.

"Bartimaeus, my friend! She is well! Healed! My daughter is here, dancing."

The patter of running, leaping, pirouetting feet confirmed the truth of Salmon's words. "Shalom, little one. You are feeling better?" Bartimaeus asked.

"Yeshua fixed my belly! It hurts no more."

"Truly?" Bartimaeus addressed himself to the lengthy shadow that fell across his face.

"Completely true!" Salmon exclaimed. "He is the greatest man who ever lived." Then, as if a thought struck him, the bodyguard added, "I must go to my master, Lord Zachai. But when he allows, I will take you to Yeshua. He will restore your eyes. I know it."

His hands nervously bobbing across cloak, coins, and walking stick, Bartimaeus crooned, "Restore my eyes? But . . . to leave here? My world is this spot by the highway between the two Jerichos. How can I go?" Then with a note of sadness he added, "And he may choose to not help me. Once before someone offered to take me to him, and I . . . I mocked him. They probably told him so. No, I cannot leave all I know and then be refused. It's too much."

"Even for . . . the light?" Salmon inquired softly.

"Yet perhaps he will come this way," Bartimaeus mused. "All prophets must appear in Yeshushalayim, eh? Perhaps he will still come."

"Perhaps, my friend. We must go home now, but I will pray you may meet this 'Son of David.'"

"Son of David? Messiah? Yes . . . please pray!"

Bathed and dressed in his Roman clothing, Zachai retreated to his private courtyard. He was once again himself—Zachai, wealthy and powerful, chief tax collector of Judea. The gold chain of his office hung around his neck. His father's signet ring was on his finger.

Yet he had changed. He took no pleasure in the insignia of rank or his great riches. He was more alone than ever. The difference was that he now understood why he would live and die alone. His money could not buy what he most longed for.

The Old Man had already prepared a table of Zachai's favorite delicacies beside a couch under the Amos tree. Zachai inhaled deeply the peace of his garden retreat. Yes. It was good to be back home . . . but he had returned to Jericho without hope.

He sank onto the couch and drew up his weary feet. Plucking a walnut-stuffed fig from the tray, he savored its taste. Thoughts flew to Shimona—beautiful, yes. Alone, dominated and isolated from human company by the will of others. Yet she remained uncomplaining and seemingly happy. There was no bitterness in her soul in spite of all she had suffered. Yeshua of Nazareth had given her a new life, she said. If only Yeshua, who could restore a leper to health, could also heal the life of a publican, diseased by greed and ambition and sin. If only Yeshua of Nazareth could, by a word, cure the rottenness of Zachai's heart. But Zachai knew somehow that it was easier to cleanse a leper than to cleanse a leprous soul.

"God who does not hear my prayers . . . God who cannot look upon the emptiness of a sinful man like me and give him hope . . . what have I learned in my journey? I have learned how I have made others suffer by my actions. They all hate me with good reason. That is the truth. How I wish my life could be different. Different than I am now. But I don't know how to get from here to there."

Hopeless, he quaffed his wine and lay back on the cushions, closing his eyes. Then the chirping of birds and the stirring of leaves high above the wall of his retreat were interrupted by shouts from the servant quarters.

Zachai sprang to his feet, suddenly wide-awake. What had happened? Had a rebel broken through his gate? An intruder come to find and kill him after all?

Then the voices of his servants proclaimed clearly, "A miracle. A miracle! Look!"

"Come quickly!"

"Look! It is Salmon and Marisha. The children. Home again!"

"Blessed be the Name of the Great One!"

"The child is alive. Alive!"

"Come quickly. A miracle has come to the servants of the House of Zachai. The child lives by the touch and the word of Yeshua of Nazareth!"

"He is coming here!" Salmon laughed and danced with Marisha high on his shoulders. Two dozen servants from the House of Zachai watched the giant in amazement. Why had Salmon come back? The road had been open. He could have returned to his land and his people. Why had he returned?

"Master Zachai. He who is the King of Heaven and Earth. He commands the demons and they fly away! He rebukes death and it dissolves! Oh, my master!" The big man turned his shining face heavenward. "No man a slave when he looks into the eyes of Yeshua. He comes to set all men's hearts free!"

Zachai blinked at the child, well and whole. He took in the grinning face of Salmon's wife and the laughing eyes of all three of his children. Something miraculous had indeed happened when they met the one called Yeshua of Nazareth. But what?

"But you came back . . . here." Zachai cleared his throat as Olabi raised his eyebrows and nodded and nodded again.

"So, my master—" the Old Man put his arm around his bountiful wife—"does this mean that I have won the wager?"

"The wager?" Zachai could not take it all in.

Olabi nodded deeply. "My freedom. If Salmon came back from this journey with wife and children, you said you would give me my freedom."

Zachai grunted in amazement. "Yes. Yes. So I did make that promise. And so you are free. You and Aphrodite. You are free from my service. Free to . . . to leave me. Salmon and his family have come back, back to this house, and you are free to go."

Salmon clapped his hands together once in delight. "Free! The Old Man is free! Praise to the Great God of Heaven! Sing joy to The One who hears every prayer. . . . Olabi is free."

Zachai could not smile. "He has you to thank, Salmon. Your faithfulness. We made a wager, you see. I did not think you would come back."

"How could I not come back?" Salmon sank to the ground before his master. The eyes of Marisha were level with Zachai's gaze.

The child said in a sweet, small voice, "Sir, the Lord . . . he is coming soon! Coming here."

"Jericho," Zachai repeated. "Yeshua coming to Jericho." Zachai could think of nothing but Shimona.

Salmon asked, "Lord Zachai, what shall we do?"

Zachai ordered Salmon, "Hurry! Go at once to the fig grove. At once! Tell Shimona the Leper—she who is no longer a leper, she who was healed by Yeshua—tell her that Zachai sends word to her urgently. Tell her Yeshua, the Messiah, is coming here to Jericho. Tell her to hurry and come to Jericho so she can see him again!"

26

The morning sky was rich blue, brushed with feathered clouds. "Like the wings of angels," Shimona said to Rose, as the kitten sat on the window ledge.

Shimona laced twine through a necklace of figs and hung them for drying. Hawk soared above the grove of trees, periodically crying out as if to alert the mice they had better find other quarters.

"A perfect day," Shimona said. "What do you think, children?" she asked the kittens playing at her feet. "Perfect, eh?"

Mingled with the shriek of the hawk came another, unfamiliar voice. A man's voice, low-pitched and resonant, shouted from far away. "Shimona! Shimona of the sukomore fig grove. A message for Shimona!"

She raised her head from her labor and stood. Setting aside her work and closing the door behind her to lock her kittens in, she emerged from the cool stone cottage.

The shout came from the direction of the road. "Shimona! Ho! Come out! I come with a message from your master, Zachai of Jericho."

Shimona cocked her head and listened. Silence. Had the messenger gone away? Her heart pounded wildly. A messenger sent from Zachai to speak to her? What could he want? Had something happened to her family? Had her father or mother died?

Shimona's mind flooded with grim possibilities as she raced through the orchard to the highway. A giant man with ebony skin stood at the verge of the grove beside the warning sign. He was beaming.

"What? What is it?" she panted.

"Shimona, Master Zachai sent me to tell you . . . hurry! Come now to Jericho!"

"Jericho? Me?"

The big man nodded. "He sent me to tell you. . . . You must hurry to Jericho. Yeshua of Nazareth is coming to us. He is coming soon!"

"A moment, please. I can't leave my little ones behind." Hurrying back to the cottage, she gathered her kittens in a square basket and tied the lid shut with twine.

The road into Jericho was clogged. Small lanes flowed into the broad highway carrying the flock of Israel searching, calling out, for the Eighth Shepherd of Israel.

High above their heads Shimona's hawk circled, moving slowly along with them.

"He's coming!"

"Son of David."

"King of Israel!"

"The Great Shepherd."

"Yeshua is coming soon!"

"He's on the way!"

"Hurry!"

Shimona clung desperately to Salmon's tunic as he forged a way through the braying throng.

Salmon, towering over all others, could see when a path seemed to open. Weaving through the press, he made better progress than those who surrounded them.

"Hold tight!" he cried to Shimona. "I see a way through the gate."

Shimona wondered if her father and the leaders of the synagogue would at last be able to meet and speak with the Good Shepherd. Would the Chazzan and the rabbi comprehend at last what Shimona had tried to explain? Would they witness the power of Yeshua's love to change the lives of Israel's lost sheep forever?

A large woman with a child on her hip stumbled and fell against Shimona's arm, breaking her grip on the giant bodyguard. Shimona cried out in pain and fear. If she was separated from Salmon now, she would never make it inside the city gates.

"Salmon! Salmon!" she shouted. He had vanished from her vision amid the thousands.

"God who hear my prayers! God who always hears! Help me find my way! Help . . . Zachai . . ."

At that instant Salmon's enormous paw reached over the heads of those who had cut her off. She clasped his hand and he propelled her forward.

"God who always hears me . . . who always knows where I am . . ."

She did not cease to pray as they inched onward. She prayed that her solitary voice would not be lost in the clamor of Jericho.

The roar was of ocean waves breaking on a rocky shore. It was the rush of a wind so powerful it uprooted groves of trees. It was the clamor of a huge throng exclaiming, "He's coming! Yeshua is coming!"

Zachai ran to the front gate of his compound, accompanied by two bodyguards. Already the highway was packed with people streaming down the hill. The lane was filled from side to side, like a river over-flowing its banks. Where had all these people come from? There were not so many in all the region of Jericho.

A human wall already ten-deep blocked Zachai's view. When his guards tried to force an opening for their master, they met fierce resistance. No one gave way for the man everyone hated.

A phalanx of synagogue officials appeared in front of the synagogue next to Zachai's estate: the rabbi, a man robed as a priest, the Chazzan, others. Their faces exhibited a wide swath of emotions: arrogance, expectation, doubt.

While Zachai stood uncertainly, wondering which way to turn, the size of the crowd increased yet again. Like a bit of driftwood tossing in the current, he was swept apart from his guards, but no nearer the street.

Another roar from down the hill, drawing nearer. Already the hum of the throng around Zachai increased with anticipation. So Yeshua was coming up the hill. He was drawing near.

But what if He turned aside? What if He went some other way? New Jericho was home to Herodians, Roman officials . . . men like Zachai. What if Yeshua chose to take another route?

What Zachai saw was a wall of cloaks and robes, angry glances and hostile looks.

"It's the publican."

"What does he want here? Can he tax curiosity?"

"Charge admission, most likely."

Where were the guards? Zachai suddenly felt surprisingly isolated while in the midst of such a multitude. He felt threatened, anxious.

The crowd, so eager to see Yeshua—might they not be equally eager to stick a knife into the chief tax collector? There was anonymity in a mob, but not for Zachai.

"Who does he think he is? Yeshua's not for the likes of him!"

"Master. Lord Zachai!"

Someone calling his name. A friendly voice amid the crush of hatred.

There! Salmon's head loomed above the rest, as much above the human barrier as Zachai was beneath it.

"I have her. She's with me."

Zachai saw rather than heard Salmon mouth the words.

Shimona! Here to see Yeshua.

The publican tried to move toward Salmon and got an elbow in the ribs. He was stalled, unable to move forward. Waving frantically, Zachai gestured toward the wall of his compound, back from the street, back from the crowd.

Salmon nodded.

It took five minutes of weaving and pushing to break through a hundred paces. At least those who recognized Zachai were willing to let him retreat. Elbows, but no daggers . . . at least not yet. By keeping close to the estate's wall he finally managed to move forward.

Shimona appeared beneath the protective shield of Salmon's arm. Just in front of Zachai's gate they met.

"You came!" Zachai cupped his hand against Shimona's ear.

She returned the gesture. "Yeshua! If you can just meet him, hear him!"

The comment was ludicrous in the setting. Zachai could barely hear someone two feet away.

"Only to see him!" Shimona continued. "Remember the Valley of Mak'ob. Some are healed just by seeing!"

See him! But how?

"Perhaps Yeshua will speak in the synagogue," Shimona persisted.

Zachai shook his head. That was no solution. The Chazzan . . . the rest . . . they would not admit their worst enemy into their synagogue. If Yeshua went there, Zachai was doomed.

"Lord Zachai," Salmon shouted, "I must see to my wife and children." He gestured toward the compound, where the household servants and their families milled about in uncertainty. Some faces mirrored the excitement of the throng; others expressed fear that the mob would turn and tear down the publican's home and them along with it.

Zachai nodded.

The crowd had left a space for the synagogue officials. The press was less there. If only Zachai could get into that opening, there was still a chance to see Yeshua.

Taking Shimona's hand, Zachai tried to move forward again. Now a score of people packed the street. Even next to the wall the way was jammed.

"Please, let me through!" Zachai begged.

He saw Shimona yell something and looked where she pointed. Her hand was outstretched toward the Chazzan, her father. "Father!" she called again.

Zachai intercepted the stare the Chazzan returned—disbelief, then deliberate disregard. He would not recognize her, would not acknowledge her.

"Please, let us pass!"

An elbow again, this time to Zachai's face.

Shimona screamed.

Zachai was knocked to the ground. Only the nearness of the wall saved him from being trampled. Even so, his hands and legs were stepped on and he was kicked once in the back.

Was he going to die here? Would he be ground into pulp under the sandals of those he had abused?

From flat on the stones Zachai looked up into the branches of the

Amos tree. The sukomore leaves waved in the breeze as if also welcoming Yeshua. As if inviting Zachai, *Come and see what we see.*

Far up in the heavens a tiny dot spiraled downward. Zachai saw a red-tailed hawk sweep in and alight on the tree's topmost branch.

"O God who won't hear me," Zachai called aloud, "if ever you will, hear me now!"

Miraculously a space appeared, allowing Zachai to breathe. Taking Shimona's outstretched hand, Zachai hauled himself upright. Once more he prayed aloud: "O God who doesn't hear me, I need to see him!" Then to Shimona: "Hold tight to my belt and follow me. Come with me!"

They came from all directions, Peniel noticed. It was not just the citizens of the two Jerichos who converged on Yeshua's path, but people from all the villages in every direction. If compass points suggested origins, there were travelers from Bethany and Bethabara and Beth-lehem.

All Judea seemed to be arriving to welcome Yeshua back to the province, back to Jerusalem. *A prophet is arriving just in time for Passover,* their demeanor suggested.

They came with the expectation of seeing miracles. There was a festive, holiday air.

Nor was it only Judeans who came.

As the band of talmidim passed the customs plaza, merchants and drovers, spice salesmen and ivory dealers, abandoned their animals and cargoes to join the rush.

Questioning shouts reverberated around the Plain of Jericho.

"What is it?"

"Is there a new emperor?"

"Is it the healer from Nazareth?"

"Will the Galilean be proclaimed king?"

"Has Messiah truly come? Is the New World dawning today?"

To each and every query the reply was the same: "It's Yeshua! Come and see him!"

Ascending the hill toward New Jericho, Yeshua's progress slowed. Pilgrims knelt at His feet. Some thanked Him for previous healings. Some lifted children to be touched. Others extended hands in supplication.

"My back."

"My hearing."

"My daughter's child."

Peniel saw Him touch them, heal them, strengthen them—all the things the Good Shepherd, the Lord God Himself, said He would perform for His human flock, according to the account of the prophet Ezekiel.

And it was not yet Passover. What would happen when all the hordes of pilgrims arrived in the Holy City for the holiday?

As the road climbed a slight prominence, Peniel saw a blind beggar sitting beside the road. It was the same blind man who had refused to go with Peniel and Zadok to meet Yeshua. The man still clung to his walking staff and begging cloak, but he was clearly anxious about all the tumult.

Peniel remembered how it felt to be blind and in the midst of an unexplained commotion—terrifying! Unable to see the cause or even judge the nature of the hubbub, the blind assumed the worst. Any moment they might be trampled underfoot or thrust aside at the point of a Roman lance.

Peniel's heart went out to the man, who was beseeching his neighbors to tell him what was happening.

He must have gotten his question answered, for suddenly he started screeching, "Yeshua, Son of David, have mercy on me!"

His cries were piercing. Those nearest him told him to be quiet, to stop shrieking. Peniel heard the man's name murmured in the crowd. *"Bartimaeus,"* they said. *"Son of Defilement."*

Some were angry at his interruption. This occasion was much greater than a blind beggar's outcry. Who did he think he was, anyway?

Bartimaeus shouted all the louder. "Son of David—yes, I proclaim it! Messiah, Son of David, have mercy on *me!*"

"Master," Peniel said, touching Yeshua's arm. "Will you . . . ?"

"Yes, Peniel," Yeshua replied. "The question is . . . will he?"

Stopping just opposite the beggar's outpost, Yeshua commanded the mob to be still. Then He called out, "Bartimaeus, come here."

Wondering words rippled back through the throng:

"He's calling the blind beggar."

"He wants the beggar to come to him."

"Bartimaeus, he's calling you! Get up, man! Go to him!"

It was then Peniel saw a wondrous thing happen and realized what a change had already come over the blind man. When Bartimaeus sprang to his feet, he cast aside his cloak. His feet scattered the coins into the dirt as he lunged forward.

The beggar had made up his mind at last. He was leaving behind his life as he knew it. Everything he was comfortably acquainted with he discarded to go to Yeshua.

"Master, we have left everything to follow you! Fishing nets . . . counting houses . . . begging cloaks!"

The crowd hummed with anticipation, but Yeshua did not immediately go to the man. He did not, Peniel saw, kneel in the dirt and make clay to anoint the man's eyes.

Instead, from several paces distant, Yeshua called loudly, "What do you want me to do for you?"

Blind, blue eyes, hazy like the cloud-streaked sky, locked onto Yeshua's voice.

There were thousands of people all around, but the blind man unerringly focused on the Healer.

"What do you want me to do for you?" Yeshua repeated.

What, indeed?

There were many in the crowd today thinking of a lifetime's supply of free bread, of never having to work again, of having positions of authority in a new king's government.

What do you want me to do for . . . you?

"Lord," Bartimaeus asked, much softer than he ever, *ever* asked for alms. "Lord, I want to recover my sight."

And Jesus said to him, "Recover your sight; your faith has made you well."

New eyes! Clear eyes! Brilliant blue as the summer sky over a placid azure Sea of Galilee.

Bartimaeus glanced around wildly, fell to his knees, grasped Yeshua's hands. "Praise the Eternal!" he shouted. "Praise the Almighty!"[43]

When Yeshua raised him to his feet again, Bartimaeus began to sing. Not in the screeching, alms-demanding voice the onlookers expected, but a clear, melodious baritone: *"Give thanks to the Lord, for He is good. His Mercy endures forever!"*

The crowd joined him in the psalm: *"Give thanks to the God of gods. His Mercy endures forever! Give thanks to the Lord of lords. His Mercy endures forever! To Him alone who does great wonders . . . His Mercy endures forever!"*[44]

Peniel made his way to Bartimaeus' side. "I'm Peniel," he said, taking both the former beggar's hands in his. "I met you before. I was blind once too! Come with me. Come with us."

Bartimaeus did not even turn back to retrieve his cloak.

Give thanks to the Lord, for He is good. His mercy endures forever!

Once inside the wall of his estate, Zachai's forward progress gathered momentum until Shimona was being dragged along after him. To each of the servants' children he passed the publican called out, "Come with me! Follow me!"

They hesitated only a moment when he pushed open the gate to his private garden. None of them were allowed there; none had ever been admitted there before.

He urged them in. "Come along! You want to see Yeshua, don't you?"

Marisha took the lead in encouraging the rest. "You must come!" she piped. "See the one who healed me!"

Zachai stood triumphantly next to the trunk of the sukomore and gestured up. "Even if he turns aside, we can see him from there." He pointed toward the limb jutting out over the wall.

Shimona shook her head. "I can't do that."

Leaping onto the limb, Zachai turned and extended his hand. "Yes, you can," he insisted.

Though Zachai shuddered when he touched the coil of rope, he thrust the accompanying thought aside. In moments the cord was tied in several places along the limb and down the tree, aiding the ascent of the children, who clambered up eagerly.

And none too soon! From his perch Zachai spotted the way the crowd parted like a wave in front of the prow of a ship. A space opened for Yeshua and His talmidim to progress.

Then, suddenly, there He was! The Man from Galilee.

Who was that next to Him? The figure walking immediately beside the Galilean appeared to be someone Zachai should recognize. Who could it be?

Then Zachai slipped and might have fallen except for Shimona's grasp on his arm.

It was Bartimaeus! Striding proudly, confidently, beside the Healer was the blind beggar of Jericho . . . blind no longer!

No walking stick, no begging cloak, no hesitant steps. Looking everywhere at everything, but always—always!—back at Yeshua's face.

"God who doesn't hear me . . ."

Zachai stopped the flow of his words. He had not been trampled in the mob. He had seen the hawk alight in the tree, had recognized the opportunity given by the limb.

"God who heard me, one thing more! I want to see! I want to *see*. Like Bartimaeus, I want to see. Open the eyes of my blind heart!"

With a glance at Shimona, he prayed, "Heal the leprosy of greed that's consuming me! Let me see *him* . . . and be healed!"

Yeshua was turning toward them, deliberately choosing the lane that ran beside Zachai's estate . . . and also beside the synagogue.

The synagogue officials were smug, arrogantly self-confident. The Healer was coming to pay His respects. The rabbi and the priest and the Chazzan stepped forward to receive this itinerant preacher who was coming to greet them.

It was the end for Zachai, and he knew it. Yeshua's ears would be filled with all the misery the most hated man in Judea had caused. Venom would flow from their mouths into Yeshua's ears . . . and it would all be true.

Zachai's eyes swelled with tears.

"O God," he called to the heavens. "Not now! Not this close and then shunned forever. Please, I beg you!"

Peniel saw the respectable citizens of Jericho waiting to receive Yeshua. Men with upraised chins and calculating eyes. *It is our due*, their expressions conveyed. *It is right for this country preacher to come to us for our seal of approval.* Like a row of rock-hard, unripe fruit in a market stall, they waited for Yeshua to acknowledge them. Unpierced by seeing their own needy souls, their hearts betrayed no sense of requiring repentance or forgiveness.

Peniel recognized none of them until his gaze lit on a thin, stoop-shouldered man and a squat, stringy-haired woman. They were one row behind the synagogue officials. Their stares were also calculating, but in a darkly murderous way.

Leaning away from Bartimaeus, Peniel said urgently to his friend, "Levi, I know those two. They tried to kill us—Miryam and Kuza and Manaen and me—back in the Galil. For them to be here means nothing good."

"Hush," the former tax collector urged. "The Master knows what he's doing. Don't you know where we are?"

Peniel wanted to shout that they were in the presence of murderers, stranglers, assassins, but he kept still. "No. Where are we?"

"More over that way. Look there. That's the home of the most hated man in Judea. Zachai the Chief Tax Collector. Once I admired him more than anyone else in the country. Later I pitied him to the same degree."

Following Levi's gesture, Peniel studied the walled compound. All around him laughter broke out. Laughter! Yeshua laughed with the rest—joyous, carefree mirth.

Peniel spotted the reason for the amusement. A massive sukomore tree behind the wall reared its ancient head over them all. Festooning its trunk, like so many plump, ripe figs, were children!

Also a woman and an anxious-appearing man.

Marching right past the row of synagogue officials, who made no move to come forward to the Healer, Yeshua stood beneath the largest branch of the tree. Stretching out His arms as if imitating the sukomore, Yeshua spoke: "Zachai! Hurry and come down. For I must stay at *your* house today."[45]

The publican trembled all over, like a sukomore leaf in a high wind. The woman seated next to him had to help him climb down from his perch.

Yeshua had addressed the publican, the chief tax collector . . . the most vile man in all Judea. Yeshua had called him by name! And they were going to his house.

The religious leaders scowled.

Some in the crowd muttered, "He is going to be the guest of a man who is a great sinner."

Judas offered apologetic looks toward the rank of priest, rabbi, and the Chazzan.

Zachai appeared, running, from his gate. His knees were scuffed from sliding down the tree trunk. His clothes were in disarray. He was panting.

A host of children, many of them dark brown–skinned, followed. One of them was Marisha, and behind her Peniel recognized her father.

Zachai almost skidded to a stop in front of Yeshua. "You called me! You didn't turn away. I thought . . . I feared . . . I almost didn't believe. . . ." Then, visibly regaining control of his emotions, Zachai declared, "A feast! A feast at my house, to honor Yeshua, Son of David, the Great Shepherd of Israel!"

Epilogue

It has been written by our brother Luke the Physician that Zachai came down from the sukomore tree and received Yeshua joyfully into his house. And when the Pharisees and the rulers of Jericho saw it, they grumbled, saying, "He has gone to be the guest of a man who is a sinner."[46]

The names of those who did not cherish and welcome Yeshua in Jericho have all been forgotten now.

You know me. I'm Peniel. I love a good story. And so I will fill in a few small details.

We gathered for a feast beneath the ancient Amos tree in the private garden of Zachai the Publican.

It was a sort of resurrection from the dead, I thought, as I saw the eyes of Zachai the Publican light up when Yeshua spoke. Things eternal had entered the tomblike house of the tax collector.

Shimona remembered me from our first encounter on the rim high above the Valley of Mak'ob.

"So you found your way home after all," I said to her.

She looked at Zachai as he spoke with Yeshua. "Yes. Yes, I have at long last found my way home."

"I am happy for you," I said.

"Zachai has asked me if I will marry him. I think I may."

"Well? Why wouldn't you?"

"I told Zachai . . . I said I would give him my answer tonight."

I sensed a change in the wind as the most hated man in Judea threw his head back in a laugh. I was certain then that Shimona's answer would be yes.

We were seated around an enormous U-shaped table. Room was made as Zachai thought of more people he wanted to invite to meet Yeshua.

The servants of Zachai prepared a great feast that night outside beneath the sukomore tree that Amos the prophet had planted. When all the food was ready, Zachai invited his servants to join us at the table.

Zadok and I sat together with the children at the far end of the table and marveled at the enormity of the ancient fig tree. Zadok declared, "Yeshua . . . here tonight. What do y' know? Like the prophet Amos, he's the Shepherd and The One who tends the fig trees of Israel."

I added, "And such a fig tree . . . it's been here all along, waiting for Yeshua to sit beneath it and pluck the ripe fruit of Israel and gather us all together in the same basket."

"Ripe fruit," Zadok mused. "Strange that there is such a lesson in this fig tree. Just like the hard, unripe heart of a proud and stubborn man, figs don't ripen unless they are wounded."

I was unable to keep my eyes from the gloomy towers of the synagogue, toward which I nodded. "*They* won't like it much."

The great synagogue of Jericho brooded empty, dark, and silent beside the blaze of lights and music in the crowded courtyard of Zachai the Publican. I considered how close the building was to Zachai's property line. No doubt the shade of the giant Amos tree fell on the members of the congregation just as it shielded the publican from the heat of the sun. As the music of the celebration drifted over the walls, the Pharisees must have discussed the fact that in the language of the Greeks the name of the *sukomore* fig tree shared its roots with the word *sycophant*.

There must have been some pleasure for them as they discussed the sinister significance that Zachai had climbed this particular tree to see Yeshua. I imagined them in their lair, applying their own interpretation to the day's events rather than understanding the true lesson of the fig tree. Zachai's heart had been wounded and at last had ripened. It was Yeshua who, with mercy and joy, harvested the fruit this night.

Shimona's kittens riding on their shoulders, Zadok's boys clambered up into the fig tree with the other children. From its branches they squealed with pleasure as the adults ate and sang and talked of marvelous deeds and wondrous things yet to come.

And there was Yeshua of Nazareth at the head of the table. Beside Him, on His right, sat His mother. Twelve surly apostles in no particular order of rank or importance came next. The Twelve still murmured and bickered as they ate grudgingly at a publican's table. I had the feeling some would have rather been seated at the table of the religious rulers of the city.

Zachai, master of the great House of Zachai, was on Yeshua's left. Beside him sat Shimona. Beside her, engaged in lively conversation, were Miryam and Marta, and their brother, El'azar. Bartimaeus, dressed in new clothes, was next to El'azar, describing every sight and telling everyone what it was like to see. El'azar, in turn, shared what heaven had been like. He exclaimed that what he had seen and heard was beautiful beyond imagination. He had left with some reluctance as the voice of Yeshua called him back to this world.

Around the great table a bouquet of faces bloomed like hastily picked flowers, mismatched and vibrant. All of us had left something behind to follow Yeshua. He demanded that we abandon much more than fishing nets or cloaks or houses or land. Yeshua called upon us to abandon the thing we most cherished . . . our own stubborn will. He asked us to leave behind all our differences and take on one heart—the heart of a servant, guided by His love. Yeshua, our Shepherd, had drawn us, His flock, near to Him by one faith in His one truth. Coming to Yeshua meant that our hearts and souls became one!

Suddenly, as I looked at all the faces gathered round, I understood that Yeshua meant for all of us, His holy people, to be united in love for all time. Slaves who had been children of slaves mingled with the wealthy followers of Yeshua. Former beggars, former lepers, and all manner of sinners sat side by side with civic rulers and leaders in business. Those once lame danced beneath the spreading branches of the sukomore fig tree while the mute sang. Zadok's dog smiled and wagged around the perimeter of the celebration.

"Was there ever such a party?" Zadok waved at his boys, who had scaled the heights of the Amos tree to peer over into the street. "Practically a wedding." He looked at Shimona, who was gazing lovingly at the host.

"I would say there will be a wedding feast soon enough," I agreed.

"Aye. Zachai has chosen well from the look of her."

"Her name is Shimona. I spoke with her when she left the Valley of Mak'ob. She said she was going home . . . home! From the Valley of Sorrows. Now look at her. Shining like a light." I downed a helping of beef. "Oh, these rich fellows! They do know how to get a bride and feed a mob well at a moment's notice."

Zachai stood and raised a golden goblet to offer a toast. "And here's to my honored guest. Most honored . . . Yeshua! The Great Shepherd of Israel who has found another lost sheep!" He placed his hand over his heart and pledged, "Lord, I have seen you coming from a great height. You have looked upon me with mercy. Half my goods I give to the poor. And if I have defrauded anyone of anything, I will restore it fourfold."[47]

Upon hearing this declaration Zadok leaned close to me and whispered in surprise, "This fellow knows the law of Mosheh and the flock: Restore four lambs for every one lamb stolen."[48]

Yeshua stood and clasped hands with the publican. "Today salvation has come to this house."

The crowd laughed at Yeshua's humor. Zadok nudged me hard, noting that Yeshua's name means "salvation," and He had indeed come to Zachai's house.

Yeshua nodded and smiled broadly, raising His cup to Zachai. "Salvation has come to this house since he is also a son of Avraham! For the Son of Adam came to seek and save the lost!"[49]

A resounding cheer arose, echoing off the dark walls of the synagogue. Everybody drank deeply. It was the best wine I had ever tasted.

"If you please, Rabbi . . . Lord Yeshua," Zachai continued. "If you would bless my household now with some word of wisdom that will be remembered and cherished forever."

Zadok whispered, "A story!"

I cradled my cup. "You know me. I do love a good story. . . ."

Yeshua sat down on His cushion and thanked Zachai. His gentle brown eyes circled the courtyard, rounding up and capturing every stray thought with a single glance.

Even now I can see His face. His smile. I can hear His voice creating a miracle in my heart with the same joy by which He must have hung the stars in place.

And then Yeshua told a parable that has been told ten thousand thousand times since that night in Jericho. But think of this . . . I was there, present at the supper the first time the story was ever told.

"There was once a nobleman who went into a far country to receive for himself a kingdom and then return . . . ," Yeshua began.

We all knew that He was speaking about Himself. Yes. Yeshua was the nobleman. He had come a long way to find us, and He told us plainly that He would return soon to the place He had come from until His Kingdom was established.

I asked myself which part I played in His parable.

"Calling ten of his servants, he gave them ten minas and said to them, 'Engage in business until I come . . .'"

Was there ever such a moment as that moment? He looked deep into our souls and spoke to each heart as though no one else could hear.

Silence fell. Children scrambled down from the sukomore tree and crowded in next to mothers and fathers. We, the flock of the Great Shepherd, heard only His voice.

"But his citizens hated him and sent a delegation after him saying, 'We do not want this man to reign over us.'"

I looked again at the dome of the synagogue of Jericho and remembered the hatred and resentment in the eyes of those false shepherds who had expected Yeshua to join their circle of power. They hated Yeshua with such a fierce hatred. Like the citizens in the story they did not want Yeshua to rule over us. The same fellows had hidden Shimona in the sukomore grove because her healing was proof of Yeshua's authority. They were even then plotting in some back room while we feasted with our King under the stars that He created in the beginning. I wondered for a moment what was ahead for us in Jerusalem.

Yeshua knew my thoughts.

He said to us all, "When the nobleman returned, having received the kingdom, he ordered these servants to whom he had given money to be called to him that he might know what they had gained by doing business. . . ."

Yeshua unfolded before us what was coming in Jerusalem and what He expected from us, His servants. But we only heard what we wanted to hear, not the true meaning of His words.

"And the first servant came before him and said, 'Lord, your mina has made ten minas more.' And the king said to him, 'Well done, good and faithful servant! Because you have been faithful in a very little, you shall have authority over ten cities.'"

All listened raptly to Yeshua's story of the returning king and servants who succeeded and servants who failed. How could we know? How could we have imagined what was to come?

I could only think to myself, *Which servant will I be when Yeshua claims his kingdom in Jerusalem?* And then I prayed, *Lord, make me like the most faithful servant. Faithful with every gift! Make me become like the man who multiplied what you gave him.*

The Twelve sat at the table with visions of power and glory dancing before their eyes, Judas Iscariot, in particular, among them.

"The ruler returned. . . ." Yeshua prophesied about His return.

And yet we could not comprehend how soon He would leave, or why, or where He was going.

Yeshua warned us that very night. He told us plainly that He was going away, but one day He will return to His Kingdom.

He taught us clearly that much would be expected of us in His absence. Hard work for the Kingdom of our Lord. Faithfulness. And when our ruler returns, there will be a moment when we will each be called before Him to give an account of what we did with the gifts we were given.

This was the parable Yeshua taught beneath the sukomore tree.[50]

I know now what Yeshua meant. I am sure the Great King will return to His land and His people, and when He does, I will be with Him.

The moment of judgment will come for me when the King will ask what I did with what He gave me.

He will look into my eyes . . . "Were you faithful?"

This story of Zachai the Publican is only the beginning.

In the years that followed, Zachai fulfilled every vow he made to

Yeshua. We came to know him very well. He made restitution according to the laws of Moses to every life he had injured.[51] The slave that had been sold in payment of debt was found and redeemed and set free. The vineyard of Elijah the Vintner was restored. The madness of poor Pella was cured by Shim'on Peter in the power of The Name of Yeshua; his olive grove was returned and his house rebuilt.

Zachai married Shimona and they had eight children, all of whom now follow and proclaim the Good News of the Kingdom to the lost.

These, then, are the words of our King Yeshua to Zachai of Jericho: "Zachai, small of stature but large in love. Well done, good and faithful servant."

The LORD is my shepherd, I shall not be in want.

He makes me lie down in green pastures,

He leads me beside still waters,

He restores my soul.

He guides me in paths of righteousness

for His name's sake.

Even though I walk

through the valley of the shadow of death,

I will fear no evil, for You are with me;

Your rod and Your staff, they comfort me.

You prepare a table before me

in the presence of my enemies.

You anoint my head with oil; my cup overflows.

Surely goodness and love will follow me

all the days of my life,

And I will dwell in the house of the LORD forever.

PSALM 23

Digging Deeper into EIGHTH SHEPHERD

Dear Reader,
Have you ever wondered if your prayers are being heard? why the heavens seem silent in the face of your heart's cries?

Have you longed for companionship in your loneliness? wondered if you will always be on the outside, looking in, wishing for acceptance and love?

Have you done so many wrong things that you feel like a black sheep? Do you wonder if it's possible for you to turn your life around? Or is it simply too late?

Do you suffer or watch someone you love suffer and wonder if—and when—God will intervene?

You are not alone.

Shimona the Leper had been physically healed by Yeshua. For twelve long years she had looked forward to returning to her home. Yet when she arrived there, she was shunned and cast out to live in solitary confinement in a sukomore fig grove. How lonely she was. How often she dreamed of companionship. . . . *Anything, Lord. Anyone. Please bring someone my way.*

Zachai the Publican had always been so powerful and successful, as well as manipulative and scheming, that he drove away all possibility of friendship. Now he was continually on the outside, looking in . . . wishing that his life could be like everyone else's and feeling powerless to change his path. Could suicide be the only answer? And would anyone care if he left this earth?

Salmon, as a slave, had no power in the eyes of the world. He was, in fact, worth little, except as Zachai's slave. Could he hope that a Messiah who did not belong to his race or religion would have mercy on his young daughter, whose life meant so little in the eyes of the world but so much to him?

What is the cry of your heart today? In what way(s) do you need to be transformed by Yeshua, the Great Healer? What kind of loving touch do you need from the Great Shepherd?

Following are six studies. You may wish to delve into them on your own or share them with a friend or a discussion group. They are designed to take you deeper into the answers to questions such as:

- Is it possible to live with hopeful expectation in the midst of life's often harsh realities?
- Is anyone ever too lost to be found?
- What prayers does God hear, and why?
- Why is it so hard for some to believe in Yeshua?
- How can you seek healing and the Healer?
- What do life and death mean, really? And how does your philosophy of these two events influence your future?

Can lives, bodies, and hearts truly be transformed? With Yeshua, *anything* is possible! Through *Eighth Shepherd*, may the promised Messiah come alive to you . . . in more brilliance than ever before.

1 LIVING WITH HOPEFUL EXPECTATION

Day after day, month after month, Shimona expected and looked for an answer to her prayer. She did not stop hoping, though she lived alone with the chickens and the goats. . . . Undaunted that her family seemed to have forgotten her and abandoned her in the fig grove, Shimona never lost hope.

—P. 10

Have you ever felt alone and abandoned? If so, when? Tell the story.

_____

_____

_____

During that period of your life, were you able to hold on to hope? Or did you lose hope? Explain.

_____

_____

_____

Who, if anyone, was your "inspiration" during that time? Why?

_____

_____

_____

Shimona's story was one of horror, tragedy, alienation, loneliness, and then happy endings. Did she ever dream, as a young girl, that she would live as a leper in the Valley of Mak'ob? that she would be driven away from her family because of fear of a disease? It's doubtful. Yet amazingly, Shimona held on to hope . . . and felt the personal touch of Yeshua.

READ

It was almost dawn. The deep shadows of the mountain relinquished their hold on Mak'ob.

Among the last to be healed was a pretty woman, about thirty years of age. Her lively brown eyes were the color of freshly turned, rich earth. Brown hair was thick and cropped short. It curled softly around her face. Skin was sun-bronzed. Still dressed in the rags of her disease, she climbed the path with certain strides. . . .

"Shalom. Shalom . . . been here long?"

"All night," I answered, moving over as she sat beside me. "A long night, eh?"

"Twelve years for me." She was breathless from the climb. She looked up as the last stars faded, then down into the shadows where Yeshua was embracing the lepers of Mak'ob. "But now . . . look . . . the sun is rising."

We stood together for a long moment. I remarked, "It will be remembered. He healed them all . . . all the lepers in Israel."

"Yes," Shimona agreed, turning away from the Valley of Sorrows. . . . "He laid hands on us. And our wounds vanished."

—PP. VIII–X

ASK

Imagine you are Shimona. You expected to die in the valley of lepers. Then Yeshua the Healer walked right into the midst of that death and disease to heal you. What would your response to Him be?

_____

_____

_____

Now you are completely healed and on your way home. What thoughts and emotions would you experience?

_____

_____

_____

READ

The one-room stone hut where Shimona the Leper lived was proof that even after happy endings, the road of life continues with unexpected twists and turns.

Shimona's father was still Chazzan of the synagogue in Jericho. He was an upright man, a righteous man, respected by all in the community. The citizens of Jericho had almost forgotten that the Chazzan's grown daughter and her husband were lepers living in the Valley of Mak'ob.

The Chazzan had been surprised to see his daughter on his doorstep after so many years of believing she was among the living dead. Shimona's mother wept to see her face but did not embrace her. The Chazzan did not allow Shimona's sisters to come near her.

She had stayed in the shed behind the house until nightfall. After dark she followed her father to the rabbi, and they called the Levite priest. At the side of the synagogue in Jericho they had listened patiently to Shimona's story about Yeshua coming to the Valley of Mak'ob and healing everyone.

"You say he healed them all?"

"Yes! He healed us all!"

"Everyone in Mak'ob?"

"Every one," Shimona declared. "Yeshua is Mashiyah! He is the Son of the Living God!"

—PP. 6–7

And then, because they weren't sure what to do with Shimona, they found a place for her . . . tending the sukomore fig grove outside of town, where no one would come in contact with her, just in case she was still leprous. There she lived out her days in solitary confinement.

ASK

What was the town's response to Shimona? Why do you think they responded the way they did?

_____

_____

_____

If you were a person in the town (a mother, say, with a child who could become ill), how would you have responded to Shimona and her story? Explain.

_____

_____

_____

Would Shimona's declaration of who Yeshua is have made you nervous, or would you have accepted it? Why or why not?

_____

_____

_____

READ

The night was thick with quiet, like cobwebs hanging from the ceiling of a deserted house.

"Mother?" Shimona cried again, hoping . . . hoping.

She drew in her breath, remembering what it had been like to hear the breath of her husband and the baby in the darkness. Strange how lonely the sound of her own heartbeat had become.

The kindness of lepers had been daily comfort in the Valley. The isolation of this stone house and sukomore grove seemed more painful to endure than the disease that had first separated her from home and kin so long ago.

"Mother?" she called, knowing her mother had long ago forgotten her. The forgetting was so complete that her mother did not want her to come back . . . not ever.

—PP. 20–21

As the evening sun sank lower and the stars appeared in the eastern sky, Shimona stood awhile within the verge of the sukomore grove and gazed at the walls of the new city of Jericho. She could plainly see where the house of her father and mother was. The lamps of distant houses shone until Shimona could not tell what was heaven and what was earth.

It was always this hour of the day when the shadow of loneliness crept over her heart. She thought about her mother and father and sisters sitting together and sharing a meal. It had been so very long since she had eaten a meal with any human company. The last time she had partaken in pleasant conversation had been the night she left the Valley of Mak'ob.

She sighed deeply, hoping that perhaps her father would feel some longing for her company as well. But she knew it had been so long . . . so very long . . . that he had probably gotten used to her absence. Daily life had flooded in where her place had been. It was as though she had died in Mak'ob and never returned home, as though she were never coming back. . . .

Was her family eating together even now? Did they look at the empty place at the table and think of her here in the sukomore grove? Or had they forgotten her?

—PP. 16–17

ASK

How was the alienation that Shimona experienced in the Valley of Mak'ob different from the alienation she felt in the sukomore fig grove? Explain.

_____

_____

_____

Have you ever felt alienated from home or family? If so, when? Tell the story.

_____

_____

_____

How did you deal with that loneliness?

_____

_____

_____

READ

Shimona sent word to the Chazzan, her father, and begged him to send a feline to help her defend the fig grove. He did not heed her request. She heard from him less and less as time passed. . . . [Then] she remembered her Father in Heaven, for whom nothing was impossible. She prayed that one day, perhaps, the Messiah would cross the creek and enter the sukomore grove with His disciples. She could see it plainly in her mind. Yeshua, the Deliverer of Israel, and His band of holy men would accept Shimona's offering of cakes of figs, and she would feed them all a hearty meal.

In preparation for that possibility, Shimona composed a song about a gray-striped cat riding on the shoulder of the Messiah. She decided that if Yeshua ever came to the sukomore grove, she would sing Him the song. Then perhaps Yeshua, who healed lepers and fed five thousand with only five loaves and two fish, would see her need for help and answer her request.

—P. 10

Shimona closed her eyes and waited for the warmth of her prayers to fill her with peace. She said to the kittens, "Someone Eternal wants to join us for supper. The Lord is coming to . . . us. Our house. Yeshua?"

Suddenly a vision filled her mind: Yeshua coming up the road to Jericho. Yeshua surrounded by a great throng, Shimona's mother and father among the faces. And . . . Lord Zachai! Trying to see him. Trying to catch a glimpse of The One who healed her leprosy.

Shimona said aloud, "Yeshua. Jericho. Close by here. Very soon." She smiled wistfully, blessed the bread, and broke it. She passed a morsel of cheese to the little ones. They clambered over one another and gobbled their supper together. Their tails were straight up and quivering with joy.

Shimona watched them eat with pleasure. Kittens. Such small things to give her such enormous joy. "Lord, who knew how lonely I was. Who would think . . ." She sighed. "Lord, I didn't know I was so lonely."

She sang the Shabbat hymns she had learned as a child from her father. The words and melody cheered her in spite of her isolation, as they did every lonely Shabbat night.

—PP. 176–177

Loneliness passed through her like a knife.

And then it came to her—a sort of revelation about Zachai the Tax Collector. They had something in common. "Lonely," Shimona remarked. "He seemed so . . . alone. Don't you think?" she asked her kittens. . . .

It would have been nice to have human company too on such a night, but the kittens . . . well? They made no demands except to be loved, and Shimona had plenty of love to give them. "God who hears my prayers always, I am not ungrateful. I thank you for sending me these three, when I only ever asked for one."

She felt a sudden ache of sorrow for Zachai, as though he were a friend. "And what about him, Lord? What about him? What kind of friends can he have? What is the rest of his life to be? And, Lord, who praises you from the grave? I know you can see Zachai even now. You know my heart and know every word I speak before it is spoken, and I ask you, in spite of how I feel about him, to have mercy on Zachai the Publican. . . .

Lily crept up to the side of Shimona's bed and cried to be let up. Rose and Gideon followed. Did the trio sense her sorrow for the lonely little man?

"Shalom, my friends. So glad you're here. I wouldn't have known what I'd missed if you hadn't come into my life. O Lord! Help him. Help Zachai. . . . He is missing so much! Missing *everything*." Rose mewed pitifully. "Yes. I know. No good being lonely, eh?"

—P. 177, 180–182

ASK

How did Shimona keep her thoughts focused on the future and envision joy instead of sadness?

_____

_____

_____

How did Shimona's loneliness increase her compassion for the unwanted kittens? for Zachai?

_____

_____

_____

How might you use your times of loneliness to anticipate the future with hope? to increase your compassion for others who are hurting?

_____

_____

_____

WONDER . . .

"I want everyone to know what happened here last night. To me. To all of us. We waited so long. Besides what we had already lost, some of us lost still more as we waited. There were so many rumors. Some went out to find him. Then he came here to find us. I want to remember what I was and remember what he has done for me. I want to tell them all. Show them all. Suffering is at an end."

  —SHIMONA (P. IX)

In spite of loneliness and ill treatment by others (including her own family), Shimona chose to live in hopeful expectation of the future and to think of others who were also suffering. As you look back on difficult times in your life, how can you remember what you were and what Yeshua has done for you?

2 | TOO LOST TO BE FOUND?

"I am too lost to be found, Shimona."

Her gaze was steady as a rock. "He is the Great Shepherd of Israel. The one we have all been waiting for. He has come to us, the lost sheep, and he will gather us in his arms, Zachai!"

—ZACHAI AND SHIMONA (P. 198)

Do you know anyone you would call "black-hearted"? Someone whose life purpose seems to be to trample others (by words, actions, or both) and try to make their lives miserable? If so, what thoughts do you harbor about such a person? Why?

_____

_____

_____

If this person suddenly changed direction, would you be happy for him or her—or angry? Explain.

_____

_____

_____

Zachai was the kind of man that everyone in Judea loved to hate. Although he was a Jew, he worked for the Roman government, extracting taxes that the people couldn't afford to pay. He was the man everyone muttered about (behind his back, of course, for fear of retribution). . . .

READ

"What makes a publican like Zachai worth anything to anyone? Everyone hates him, even his Roman masters."
  —LAMECH (P. 62)

The name of Zachai, the chief tax collector, conjured only disdain and insults in the hearts of all within the district of Jericho. He was short of stature and had a big voice and a jovial laugh. He might have done well as a jester in the court of Herod or as a comic actor in a Greek play. He was cocky in his manner, wore a perpetual smile, and exhibited no shame when making a demand for overpayment.

Loathing and earnest curses for Zachai were woven into the bedtime prayers of little ones taught by their parents.

> "Blessed are you, O Lord, who hates thieves and liars and extortioners and collaborators and tax collectors. Blessed are you who hates Zachai, who is all these things and more. Please crush our much-loathed enemy, Zachai the Tax Collector, who stole my father's vineyard. Do unto him what he and his fathers before him have done to our father and his fathers. Omaine!"

The Jewish elders of Jericho were counting on the fact that the God of Israel heard and answered the prayers of children. Like the citizens of Jericho, Jewish Zealots who met in secret and carried daggers beneath their cloaks hated Zachai more than they feared him. He and his fathers before him had grown wealthy by betraying their own people, had they not?

Collaboration with the enemy made Zachai very rich and, therefore, a greater enemy than the Gentile overlords he served. Little wonder rebels covertly watched the bronze gates of Zachai's estate and took down his every move. They plotted and waited for their opportunity to murder Rome's chief tax collector in Judea.

This reality made Zachai a man who sensibly lived in fear for his own life.
  —P. 12

Hatred demanded retribution.

"It is only a matter of time," the Zealots whispered.

—P. 13

"He is a leper inside, just as I was once a leper outside. Lepers have no feeling when their flesh dies. So it is with the heart of a man like Zachai, I think. No feeling for anyone but himself. He steals a vineyard of another and is strangely proud that he has stolen what another man worked his life to build. How false all his accomplishments are."

—SHIMONA ABOUT ZACHAI (P. 181)

ASK

Put yourself in Zachai's shoes. What would it be like to be so extremely successful in your career, but also tremendously loathed? Would this bother you? Why or why not?

_____

_____

_____

What would an average day be like for you? Would you live in fear or confidence, surrounded by your guards? Explain.

_____

_____

_____

READ

Even Zachai's slave could openly cross the Jordan and seek Yeshua with a petition. Zachai was a prisoner within the walls of his own home. The mansion he had built was a beautiful cage, but it was an empty, lonely cage all the same.

—P. 80

"Well done, bird." Zachai applauded. "Excellent. In the dark no one could tell you from a plover."

The blackbird acknowledged the compliment by mimicking the dove, which abruptly flew away.

"Need more practice on that one," Zachai noted. "Just like I could fool people now who don't really know me . . . but not many. And hear me, bird: While you're learning to fool others, don't forget who you really are, eh? . . . A good lesson. Even when I'm not recognizable, it won't change who I am, will it?" . . .

If Zachai were gone, would anyone miss him? Would anyone remark that he left an empty space, or would some newly appointed tax collector suddenly succeed to the title of most hated man? Would anyone spare him even as much sorrow as he felt when a bird flew away? . . .

"Would anyone recall my name a year after my death, except with satisfaction that I was gone?" . . .

Zachai studied the branch. "It'd be easy to climb," he said to the tree. "And plenty strong enough to hold me all the way out to that open space just inside the wall, where the smaller branches thin out. I wonder if there's any rope in the garden shed."

He shook his head, and something felt like it rattled within his skull. "Not tonight," he told himself aloud. "I won't go see about the rope just yet. Not tonight, anyway."

—PP. 141–142

"Please, Shimona. I didn't mean to . . . deceive."

"Deceive?" On her lips the word clanged like a gong. Denying his deception was itself a great and terrible lie.

"Well, I did. I meant to . . . I *hoped* to find some kind word about myself, my life. Even one friend who would speak well of Zachai of Jericho."

She smiled, knowing. "There is only one time in a man's life when everyone speaks well of him. That is at his funeral."

"Even then—" Zachai sighed—"no one will speak well of the House of Zachai."

"What did you expect? That people you oppress would enjoy the power you wield over their lives?"

"Power. It has its benefits."

"Love is not among them."

"Then it demands its privileges."

Shimona replied quietly, "Gratitude and personal friendship are not among them." . . .

"What am I?"

"Can't you answer that yourself?"

He paused. "A tyrant, I suppose. A thief."

She changed the subject. "Did you find whatever you were looking for
. . . out there?"

"I found myself as others see me."

"And?"

"I did not find any answers. How I might be someone else. Change and
become changed. Someone worthy of being . . . Worthy of love."

   —PP. 196–197

ASK

How does Zachai see himself? What has he lost in the way he's chosen to
live his life? What has he gained?

_____

_____

_____

If you could disguise yourself, as Zachai did, and find out what people really
thought of you, would you do it? Why?

_____

_____

_____

It took Zachai literally coming to the end of his rope—experiencing the
horror of a night with the mad hermit and the tender ministrations of
Shimona, who knew who he really was, yet saw through to his hurt—for him
to realize how much his heart needed to be transformed.

READ

"You can't change on your own. You are a hawk, addicted to wealth and power. You take what someone works for and call it your own. You celebrate the death of his dreams as if you have won some game by destroying him. You pounce on whatever moves. Kill the mice of this world and kill the kittens with the same pleasure."

He lowered his chin and sat in silence for a long moment. "That is the way of all men."

"Not all. Not Yeshua. He teaches a better way. Instead of discouragement, he teaches us how to hold each other up and encourage one another. He taught us that anything not done out of love is not of God. A simple self-test. Actions that are vindictive or envious or destructive are not love. Assuming power and control over the life and calling and God-given talents of another man is not love. You can have all the money in the world, but without love you are eternally destitute."

"What is love, Shimona? I do have everything but I have never known love."

"Yeshua teaches this: Love is kind. And patient. It doesn't envy and steal and claim the talents and possessions of another man. Love keeps its promises even when it hurts. Love does not boast or crow when it is victorious in battle. Love heals the wounded rather than destroys the weak. Love is not motivated by injured pride to destroy the life and work of another. Love builds up. It does not tear down. Love isn't rude or thoughtless in actions or words. Love is not ambitious or self-seeking or addicted to flattery. It does not lie and claim it is somehow serving God. It keeps no record of wrongs or plots ways to take vengeance. Love is not easily angered, yet neither is it silent when confronting evil. It does not accept or delight in the actions of an evil man that hurt the innocent. Love does not defend a lie or accept the persecution of the innocent for the sake of remaining in control. Love rejoices in the truth. It always protects. Always trusts. Always encourages. Always hopes. Always perseveres. Yeshua teaches us that Love never fails. God's love heals all wounds."

"Do you believe I want to turn my life around? For you . . . for love . . . I think I could."

"For me?" she asked in delight. "I had stopped hoping I could be loved . . . long ago. I put away my expectations and found joy in each day's surprises. You, Zachai, are a surprise I can embrace. I love you, though you are not a safe man to love. What I feel for you frightens me because I know the truth about you."

"I could change if you loved me," he declared.

"Not for love, nor for money, can any man heal the leprosy of his own, inward, hidden life. Sin is a sort of leprosy in a man's heart, you see? And you have the disease, Zachai."

"Shimona, I came here hoping . . . if you could only tell me how . . ."

"If it's truth you're after? I can only point you to The One who never lies. Yeshua of Nazareth will show you the truth! He alone can heal your wounds."

"If only I could meet with him. Speak to him. Ask him so many questions . . ."

She sighed and smiled. "He is the only one I know who can heal all the lepers in Israel, yet you still think he can't heal your heart!"

He clasped her hands in his and kissed her palm. "I want him to, Shimona. God cannot hear my prayers. I know that. I am too black-hearted."

"But he *can* hear you. He *does* hear you! Zachai, if only you could just see him with your own eyes! There is a look in his eyes so deep, so filled with love and compassion. When you see him for yourself, then you will know he loves you and can forgive anyone who asks him."

—PP. 197–198

ASK

Have you ever tried to change to please someone else? Did it work? Why or why not?

_____

_____

_____

What does love mean to you? Explain.

_____

_____

_____

Do you think anyone is too lost to be found? Why or why not?

_____

_____

_____

WONDER . . .

"Every day of your life you go out, hoping to find yourself. But you're right about one thing: You are truly lost, Zachai of Jericho. Only Yeshua, Son of David, Shepherd of Israel, is The One you have been looking for. And here is the funny thing: When you finally come face-to-face with him, when you look into his eyes, you will know all the truth about yourself. On that day you will not be able to hide what you have been hiding. It is a frightening thing, I think, that there will be no more human disguises when he comes to rule over us. This is the truth: He came here to show you who he meant for you to be from all eternity."
    —SHIMONA TO ZACHAI (PP. 198–199)

Do you go out each day, hoping to find yourself? Have you come face-to-face with Yeshua? Do you know who you are meant to be from all eternity?

_____

_____

_____

"I will pray for you. I will. I promise. And I will pray you may soon meet your Shepherd face-to-face one day and be healed as I am healed."
    —SHIMONA TO ZACHAI (P. 199)

3 | GOD WHO HEARS OUR PRAYERS?

"God who hears my prayers . . . oh! God of Heaven and Earth."
—SHIMONA (P. 18)

God of Israel who does not hear the prayers of a sinner like me,
I am so alone.
—ZACHAI (P. 80)

Do you believe that there is power in prayer? that when you pray to God, He hears you and answers? Why or why not?

_____

_____

_____

What experiences have led you to believe what you do?

_____

_____

_____

Are you more like Shimona or Zachai? Explain.

_____

_____

_____

Both Shimona and Zachai constantly talked to God. But there was a vast difference in the way that they approached the Almighty. . . .

READ

"God who hears me . . . always . . . always you hear me. I am so alone now, God. Did you heal me only to suffer this? At least when there were others sick and dying all around me, we loved one another. Though our bodies had no feeling, our hearts were full of wishing the same wish. . . . God, Lord! You who hear my every thought. I know you remember what I remember. I knew fear that was like the low, dark entrance to a tomb. Enter the blackness and there was no way out." She covered her face with her hands. "Though I was set free, I am still a prisoner. Trapped in a dungeon. Needing to hear the voice of my mother . . . my mother."

Raising her face to the patch of starry heaven that gleamed through the window, she cried, "I miss Mak'ob! I miss the lepers of the Valley of Sorrows who moved my heart, though I was a disease. Oh, Lord, where are they all now? Where is Yeshua? Oh, please! I don't believe you healed me, Lord, only so I could suffer a deeper wound."
—SHIMONA (P. 21)

God of Israel who cannot hear my prayers: Oh, how I long to marry this woman and bring her home to fill my wide, but empty, house. . . . God who does not hear me, I am the most hated man in Judea. I am a fool to love or ever think I could be loved. I am a fool to think it could be otherwise.
—ZACHAI (PP. 19–20)

ASK

What words does Shimona use when she talks to God? What emotions does she express?

_____

_____

_____

What words does Zachai use when he talks to God? What emotions does he express?

_____

_____

_____

How does the wording of each reveal his or her life philosophy?

_____

_____

_____

READ

As a child Shimona had played the harp quite well. As a leper without fingers the talent had been useless, so she sang throughout her waking hours to help retain her sanity. The habit of song had come away with her when she left the Valley of Lepers. There were times, like tonight, when she studied her ten fingers in the firelight and wondered if they might easily pluck the strings of a harp again.

"Lord of Heaven and Earth, Lord of song who dances with the angels, someday perhaps when my father the Chazzan remembers me and brings me home, I will play the harp again. Lord who hears my prayers always, I implore you to remind my father that I am here, waiting. Make some old tune he hears bring my face to his thoughts, please, Lord. And then I will play the harp for him and sing such a song of joy for you . . . such a song of coming home and embracing my family as I have dreamed for so long."

The loneliness might have crushed her except for the hope that one day soon her father and the rabbi and the priest would come to the grove and pronounce her well and healthy. Perhaps they would come soon and she would be free again, like other women. She imagined sitting by the well of Jericho, drawing water and talking about the weather and their children. How she missed the sound of human voices this time of night!

"God who hears my prayers . . . oh! God of Heaven and Earth . . . free again," she sighed, gazing through the bars of the window to the starry sky.
—P. 18

Each day she woke up before dawn and said, "God who hears my prayers and sees to every need, I love it here!" Then she sang songs of praise that she made up as she went along.

Each morning and night she looked at her smooth skin and knew that she was indeed healed—whole, well! And she thanked the Almighty One for sending Yeshua into the Valley of Mak'ob.

Of course, there were small irritations, including the army of field mice that lived in the grove. Shimona called the rodents "Philistines" and fought a constant battle against them. Sometimes they snuck into the house and spoiled her flour. They chewed her clothing as she slept. She set traps and captured a great number every day. But there were always more.

She prayed, "Blessed are you, O Lord, God of the Universe. You hear my every prayer. You know my needs before I ask. So, Lord of Heaven and Earth, if you will not banish the Philistines from this sukomore grove, please send me a cat! Please. Lord who hears all my prayers and knows my needs, please, O Lord! Send a cat to keep me company. A cat with sharp teeth and keen eyes to hunt and catch the horde of Philistines who are my enemies and the enemies of this orchard, which my father has rented."

But no cat came to the orchard.

Day after day, month after month, Shimona expected and looked for an answer to her prayer. She did not stop hoping. . . . She fought the army of Philistines on her own.
—PP. 9–10

Hawks were familiar to Shimona. Years ago in the Valley of Mak'ob, Lily's husband, Cantor, had trained a red-winged hawk to hunt pigeons and bring them back to him for supper. The relationship between that enormous bird and the man had seemed a sort of miracle to Shimona when she watched them work together.

Today the whoosh of the raptor's wings was an angel's voice speaking to Shimona's heart: *God cares for you. Though your earthly father did not heed your request for a cat, your Heavenly Father knows all your needs. He loves you enough that He has sent His friend to drive away your enemies. . . . The mice in the sukomore grove will not remain to torment you or steal from you. The Lord Himself covers you and your work with the protection of His wings.*

The hawk did not fly away from the grove. He landed on the highest branch of the tallest sukomore. Bobbing on the fragile limb, he devoured his prey in full view of Shimona.

So it will be even with small worries, Shimona thought. *O Lord, who answers my prayers in ways more perfect than I know to pray . . . I thank you for sending this ally, who has come to help me. I never thought to ask you for a hawk.*

Then she addressed the bird. "So, Hawk, it's plain to see you are a friend of the Almighty. The Lord has told you to come here to hunt. I know that. Thank you for listening to his voice. I suppose that men are the only creatures in creation who do not listen to him." She sighed. "So, I need help, but it won't come from man. There's lots of game here in the sukomore grove for you. Stay with me, Hawk," Shimona whispered. "I will harvest the figs, and you will harvest the mice. We will praise the Lord together for his bounty, you and I."

—P. 34

ASK

What things did Shimona thank God for in the above passages?

_____

_____

_____

What small things do you need to thank God for—even in the midst of larger worries?

_____

_____

_____

READ

"You who are the God of Truth—all truth without a shadow of deception—help this wicked man see himself as he truly is. Then turn him around by the power of your love. Restore life and feeling to his dead heart. Have mercy. Guide him back from the brink of hell to repentance and change."

It was a good prayer, Shimona thought, as she lay down to sleep that night. The Lord of Heaven and Earth loved to hear the righteous ask for mercy for the wicked. The righteous were blessed when they asked for mercy for those who wronged them. Repentance in a great sinner like Zachai would be a blessing to every person he had wronged.

She smiled, knowing something terrible was about to happen to the publican. She wondered what unhappy shipwreck Zachai had caused that God would now show him. What shore of human suffering had Zachai created upon which he would now wash up? What broken man would the Lord send to show Zachai the effect of his terrible pride? How would the publican's leprous heart feel when it was pierced by the truth that his lies were directly responsible for the misery and ruin of so many?

How many had Zachai betrayed over the years? He had forsaken friendship and love all for the sake of power over others. He had sold love for money. Honorable accomplishments had been replaced by his own distorted perception of success. Was there any way back from such a life?

Shimona closed her eyes. "Yes, Lord, it's always good to ask you to show mercy and bring repentance to the hearts of the greatest sinners."

—P. 181

ASK

What do you think Shimona's motivation was in praying for Zachai?

_____

_____

_____

Given the same situation, what would your motivation be?

_____

_____

_____

READ

It is only after his horrific night with the hermit (the same night that Shimona prays for Zachai to repent!) that Zachai prays and admits his sinfulness:

Raising his eyes briefly heavenward, he prayed, "Thank you, God of Avraham, Yitz'chak, and Isra'el . . . God whom my fathers did not worship. Though you cannot hear the prayer of one as sinful as I am, I thank you this morning, all the same, that I am alive. God who knows everything, don't lay the guilt of my father and grandfather in the matter of the House of Pella on my soul. Poor fellow, poor mad fellow. God who does not hear me, I am sorry for him. Hopeless. Hopeless. But look not upon the sins of my grandfather against his grandfather. Do not lay that deed upon my tally of sins. I have plenty of my own sins to answer for."
—PP. 182–183

ASK

How did God use Shimona's prayers to bring about transformation in Zachai's life?

_____

_____

_____

How has Zachai's heart changed, in just one night? Explain.

_____

_____

_____

WONDER . . .

The Lord detests the sacrifice of the wicked,
but the prayer of the upright pleases Him.
—PROVERBS 15:8

For the eyes of the Lord are on the righteous
and His ears are attentive to their prayer,
but the face of the Lord is against those who do evil.
—1 PETER 3:12

What do you need to pray for today? In what way(s) does your heart need transformation or restoration?

4 | WHY NOT BELIEVE?

"People outside don't want to believe." I shrugged. "Just a warning. I was born blind . . . healed . . . then they threw me out of the synagogue. Even my mother and father disowned me. You see, everyone with human power is afraid of Yeshua's power. They have a lot to lose."

I felt sorry for Shimona. She had suffered so long she couldn't understand that there were many outside who would look at her and resent Yeshua for the miracle that had brought a leper back from the grave.

—PENIEL (P. IX)

How easy is it for you to believe in Yeshua's ability to perform miracles, like healing the blind Peniel? Explain.

_____

_____

_____

Why would people be afraid of Yeshua's power? In your opinion, what would they have to lose?

_____

_____

_____

The four gospels of the Bible (Matthew, Mark, Luke, and John) are filled with true stories of Yeshua, the miracle worker. Of Yeshua, the great and loving Shepherd who cared for and disciplined His sheep for their own well-being. But whether you believe these events or not all comes down to you, personally.

There are all kinds of reasons for choosing not to believe in Yeshua. . . .

READ

Something had happened. The normally stoic Salmon trembled slightly. He wiped his cheeks with the back of his hand and wagged his massive head like a sorrowing child. . . ."My child. The middle one. Marisha. She is dying."

Marisha was a pretty little thing. Quick and happy in school even at five years old. "Dying? Your Marisha? The bright one? What? When? Why wasn't I informed about such a thing? She is the property of the House of Zachai. Speak up!"

Salmon stammered, "For some time now she has been unwell. Two months she has declined. Her mother has tried everything. Marisha's belly swells. She bleeds at the nose. She cannot eat. She has gone very weak and given up. She cannot walk. Last night she will not sip broth. . . . Something grows inside her, eating her flesh, [the doctor] says. Hopeless, he says."

"Then what is to be done?" Zachai sat down hard on the stone bench beside the fig tree. "What?"

Salmon looked to his troop for support. "Master, we have one hope. A dream. One in your household dreamed that I carried my child over Jordan and into the camp of Yeshua the Nazarene. In the dream I brought Marisha to Yeshua. In the dream, Master, I carried her on a brief journey. When I returned home she came riding upon my shoulders."

Zachai frowned. "You are a good fellow, Salmon. You know they say this Yeshua only heals the sheep in Israel's flock. You know well that unrest in Judea grows because of him. I have been cut off from the flock of Israel. And you . . . are of my house."

"I have heard these things. But, my lord, we have no other hope. No choice but to approach him. If he truly is the King, will he not grant grace to all people who come to him? I must beg him to touch her and give my child back to us." . . .

"Take her, then," Zachai said. "But know that this miracle worker Yeshua hates men like me. He only helps the sons of Avraham. His sheep are not black. His sheep are not slaves. His sheep are not . . . publicans . . . or the slaves of publicans."

—PP. 64–66

Crossing Jordan for a valuable slave like Salmon could well end in his disappearance and loss. His request to travel to the camp of Yeshua took him far beyond the jurisdiction of Judea. . . .

Zachai had the power to let Salmon cross the river and possibly escape in his attempt to make the child well. Zachai had the right to keep him here and let his child die. Salmon was worth much more than the child. Suppose she died on the way and he never returned?

—P. 66

"God of Israel, God of my fathers but not of myself, though I am unworthy of your forgiveness, I . . . regret . . . what I did to Elijah the Vintner."

Zachai cleared his throat uneasily as so many other names and faces of those he had cheated over the years came to mind. He shrugged at the hopelessness of the pit he was in. The thought came, *Ah well, what is one more? More or less.*

—P. 166

ASK

What about Salmon could have made him "unacceptable" to Yeshua? Why did Salmon not let this stop him from seeking Yeshua?

_____

_____

_____

What reason(s) could stop Zachai from allowing Salmon to pursue Yeshua?

_____

_____

_____

What reason(s) could Zachai give for refusing to seek out Yeshua for himself?

_____

_____

_____

READ

When El'azar of Bethany emerged from his tomb at the behest of Yeshua of Nazareth, the event was witnessed by many more onlookers than just Yeshua's talmidim and El'azar's family. Dozens of mourners were on hand when the miracle occurred.

The news had broken over Judea like a clap of thunder, and its implications reverberated among the ruling classes like an earthquake. Though an hour of wrangling had already elapsed, there was still a stormy session inside the cedar-paneled hall of the Sanhedrin's council chambers on the Temple Mount in Jerusalem. It seemed everyone was speaking at once.

"What are we to do?"

"What *can* we do? The man from Nazareth performs many . . . signs."

"Dead four days! El'azar was *stinking* dead! Widely reported by reputable members of my own sect."

Until now High Priest Caiaphas had maintained a brooding silence. . . . "Your quarreling accomplishes nothing. We have already looked into the claims of this man. Some choose to believe. But belief or not is no longer important."

"How can you say such a thing? If we let him go on like this, everyone will believe in him! Then the Romans will come and take away both our place . . . and . . . our nation!"

Renewed murmuring swept the chamber, but it was much subdued. Every man present enjoyed wealth and prestige—much of it connected with Temple worship. The Sadducees, like Caiaphas, profited directly.

Imperial Rome appointed the high priests. So long as the emperor received his cut of the profits and the province remained peaceful and profitable, Governor Pilate had no reason to upset the status quo.

But if all the *am ha aretz* truly welcomed Yeshua as Messiah, two dreadful things would happen: The common folk would stop paying exorbitant fees for sin offerings and fellowship offerings and cease buying overpriced lambs for sacrifice. Perhaps Yeshua would lead them all to worship somewhere else completely.

Many in the room recalled the time a couple of years earlier when a then little-known Yeshua had stormed around the Temple Mount stalls, overturning tables of money changers and disrupting commerce.

No, Yeshua of Nazareth could not be counted on to keep the money flowing into the coffers of the priests and the Temple officials. If all the peasants ran after Yeshua, Imperial Rome might choose to deal with Him, rather than with the council at all.

This worry was clearly uppermost in the minds of many.

That the Romans would take away the Jewish nation was added as a patriotic afterthought.

If Yeshua led an uprising against Rome—as most believed Messiah would do to free His people—not one on the council believed such a rebellion would succeed.

It would be a bloodbath, followed by mass executions and deportations into slavery.

And it would be bad for business for a long time to come.

—PP. 21–23

The high priest of Israel planned to murder the one who Nakdimon, and many others, believed was the Messiah! "So I'm to warn him? send him to safety?"

"Not just Yeshua," Gerar stressed. "They plan to kill El'azar too. A man brought back to life! They fear this power, this fame, Lord Nakdimon. And fear makes them willing to do murder . . . *many* murders."

—GERAR TO NAKDIMON (P. 26)

Ben Dives had shuddered when he met them but once again set aside his scruples in the name of ambition. Besides, how wrong could it be if the religious shepherd, Caiaphas, and Herod Antipas, the son of the royal house, both approved this action? This night's work should certainly fix him firmly in the high priest's favor.

—P. 30

"Shimona will live in isolation until such time as Yeshua is proved a prophet or a devil, and she is pronounced free from leprosy or sent back to the Valley of Mak'ob!"

—THE RABBI OF JERICHO (PP. 8–9)

ASK

Why do the religious leaders choose not to believe in Yeshua?

_____

_____

_____

What were Bera Ben Dives' reasons?

_____

_____

_____

What was the rabbi of Jericho's stance toward Yeshua?

_____

_____

_____

READ

There was one beggar known to all the residents of both Jerichos. He had been a fixture of the settlement forever. . . . Bartimaeus was in the sixth decade of his life—almost a record for a blind beggar. . . .

Encountering Bartimaeus for the first time made pilgrims uncomfortable. The fixed gaze he unerringly turned toward any footstep or spoken word seemed uncanny. Even if a group of several passersby approached, he managed to stare at each of them in turn, crying out in a high-pitched voice: "Good sirs, have pity on a poor, blind man. Have pity! A copper or two for the good of your soul, eh?" This he continued without ceasing, but at an ever-increasing volume and intensity.

—PP. 15–16

When Peniel and Zadok travel by Bartimaeus and give him only two pennies, he looks reproachful. Yet he is also intrigued when he finds out from Peniel:

"We are followers of Yeshua of Nazareth. Let us take you to him. It's better than money. He can heal you."

"From Nazareth?" Bartimaeus repeated scornfully. "In the Galil? Ha! Who's he, anyway?"

"He is Messiah," Zadok replied stoutly. "Son of David."

"Son of David!" Bartimaeus mocked. "Another messiah to run after into the desert. I've heard people speak of him. I've also heard—" he lowered his voice—"Herod Antipas wants him dead." Then, louder again, "No, thank you! Better a live beggar, even blind, than a dead fool."

Zadok bristled at the affront, but Peniel still spoke kindly. "You do not know me, but I'm Peniel. I used to be the blind beggar of Nicanor Gate. Yeshua healed me . . . me! Blind from birth. He'll do the same for you. Leave your begging cloak and come with us."

"Leave my cloak?" Bartimaeus said incredulously. "Give up my livelihood to chase moonbeams? Thank you for your pennies, but you may keep your advice. And if you'll take some counsel from me, your best chance of keeping your throats uncut is to keep away from the Nazarene. He's trouble."

Peniel was dejected as he and Zadok trudged away from the beggar and entered Old Jericho. "I can't understand why he wants to stay blind," he lamented.

"There's many has the use of both eyes who are eager t' stay blind in other ways," Zadok reminded, "or so the Master says. Y' cannot force someone t' want what's best for them, eh? . . . Mark this: Yeshua'll never make y' give up anything y' need, nor leave y' long without filling that need. But a whole lot of folks wander about carrying loads of unneeded things that hold 'em back on their journey."

—PP. 38–39

ASK

Why did Bartimaeus refuse to leave his place in the road to search for Yeshua?

_____

_____

_____

Have you ever found it more comfortable to stay in a rut than to risk change? If so, when? Tell the story.

_____

_____

_____

WONDER . . .

> *"He who has clean hands and a pure heart,*
> *who has not lifted himself up to falsehood*
> *nor sworn deceitfully.*
> *He shall receive blessing from the Lord*
> *and righteousness from the God of his salvation"* (Psalm 24:4-5). . . .

All men stood in need of repentance and forgiveness. . . . Nakdimon remembered how he had gone to Yeshua's camp by night. *I am part of the generation seeking the God of Jacob*, he reflected. *Many of the people seek him. Why not the council?*
—PP. 24–25

What a great privilege was his! To be a worshipper of The One, the Almighty God, in His Holy City, before the Temple of His Name!

> *"Who shall go up into the mountain of the Lord?*
> *Or who shall stand in His Holy Place?"* (Ps. 24:3)

Who indeed? Nakdimon reflected. When the high priesthood was bought and sold; when the House of Annas was mocked in street songs for the wealth they had accumulated because of it; when so many family members, including Lord Caiaphas, occupied the office in their turns . . . who indeed?
—P. 24

If you have not yet chosen to believe in Messiah, what holds you back?

- Do you worry you won't be accepted?
- Do you feel unworthy?
- Do you fear a life change or loss of income?
- Are you afraid of losing power over your life?
- Are you concerned about losing popularity?
- Do you want God to "prove His power" first?
- Do you fear the unknown?

Is it time to examine your heart for the reason(s)?

5 | SEEKING THE HEALER

This is the generation of those who seek Him,
who seek Your face, O God of Jacob.
—PSALM 24:6

Do you know a person who earnestly seeks after God? If so, what qualities does that person have that make you so certain of his or her relationship with God?

_____

_____

_____

When your life grows difficult, whom do you turn to first? Why?

_____

_____

_____

When Shimona was in the Valley of Mak'ob, the valley of suffering and death where all the lepers were sent to live out the rest of their days, a minyan of lepers left to search out the rumors regarding the supposed Messiah. If it was true that a great Healer walked the earth, might He have mercy on the valley of lepers? Might the Great Shepherd stoop to gather these needy ones into His flock and heal them?

It was a long time later that Shimona, in her alienation in the sukomore fig grove, recognized the desperate beggars who stumbled close to her home. . . .

READ

It was Carpenter, leader of the ten lepers who had left the Valley of Mak'ob in search of Yeshua so long ago! With him was the Samaritan Fisherman, the Crusher, the two Cabbage Sisters, the four young Torah scholars from the camp of boys, and one more Shimona did not recognize. Clearly their search for Yeshua the Healer had been in vain.

Shimona cried out as she ran to them, "Carpenter! Crusher! Look—all of you! It's me, Shimona. Daughter of the Chazzan." She embraced the two Cabbage Sisters, who tried to fend her off.

"Please! We're *tsara*. Unclean. Defiled. Woman, don't touch us!"

Laughing and crying at the same time, Shimona showed them her unmarred hands. "But I was one of you. In the Valley. Yeshua came! He came to us one evening and—"

Carpenter, his noseless features hidden behind a strip of fabric, said, "It is Shimona. I know the voice. But why are you here? And you're restored but . . . what is that sign posted there?"

"The people are afraid their eyes are bewitched. They can't accept that I've been healed. So I'm here. Until, well, I don't know how long. But they want to be certain."

Fisherman muttered, "We've been looking for the Healer. But every time we hear he's one place and go there, he's gone to another place. He was in Bethany. Raised a dead man to life, they say. But then the high priest got wind of it and put a price on his head. They want to kill Yeshua and the man he raised as well."

Shimona's words spilled out in a rush. "Kill him? Kill? Oh, Carpenter, you must find Yeshua. He is life to us!"

Crusher shook his head slowly. "We are afraid they will kill him before we find him. What then?"

The Cabbage Sisters cried, "Our only hope!"

Shimona sighed. "Friends! Yeshua healed everyone in the Valley. Everyone. It's not a fable. Everyone who came near . . . he healed them all. He laid hands on us and healed us and sent us out of the Valley and to our homes. But my family was afraid. My mother wouldn't touch me. The rabbi and the priest and my father . . . they don't believe what they see, even though their eyes tell them I have no spot or sign of sickness. They are afraid it is witchcraft. So I have been here in isolation according to the law of Mosheh for all these months. . . . Every day I pray, 'When is Yeshua going to set up his Kingdom?'"

Crusher raised fingerless hands to the heavens. "Omaine to that. Omaine! Oh, that Yeshua would come to Yerushalayim soon! The oppression of Herod and the Romans grows worse every day. Taxes. There's nothing left over to share with a beggar."

Fisherman agreed. "The people are desperate. Hopeless but hoping Messiah will restore the throne of David. So many believe Yeshua will overthrow the Romans. At least they are hoping. Hoping he'll call down fire . . . you know. Like Elijah."

—PP. 40–42

ASK

If you were Shimona, now healed from leprosy, would you have responded the same way to the minyan of lepers? Why or why not?

_____

_____

_____

The lepers had been traveling a long time, at great sacrifice to themselves, to seek the Healer. If you were these lepers, would you be as determined to find Yeshua? Explain.

_____

_____

_____

READ

Carpenter answered, "We must go on. We have heard that Yeshua is hiding from the authorities over the Jordan. The place where Yochanan the Baptizer used to preach. We're going there to find him. Shimona—come with us!"

"I can't. . . . I made a vow that I would stay here and work, that I would not cross the boundary and leave the grove. I'm happy. Really." Shimona opened the basket, which contained heaping loaves of bread. "I don't have money, but take what I have. Here. There's plenty to get me through the month. Take it, my dear friends, and go quickly. Cross the Jordan. Find the Lord and you will find life!"

Shimona remained fixed behind the boundary of her vow. She moaned inwardly as her friends left her. Was it a contradiction, she wondered, to say that her heart was filled with emptiness at their going?

The ten topped the rise of the road. Shimona, hungry for one last look, scrambled up the tallest sukomore tree. Clinging to the branches, she stared after them until their individual identities were indistinguishable in the distance. Her beloved friends, linked together by the common bond of suffering and longing, seemed no longer to be ten lepers, but one dark unity, moving forward, searching for Yeshua the Savior. Thus they remained in her vision, framed against the slope of a hill until it was too dark to see them anymore. . . . "O God who hears our prayers and knows our suffering, my heart travels with them."

Shimona carefully climbed down from the tree. She groped her way through the darkness to her little house. "O God who sees their suffering, you see that I am also alone and forgotten. Send angels to this sukomore grove. Keep me company in my long, unending night."

—PP. 42–43

ASK

Again, put yourself in Shimona's shoes. Would you have gone with your leper friends? Or stayed behind in the olive grove? Explain.

_____

_____

_____

How would you have felt, being left behind—alone once again?

_____

_____

_____

Have you faced your own "long, unending night"? If so, how did you handle it? Have you seen any light of morning yet?

_____

_____

_____

READ

Zachai stood and raised a golden goblet to offer a toast. "And here's to my honored guest. Most honored . . . Yeshua! The Great Shepherd of Israel who has found another lost sheep!" He placed his hand over his heart and pledged, "Lord, I have seen you coming from a great height. You have looked upon me with mercy. Half my goods I give to the poor. And if I have defrauded anyone of anything, I will restore it fourfold."

Upon hearing this declaration Zadok leaned close to me and whispered in surprise, "This fellow knows the law of Mosheh and the flock: Restore four lambs for every one lamb stolen."

Yeshua stood and clasped hands with the publican. "Today salvation has come to this house."

The crowd laughed at Yeshua's humor. Zadok nudged me hard, noting that Yeshua's name means "salvation," and He had indeed come to Zachai's house.

Yeshua nodded and smiled broadly, raising His cup to Zachai. "Salvation has come to this house since he is also a son of Avraham! For the Son of Adam came to seek and save the lost!"

—P. 224

ASK

What changes do you see in Zachai's heart? How do they spill over to his personality and actions?

_____

_____

_____

What does Yeshua's name—"Salvation"—mean to you?

_____

_____

_____

WONDER . . .

"Though they seem to be only one, you know them each as individuals. You love us one at a time and all together as we search for your Son."

—SHIMONA (P. 42)

What do you long for? What kind of healing do you need?

6 | A NEW WAY OF LOOKING AT LIFE AND DEATH

"It is a bright, clean cup we drink from today. A new way of looking at life and death. And yet, here is the dark crack that runs through the cup of our joy: They will fight harder, I think, to kill the man who has returned from death. They will plot secret ways to kill Yeshua, who we know now is the source of life."

—PENIEL'S FATHER (P. 4)

If you saw someone walk out of a grave—*alive and healthy*—what would your reaction be? Joy? Disbelief? Shock? Why?

_____

_____

_____

Why do you think someone would want to kill a person who has proven to be "the source of life"?

_____

_____

_____

What dark crack, if any, runs through the cup of your joy today?

_____

_____

_____

Peniel's father, who has come full circle in the A.D. Chronicles—from denying that Yeshua healed his blind son to believing in Yeshua—rejoices in the incredible miracle of Yeshua raising El'azar from the dead. However, he also knows that not everyone will be happy about the miracle. . . .

READ

"Be careful, Son."

Peniel embraced his father at the gate. "What do you mean, Father?"

"You know well how they put you out of the synagogue when Yeshua gave you eyes. I have heard that in other towns lepers healed by Yeshua's command and returned home from the Valley of Mak'ob have been banished as well, put away as though they are still bearing the disease. There is a rumor about the daughter of the Chazzan of Jericho. Banished, though she is plainly healed. They don't want anyone to know what Yeshua is capable of."

Peniel peered at the circling hawk and wondered about Shimona. "He tells everyone he heals not to speak of it."

"Too late. The cat is out of the bag, as they say. The dead man out of the tomb. The secret is shattered like a clay pot and everyone knows. . . . Everyone!"

—P. 4

ASK

When have you tried—and failed—to keep a secret? What happened as a result?

_____

_____

_____

Why would someone try to downplay a miracle? Does it work? Why or why not?

_____

_____

_____

READ

Inside the walled compound a great feast was prepared for Yeshua and His band of followers. The talmidim looked proud of their Master as they sat at the table with the family. They seemed more confident now than at any time in their travels with Yeshua.

"Let them come," Thomas boasted with his hand on the hilt of his sword. "And even if they kill us, what of it?"

John agreed. "They're beaten now for certain. What can Rome do? Or Herod Antipas? Caiaphas, the high priest, and his puppets are beaten. Yeshua will raise us up again, though they kill us a hundred times!"

—P. 4

Ezra, the youngest ben Dives, inquired, "Is it true that Ra'nabel was investigating the charlatan Yeshua of Nazareth?"

"You are not to mention that name!" Bera rebuked Ezra sharply. "Wild stories! Rumors! Gossip! That deluded blasphemer El'azar of Bethany returned to life when our worthy and noble brother lies here?" Bera put the palm of his hand on the sealing stone in a dramatic gesture of bereavement. He betrayed no sense of irony when in almost the same breath he accused Yeshua of trickery and then credited the man with bringing the dead back to life.

"They say he works miracles," sixteen-year-old Ezra persisted.

"Superstition! Poison, more likely!" Bera exclaimed. "Perhaps El'azar and the Nazarene conspired to kill our brother. From perfect health to stone-cold dead? Is it reasonable? Is it likely?"

—P. 6

Bera ben Dives consulted with the pair of assassins in their rooms at an inn at Jericho. "It's now certain the Nazarene is returning to Yerushalayim.

Discretion must be used near the Holy City. Since I'm known to be in the high priest's employ, I mustn't be connected to his death or Lord Caiaphas might be blamed. It could cause a riot in Yerushalayim."

Ona patted ben Dives' arm. "My methods don't leave connections behind," she affirmed, fingering a glass vial hanging from a cord around her neck.

Her husband grimaced. "I don't know why we don't start picking them off one at a time as soon as they come out of the wilderness. That boy . . . the blind beggar? He's alone, away from the others at times. An easy target."

"Or El'azar of Bethany," Ona suggested. "Stories about a dead man alive again are what keep the crowds coming to see the Galilean."

Ben Dives shook his head. "You really don't understand, do you?" he argued. "Trickery, magic, sorcery—call it what you will. But we have to eliminate Yeshua first. Otherwise, what if he just brings them back to life? His fame will be even greater; things will be worse than ever. No, it must be Yeshua who dies first."

—P. 183

ASK

What are the views of the following people toward life and death?

- Yeshua's disciples Thomas and John
- Ezra ben Dives
- Bera ben Dives
- Ona and her husband—the assassins

READ

"Yeshua is Mashiyah! He is the Son of the Living God!"

[Shimona's] declaration shocked the Chazzan, the rabbi, and the ⬅ priest. The rabbi made the sign against the evil eye and turned his back on Shimona, commanding her to be silent.

The officials conferred together in the synagogue by lamplight while Shimona waited outside beneath the stars.

When they emerged at last, neither Shimona's father nor the rabbi nor the priest in Jericho believed her story. Every word must be tested, they declared. Shimona had been irrefutably pronounced unclean—she and her leprous husband. Had her husband not perished horribly in the dying cave of Mak'ob?

How could Shimona, so near to death, have been healed? Though she had returned home in the stinking rags of a leprous beggar, the dread disease did not seem to be evident.

Was there a possibility that Shimona had indeed been healed by Yeshua of Nazareth? And that the one some proclaimed a charlatan was actually a miracle worker? Yet the high priest himself had declared Yeshua a fake Messiah in league with the devil.

What if this was a trick? What if Shimona the Leper was not truly healed? What if the eyes of those outside the Valley of Lepers who beheld her were bewitched and blinded to the truth by a demon? Perhaps Shimona the Leper had been sent back to Jericho by Yeshua to infect all who came near her!

The rabbi of Jericho had said, "Perhaps . . . just perhaps . . . Shimona is like a fireship in a battle, sent among our ships by the enemy to set us on fire."

Shimona's father had stared at her in fear as he considered his other children, his home, and his reputation. "What shall I do with her, Rabbi? How can we be sure?"

The rabbi considered the danger for a moment before he replied. "Torah and Mosheh command that anyone suspected of leprosy be isolated from the congregation of Israel. How could we know for certain, unless she is isolated for a time? Say, perhaps a year or so? Does Torah not command Shimona the Leper to live apart until her wellness can be proved without any doubt?"

—PP. 7–8

ASK

How did the Chazzan, the rabbi, and the priest respond to Shimona's return from the Valley of Mak'ob, which no one came back from alive? What were their fears? their suspicions about Yeshua?

_____

_____

_____

What did they require as proof of her new life?

_____

_____

_____

READ

It is written that the pit of human anguish was, for the Son of God, a wondrous mine of human souls. Throughout the night the cauldron of Messiah's love glowed golden, promising new life.

The people of Mak'ob drew near to Yeshua. One at a time they approached: those hobbling on crutches, the sightless, the lame. Half hands. Faceless faces. Legless stumps.

And Yeshua embraced each one, called each by name. One at a time He healed them all—rebuilding limbs and features, renewing blind eyes with radiant revelation, restoring lips with which to praise the God of Heaven.

—PP. VII–VIII

Around the great table a bouquet of faces bloomed like hastily picked flowers, mismatched and vibrant. All of us had left something behind to follow Yeshua. He demanded that we abandon much more than fishing nets or cloaks or houses or land. Yeshua called upon us to abandon the thing we most cherished . . . our own stubborn will. He asked us to leave behind all our differences and take on one heart—the heart of a servant, guided by His love. Yeshua, our Shepherd, had drawn us, His flock, near to Him by one faith in His one truth. Coming to Yeshua meant that our hearts and souls became one!

Suddenly, as I looked at all the faces gathered round, I understood that Yeshua meant for all of us, His holy people, to be united in love for all time. Slaves who had been children of slaves mingled with the wealthy followers of Yeshua. Former beggars, former lepers, and all manner of sinners sat side by side with civic rulers and leaders in business. Those once lame danced beneath the spreading branches of the sukomore fig tree while the mute sang. Zadok's dog smiled and wagged around the perimeter of the celebration.

—PP. 223–224

In the years that followed, Zachai fulfilled every vow he made to Yeshua. We came to know him very well. He made restitution according to the laws of Moses to every life he had injured. The slave that had been sold in payment of debt was found and redeemed and set free. The vineyard of Elijah the Vintner was restored. The madness of poor Pella was cured by Shim'on Peter in the power of The Name of Yeshua; his olive grove was returned and his house rebuilt.

Zachai married Shimona and they had eight children, all of whom now follow and proclaim the Good News of the Kingdom to the lost.

These, then, are the words of our King Yeshua to Zachai of Jericho: "Zachai, small of stature but large in love. Well done, good and faithful servant."

—PP. 226–227

ASK
How did the following people or groups change their perspectives about life and death because of the transforming touch of Yeshua?

- The lepers of Mak'ob
- All those gathered around Zachai's table
- Zachai

_____

_____

_____

WONDER . . .
The moment of judgment will come for me when the King will ask what I did with what He gave me.

He will look into my eyes. . . . "Were you faithful?"

—P. 226

Are you faithfully seeking Yeshua? Have you been faithful in what He has given you, small or large? How has your perspective on life and death changed?

_____

_____

_____

Yeshua waits to extend to you the promise of life . . . life forever with Him. Will you accept it?

Dear Reader,

You are so important to us. We have prayed for you as we wrote this book and also as we receive your letters and hear your soul cries. We hope that *Eighth Shepherd* has encouraged you to go deeper. To get to know Yeshua better. To fill your soul hunger by examining Scripture's truths for yourself.

We are convinced that if you do so, you will find this promise true: *"If you seek Him, He will be found by you."*

— I Chronicles 28:9

Bodie & Brock Thoene

Scripture References

1 Ps. 24:1-2
2 Ps. 24:3
3 Ps. 24:4-5
4 Ps. 24:6
5 Ps. 24:7
6 Ps. 24:8
7 Ps. 24:10
8 Luke 17:11-19
9 Luke 10:27
10 Matt. 19:16-30
11 Matt. 19:27
12 Matt. 19:29
13 Matt. 6:25-34; Luke 10:1-8
14 Ps. 5:1-2
15 Ps. 5:3
16 Matt. 20:1-16
17 Luke 17:7-10
18 Gen. 4:2-8

19 Gen. 25:19-34; 26:34-35; 27:1-46; 28:1-9; 32–33
20 Gen. 37
21 1 Sam. 16:1-13
22 Matt. 20:18-19
23 Matt. 16:21-23
24 Gen. 33:17
25 Luke 17:3-4
26 Luke 17:5
27 Luke 17:6
28 Luke 18:16
29 Luke 18:17
30 Luke 13:18-19
31 Amos 5:11-12
32 Matt. 20:20-21
33 Luke 9:51-56
34 Matt. 20:22-23
35 Matt. 16:17-19

36 Ps. 106:1
37 2 Chron. 20:1-21
38 Ps. 5:9
39 1 Cor. 13
40 Ezek. 34:3-4
41 Ezek. 34:18, 16
42 Ezek. 34:11, 15
43 Mark 10:46-52
44 Ps. 136:1-4
45 Luke 19:1-9
46 Luke 19:7
47 Luke 19:8
48 Exod. 22:1
49 Luke 19:9-10
50 Luke 19:11-27
51 Exod. 22

Authors' Note

The following sources have been helpful in our research for this book.

- *The Complete Jewish Bible*. Translated by David H. Stern. Baltimore, MD: Jewish New Testament Publications, Inc., 1998.

- *iLumina*, a digitally animated Bible and encyclopedia suite. Carol Stream, IL: Tyndale House Publishers, 2002.

- *The International Standard Bible Encyclopaedia*. George Bromiley, ed. 5 vols. Grand Rapids, MI: Eerdmans, 1979.

- *The Life and Times of Jesus the Messiah*. Alfred Edersheim. Peabody, MA: Hendrickson Publishers, Inc., 1995.

- Starry Night™ Enthusiast Version 5.0, publishing by Imaginova™ Corp.

About the Authors

BODIE AND BROCK THOENE (pronounced *Tay-nee)* have written over 45 works of historical fiction. That these best sellers have sold more than 10 million copies and won eight ECPA Gold Medallion Awards affirms what millions of readers have already discovered—the Thoenes are not only master stylists but experts at capturing readers' minds and hearts.

In their timeless classic series about Israel (The Zion Chronicles, The Zion Covenant, and The Zion Legacy), the Thoenes' love for both story and research shines.

With The Shiloh Legacy and *Shiloh Autumn* (poignant portrayals of the American Depression), The Galway Chronicles (dramatic stories of the 1840s famine in Ireland), and the Legends of the West (gripping tales of adventure and danger in a land without law), the Thoenes have made their mark in modern history.

In the A.D. Chronicles they step seamlessly into the world of Jerusalem and Rome, in the days when Yeshua walked the earth and transformed lives with His touch.

Bodie began her writing career as a teen journalist for her local newspaper. Eventually her byline appeared in prestigious periodicals such as *U.S. News and World Report, The American West,* and *The Saturday Evening Post.* She also worked for John Wayne's Batjac Productions (she's best known as author of *The Fall Guy)* and ABC Circle Films as a writer and researcher. John Wayne described her as "a writer with talent that captures the people and the times!" She has degrees in journalism and communications.

Brock has often been described by Bodie as "an essential half of this writing team." With degrees in both history and education, Brock has, in his role as researcher and story-line consultant, added the vital dimension of historical accuracy. Due to such careful research, the Zion Covenant and Zion Chronicles series are recognized by the American Library Association, as well as Zionist libraries around the world, as classic historical novels and are used to teach history in college classrooms.

Bodie and Brock have four grown children—Rachel, Jake, Luke, and Ellie—and seven grandchildren. Their children are carrying on the Thoene family talent as the next generation of writers, and Luke produces the Thoene audiobooks. Bodie and Brock divide their time between London and Nevada.

For more information visit:
www.thoenebooks.com
www.familyaudiolibrary.com

suspense with a mission

TITLES BY

Jake Thoene

"The Christian Tom Clancy"
Dale Hurd, *CBN Newswatch*

Shaiton's Fire

In this first book in the techno-thriller series by Jake Thoene, the bombing of a subway train is only the beginning of a master plan that Steve Alstead and Chapter 16 have to stop . . . before it's too late.

Firefly Blue

In this action-packed sequel to Shaiton's Fire, Chapter 16 is called in when barrels of cyanide are stolen during a truckjacking. Experience heart-stopping action as you read this gripping story that could have been ripped from today's headlines.

Fuel the Fire

In this third book in the series, Special Agent Steve Alstead and Chapter 16, the FBI's counterterrorism unit, must stop the scheme of an al Qaeda splinter cell . . . while America's future hangs in the balance.

Available from www.thoenebooks.com and www.familyaudiolibrary.com

CP0025

THOENE FAMILY CLASSICS™

✪ ✪ ✪

THOENE FAMILY CLASSIC HISTORICALS
by Bodie and Brock Thoene
*Gold Medallion Winners**

THE ZION COVENANT
*Vienna Prelude**
Prague Counterpoint
Munich Signature
Jerusalem Interlude
Danzig Passage
*Warsaw Requiem**
London Refrain
Paris Encore
Dunkirk Crescendo

THE ZION CHRONICLES
*The Gates of Zion**
A Daughter of Zion
The Return to Zion
A Light in Zion
*The Key to Zion**

THE SHILOH LEGACY
*In My Father's House**
A Thousand Shall Fall
Say to This Mountain

SHILOH AUTUMN

THE GALWAY CHRONICLES
*Only the River Runs Free**
Of Men and of Angels
*Ashes of Remembrance**
All Rivers to the Sea

THE ZION LEGACY
Jerusalem Vigil
Thunder from Jerusalem
Jerusalem's Heart
Jerusalem Scrolls
Stones of Jerusalem
Jerusalem's Hope

A.D. CHRONICLES
First Light
Second Touch
Third Watch
Fourth Dawn
Fifth Seal
Sixth Covenant
Seventh Day
Eighth Shepherd
Ninth Witness
and more to come!

THOENE FAMILY CLASSICS™

✪ ✪ ✪

THOENE FAMILY CLASSIC AMERICAN LEGENDS

LEGENDS OF THE WEST
by Bodie and Brock Thoene

Legends of the West, Volume One
Sequoia Scout
The Year of the Grizzly
Shooting Star
Legends of the West, Volume Two
Gold Rush Prodigal
Delta Passage
Hangtown Lawman
Legends of the West, Volume Three
Hope Valley War
The Legend of Storey County
Cumberland Crossing
Legends of the West, Volume Four
The Man from Shadow Ridge
Cannons of the Comstock
Riders of the Silver Rim

LEGENDS OF VALOR
by Luke Thoene

Sons of Valor
Brothers of Valor
Fathers of Valor

✪ ✪ ✪

THOENE CLASSIC NONFICTION
by Bodie and Brock Thoene

Writer-to-Writer

THOENE FAMILY CLASSIC SUSPENSE
by Jake Thoene

CHAPTER 16 SERIES
Shaiton's Fire
Firefly Blue
Fuel the Fire

✪ ✪ ✪

THOENE FAMILY CLASSICS FOR KIDS

BAKER STREET DETECTIVES
by Jake and Luke Thoene

The Mystery of the Yellow Hands
The Giant Rat of Sumatra
The Jeweled Peacock of Persia
The Thundering Underground

LAST CHANCE DETECTIVES
by Jake and Luke Thoene
Mystery Lights of Navajo Mesa
Legend of the Desert Bigfoot

THE VASE OF MANY COLORS
by Rachel Thoene (Illustrations by
Christian Cinder)

✪ ✪ ✪

THOENE FAMILY CLASSIC AUDIOBOOKS

Available from
www.thoenebooks.com or
www.familyaudiolibrary.com

CP0064